Praise for
The Sister Season

"A really wonderful book and a pleasure to read."
—*New York Times* bestselling author Jen Lancaster

"Emotionally honest and psychologically astute, *The Sister Season* is ultimately an uplifting story about the pull of the past, the need for forgiveness, and the redemptive power of familial love."   —Liza Gyllenhaal, author of *A Place for Us*

"*The Sister Season* is a powerful, honest look at the harm that ripples out from every unkindness, and the strength inherent in the sisterly bond."
—Heidi Jon Schmidt, author of *The Harbormaster's Daughter*

"The perfect book to curl up with on a nice snowy day!"
—Open Book Society

"Jennifer Scott deserves accolades. . . . These sisters have to learn to face each other with care . . . forgive (although one could never forget what they have endured), and be there for each other as well as their mom. The book is carefully crafted, with pivotal moments carefully placed in a solid plot that moves. . . . Nice writing and very appropriate themes as the holidays approach for families of all!"   —The Best Reviews

continued . . .

Written by today's freshest new talents and selected by New American Library, NAL Accent novels touch on subjects close to a woman's heart, from friendship to family to finding our place in the world. The Conversation Guides included in each book are intended to enrich the individual reading experience, as well as encourage us to explore these topics together—because books, and life, are meant for sharing.

Visit us online at penguin.com.

D0067789

THE ACCIDENTAL BOOK CLUB

Jennifer Scott

NAL
ACCENT

NAL Accent
Published by the Penguin Group
Penguin Group (USA) LLC, 375 Hudson Street,
New York, New York 10014

USA | Canada | UK | Ireland | Australia | New Zealand | India | South Africa | China
penguin.com
A Penguin Random House Company

First published by NAL Accent, an imprint of New American Library,
a division of Penguin Group (USA) LLC

First Printing, May 2014

LIBRARY OF CONGRESS CATALOGING-IN-PUBLICATION DATA:

Scott, Jennifer, 1972–
    The accidental book club/Jennifer Scott.
        pages cm
    ISBN 978-0-451-41882-1 (pbk.)
    1. Book clubs (Discussion groups)—Fiction. 2. Middle-aged women—
Fiction. 3. Widows—Fiction. 4. Mothers and daughters—Fiction. 5. Domestic
fiction. 6. Psychological fiction. I. Title.
    PS3619.C66555A64 2014
    813'.6—dc23   2014000337

Printed in the United States of America
10 9 8 7 6 5 4 3 2

Set in Bembo
Designed by Spring Hoteling

For Scott

ACKNOWLEDGMENTS

It takes so many people to put together a book, it's sort of like a book club all its own. I'd like to give special thanks to these, the members of *The Accidental Book Club*'s book club.

Thank you to Cori Deyoe, my trusted agent and beautiful friend. For you, I will bring out the fancy veggie tray.

Thank you to my amazing editor, Sandy Harding, whose advice and suggestions made me fall even more in love with my characters. Also, huge thanks to Elizabeth Bistrow, Kara Welsh, Claire Zion, Daniel Walsh, Jane Steele, and everyone else at NAL who had their hands and hearts in my manuscript. Cheesecake squares for all!

A special thanks goes to Maryellen O'Boyle, who makes covers so beautiful I want to sleep with them under my pillow. I'll break out the chocolate wine for you.

Thank you to the many book clubs I've visited for inviting me into your libraries, bookstores, offices, and homes, and for sharing your thoughts, your best dishes, and your wine with me. You are all the best book club I've ever been to. I made secret-recipe macadamia-nut brownies just for you.

Thank you, and bread with real butter, to my mom, Bonnie McMullen, for taking me to libraries and always indulging my love of reading.

And, of course, thank you to my family. Scott, Paige, Weston, and Rand, you are the roasted red peppers in my macaroni and cheese. I would be so plain without you.

THE ACCIDENTAL
BOOK CLUB

PROLOGUE

May 2

NEW YORK, NY—Crowds are lining up across the country for the midnight release of Pulitzer Prize–winning author R. Sebastian Thackeray III's newest novel, *Blame*.

"We've been here since nine o'clock this morning," thirty-four-year-old mother of two Wendy McMickle said. "There were a lot of people already here. Somebody said the woman in the front of the line got here two days ago. I feel like we're meeting the president or something."

Blame, which chronicles the struggles of three generations of suffering women, is the most highly anticipated novel of the year, with sales expected to be well into the millions.

Bookstore owner Lavitia Jones called the release of

a Thackeray book "Christmas, no matter what day of the year it is."

"We will sell as many books tonight as we did during all of the previous quarter," Jones said. "People have been calling for months asking about it. Everybody wants *Blame*. The reviews have all been so great. Some say Thackeray will win a Nobel for this one, and I would say he deserves it."

While some feminist groups are questioning the novel's bleak look at women, reviews have lauded *Blame* as the only true great American novel to have ever been written, with one reviewer proclaiming it "so honest, it will break your heart with clarity," and another calling Thackeray "a leading light of human behavior."

"Yes, I've read *Blame*," Jones said. "I don't want to give any spoilers, but just expect your eyes to be opened. Everything you ever thought about life will be proven false; mark my words."

Thackeray himself, however, is too humble to talk of big prizes and record-breaking sales. The author is notoriously reclusive, rarely granting interviews or making appearances, and that doesn't appear to have changed with the release of his newest tome. Thackeray does not participate in social media, has no Web site, and is said to refuse fan mail. So it is anyone's guess what he makes of *Blame*'s initial success, though in the past he has been known to call his work simply "common sense in pretty packages."

"Whatever you call it, I want it," McMickle said. "I have been dying to read this book since I heard he was writing it. I'm pretty sure I've read everything he's ever written. If he wrote a grocery list, I'd read that too. I even named my son Sebastian. He's just that amazing."

ONE

Jean Vison dumped a fistful of chopped roasted red peppers into a pan of macaroni and cheese, and stirred, hoping doing so would make her dish pass as "gourmet." This was her battle the second Tuesday of every month—calling on her minimal Food Network knowledge in an attempt to upscale her simple cooking and make it book club–worthy. Make it an offering that could sit alongside Dorothy's chicken with lemon caper sauce or May's salsa cruda or Janet's crème fraîche something-or-other without Jean feeling embarrassed. Whereas her friends seemed to have actual recipes that called for fennel bulbs and chili threads and things scooped into quenelles, Jean seemed to rely on simply tossing soggy clumps of jarred peppers into her pasta and hoping for the best. She'd never been anyone's chef.

Besides, it was a *book* club, she told herself. They were

there for the books, not the food. But she knew that was a lie. Her book club may have once been about rekindling a love of reading, not to mention a welcome distraction from her lonely life, but it was now as much about the saffron risotto and the flourless tortes, and even the macaroni and cheese with soggy peppers, as it was about reading. Not that she was complaining. The meals were always amazing—sometimes far more amazing than the book they'd read. Sometimes they spent more time talking about how to get the brown sugar icing just right on Mitzi's bananas Foster bars than they did about plot development or symbolism. And the sitting and talking while digging into a quiche so velvety it felt like sin was really the only thing that kept Jean going most months.

It was never just quiche or capers or a balsamic drizzle. It was one of Dorothy's clan of riotous sons in jail once again for stealing a DVD player ("A DVD player, for crying out loud," Dorothy had railed. "You'd think if he was going to risk jail time, he'd at least be smart enough to steal better technology."). It was Dorothy's divorce and her ex's new girlfriend, who wore a thong to the country club pool despite being far beyond thong age and, to hear Dorothy tell it, had "more hail damage on those thighs than a used-car lot in the springtime." It was Mitzi's political rants. It was Loretta's off-color jokes that made everyone choke on their Sangiovese. It was poor, skittish Janet, so nervous she chewed her top lip flaky and chapped, her raw fingers making the fork or the book page or the ice in her water glass shiver while she tried desperately to join in the conversation. It was May's dating woes.

It was the way nobody ever mentioned Wayne.

It was the way Jean never even thought of him during those meetings.

For two hours, once a month, Jean wasn't Wayne's widow. She was just Jean, the one who thought a shaved piece of mushroom or a chopped shallot elevated her cooking. She was just Jean, the one who bought three expensive bottles of Shiraz to go with May's venison cutlets, the one who carried a printed list of all the bestsellers in a fat notebook where she kept a record of attendance, as if anyone bothered to worry about attendance. She was just Jean, the one who had it all quietly and delicately under control.

On a whim, she dumped a carton of feta cheese into the pasta and stirred. Now it was Greek macaroni and cheese. Now she had a foreign country to pin it to, which automatically made it exotic. If only she had some fennel to add—not that she could guess what that would do to make a difference in flavor, just that she'd heard a TV chef once say that feta cheese and fennel were like peanut butter and jelly. She knew much more about peanut butter and jelly than fennel and feta, but nobody needed to know that.

She popped the macaroni into the oven, uncorked the first bottle of Signorello, and placed it on the island, surrounding it with a cluster of sparkling wineglasses.

"Halloo?" called Loretta, Jean's next-door neighbor and best friend of many years, from the front door. Loretta was, technically, the oldest of the group, but in numerals only. She liked to call herself "a born-again twentysomething," and proved it just about every time she opened her heavily lipsticked mouth.

"In the kitchen," Jean called back, and poured a bowlful of chocolate candies, which she slid into the middle of the massive dining room table. These would go untouched at first, but if the conversation was lively enough and long enough, they would soon be devoured, yet nobody would admit to having eaten a single one. She double-checked the notes that she had placed at her seat, double-checked that she had her copy of *The Marriage Plot* at easy disposal. She had so many thoughts about this book, so many things she wanted to say. She was excited about their meeting today. She turned back toward the kitchen in time to see Loretta pull a giant loaf of some sort of bread out of a paper bag.

"Let me tell you, Jeanie," she said, holding the loaf between fingernails manicured to match the deep red of her lipstick, "this bread is better than sex. The best thing I've put in my mouth since college. And, trust me, I put some pretty amazing things in my mouth in college. A whole phone book of amazing things, from Adam all the way to Zachariah."

Jean lifted the loaf to her nose. It smelled sweet and like something else—maybe anise?—and like it might just go perfectly with her macaroni and cheese. "Butter," she said, and went to the refrigerator to find a stick.

Meanwhile, Loretta had poured herself a healthy glass of wine and had commandeered her usual spot at the dining room table, just at Jean's right. "I'm starving," she moaned, plucking at the front of her button-down to get it just perfect. "Whatever you're cooking smells wonderful."

"Greek macaroni and cheese," Jean called from the kitchen, where she was rummaging for a butter dish, and smiled. Yes, it did sound gourmet when she said it out loud like that.

"Well, then *opa*! I hope May brings some of those cheesecake things again," Loretta said. "I'd like to walk barefoot through a field of those."

Jean popped her head around the corner. "Let me know if you run across a cheesecake field and I'll be first in line to buy it. And I'm sure she will. You practically ordered her to never bring anything but."

"For good reason. Those are worth the extra protein."

Jean snickered. May was legendary for two things—her beautiful, white-blond, thick, curly hair and her food, which always contained equal parts food and beautiful, white-blond, thick, curly hairs. Loretta had been known to call her out on it on multiple occasions, but May, God bless her, only chuckled and told Loretta to "can it and make her own dessert," and they went back to their lunching and book dishing and pulling hairs out of delicious cheesecake.

There was a knock on the door, followed by the sound of it opening, and Jean could hear animated chatter coming from the entryway. Dorothy and Mitzi, friends and coworkers at American Dollar Bank, rounded the corner, juggling their dishes and books. Mitzi, the younger of the two, and life-dedicated conservative radio talk show listener, was going on, as usual, about something that sounded political.

"Hello," Jean called out when they reached the kitchen, but neither of them had heard her over their own talking, and simply went on about their conversation, distractedly setting their dishes next to Loretta's bread and uncovering them.

"Good riddance, that's what I say. We can't allow ourselves to continue to be governed by males who can't keep their pants buckled. I can't believe voters are so stupid as to keep him in office for as long as they have . . . ," Mitzi continued.

"I sure didn't vote for him," Dorothy said.

"Well, of course not, because you have a brain. That's why you dumped Elan."

Dorothy tried to corral her frizzy graying hair behind one ear. Jean noticed a small hole in the armpit of her dress when she lifted her arm. Newly divorced and left with five out-of-control boys to wrangle, Dorothy was doing good to just get dressed in the mornings. Some meetings, Jean thought, Dorothy looked as if she might nod off right there at the table. "Ugh, don't mention his name. And, technically, Elan dumped me."

The door opened again and May came in, and not long after, so did Janet, reminding Jean of a doe the way she practically tiptoed into the room, looking apologetic, round-eyed, and afraid.

"Hey, Dot, I saw Elan and his stripper at the furniture store—did I tell you that?" Loretta called from the other room.

May, licking her thumb, which she'd accidentally pressed into a cheesecake bite while uncovering it, gave Jean a quick sideways hug, then headed straight toward the dining room. "What were you looking for at the furniture store, Loretta? Something for your reading room?"

"Oh, you know, that damn recliner of Chuck's has crapped out again. The man's killed more chairs than shoes—I can tell you that much. I should have asked Elan's stripper if she was shopping for a new pole," she called to Dorothy.

"You know, Dorothy, you should really see about going to the rally with us on Saturday . . . ," Mitzi was saying, but Dorothy had plopped into a chair and was patting the back of her hair distractedly. Tired, Jean thought. She just looked so tired.

"More power to her. If she's stupid enough to think he won't cheat on her after he cheated on me with her, she deserves what she gets," Dorothy said.

May returned to the kitchen and surveyed the counter. "Oooh, that casserole looks delicious. What's in it?"

"That's cowboy casserole," someone—Jean couldn't

determine who—shouted from the dining room, and she heard scrapes of wood on the floor as they made their way toward the food.

"Come in, come in," Jean said to poor, hovering Janet. Then she set out the plates as everyone else busied themselves with catching up while pulling plastic wrap off dishes, rummaging for serving spoons, and pouring wine.

As she always did, Jean took a moment to lean back against the counter and just listen. The house was far too quiet with Wayne gone, but it seemed she never noticed until it was full again. Wayne had liked to entertain. Back when the kids were young and they felt like they had all the time in the world, they put off having parties, but when they did have one, it was a *party*—so loud everyone had to shout to be heard. Wayne's laughter carried the party to success.

She probably wouldn't be able to handle a party without Wayne's laughter now. She'd passed up the few invitations she'd been offered since he died. But this . . . This was a close second. This was the kind of party she could control, rather than a party that would take control of her. That was what she needed more than anything in her life right now. She'd been out of control for so long—everything had been out of her control. This felt good.

If two years ago someone had told Jean that a day would come when her only thought would be whether the roasted red peppers would be a good enough addition to the macaroni and cheese, she never would have believed it.

Jean pulled the macaroni and cheese out of the oven and added it to the buffet, and the ladies began loading up their plates, the conversation slowly and naturally turning toward the book, as it always did.

"I didn't want this one to end," Janet practically whispered over her plate, which had teeny mounds of food on it, more like samplings than actual portions. Jean had noticed this about Janet, who was so heavy, most of her bottom fell over the sides of the dining room chairs, her ankles often looking spotty and blue underneath the cuffs of her pants as she stood up to leave. "What a realistic look at love."

Dorothy made a noise. "In my experience, a realistic look at love is when your husband of thirty years follows his doohickey to a woman who uses the word *whatevs* in every sentence."

"Not every man is like that. You got a bad one is all," May said. "I agree with Janet. I thought this was realistic. And . . . pretty."

"Pretty? How is mental illness pretty?" Mitzi asked, jumping right in, as always.

May shrugged, her delicate shoulders pushing up her spirals. "I don't know. Maybe it's the writing that's pretty. It seemed like it had something more to say. I keep wondering what I would have done if I were Madeleine."

"I didn't realize that a *marriage plot* was an actual term," Loretta said. "I just thought it was a good title."

Mitzi nodded. "A literary term, right? I didn't know that, either."

"I'm pretty sure it was a term used in the 1800s, because it was a kind of new idea back then," Janet said. "I think maybe the title was supposed to be a double entendre." She stumbled over the ending of the word and immediately ducked down to her plate again.

Jean took a sip of wine. "It was nice to read a meaty romance," she said. "I guess you can call it a romance?"

"Beats me. I don't write 'em; I just love reading 'em," Loretta said.

"Well, I think so," Mitzi said. "If a marriage plot is literally about the plot, and the plot is about marriage, then isn't it romance?"

"Not in my marriage, it wasn't," Dorothy grumbled. "And that sentence made my brain hurt, Mitzi."

"Mine too," Loretta said.

May nodded. "We may be overthinking things. More wine!"

"Either way, I would read more of this guy's books," Jean said.

"Hey, Jean, why didn't we ever read *Middlesex*?" Dorothy asked. "I think we may be the only book club in the world that didn't."

"And it has Loretta's favorite word right there in the title," May said.

"What? *Middle?* Absolutely! I love the word *middle*. Especially when the other words are *fireman* and *sexy cowboy*," Loretta said, and held her wineglass up, toast-style. May giggled and clinked her glass against Loretta's.

"Well, I wouldn't read more," Dorothy said. "I didn't like it."

"Oh, Dot, you just didn't like it because you're burned by romance right now," Mitzi said. Mitzi had a way of speaking bluntly to Dorothy, and sometimes Jean thought she was right on the edge of rude. But Dorothy didn't seem to mind. *Our friendship is honest,* she'd been known to say. *As honest as a slap in the face.*

Dorothy shook her head. "I didn't like Madeleine. I thought she was . . . I don't know. Annoying."

Mitzi reached over and patted Dorothy's hand. "She's young. You're going to find any young girl annoying right now. And for good reason."

"Absolutely," Jean agreed. "You'll come back to romance. When you've gotten some distance." *Like me,* she almost added, but knew that wouldn't be the truth. She still had to read romance as an outsider. She still had to skim over the more tender scenes, the scenes that made her think too hard about Wayne.

"Oh, Dorothy, I almost forgot," Mitzi said, changing the subject. "My neighbor is convinced that your oldest son, Leonard, is the one who stole the hood ornament off his vintage Mercedes. He is seven shades of pissed. You're probably going to have the cops on your doorstep soon. Just a heads-up."

Dorothy groaned. "Just what I need—more cops. Those boys . . ."

"Send them to church. A good pastor will turn them

around," Mitzi said. "Send them to *my* church. *I'll* turn them around."

"Let me at 'em. I'll take care of 'em," Loretta offered. "God, this wine is good, Jeanie."

"You'll forgive me if I don't want you defiling my Leonard," Dorothy said.

Loretta faked indignation. "Well, I never!"

"Oh, yes, you have!" Mitzi and May said together, and everyone, including Loretta, burst into laughter.

Jean placed her plate on the table and eased into her chair. She cleared her throat. "Okay, okay, before we get too sidetracked, we need to discuss our next read. Any suggestions?"

Everyone looked at one another, munching, eyes wide. Jean always asked for suggestions but rarely got them. "All right," Jean said. "I printed out this list." She held up the list and waved it around, then looked at it again. "I was wondering about R. Sebastian Thackeray's newest one. *Blame*, I think it's called?"

"Oh, I've heard good things about that one," Loretta said around a bite of Dorothy's famous tabouleh salad. "Everyone's raving."

"Not everyone. I heard some feminist groups have been giving him grief over it," Janet said.

"Eh, everyone knows feminists are always looking for something to be pissed off about," Mitzi said.

Dorothy rolled her eyes. "Oh, goodness, don't get her started on the feminists."

"But we liked that one of his that we read last fall. What was it called?" May asked.

"Something about crime lines," Dorothy said. "It was pretty good. He can write."

"*No Crime in Timelines,*" Jean corrected. "And yes, we all liked it, which was why I thought—"

The phone rang, interrupting her. Since Wayne died, her phone didn't ring very often. Only the book club members ever called, really. Or the occasional telemarketer.

She excused herself from the table and rushed to the kitchen to answer it.

"Jean?"

"Yes?"

"This is Curt."

Jean blinked. As long as it had been since anyone had called her, her son-in-law Curt had never called her in the seventeen years since he'd married her daughter, Laura, and whisked her away to the other side of the state. "Yes, yes, how are you?"

"Uh, not good. I'm afraid there's a little problem."

"A problem? What kind of problem?" Jean laid the book list on the counter.

"It's Laura. She's in the hospital. I think maybe you should come."

TWO

Jean hadn't seen her son-in-law in ages, and she almost didn't recognize him as the graying man pacing the hospital corridor in a suit and tie, a cell phone plastered to his ear.

She stood in front of him, her purse looped over one wrist. With her other hand, she pushed the purse into her stomach uncomfortably, trying to suppress the jittery feeling that she needed to Do Something. He glanced at her, held up one finger, and continued talking, turning to pace away from her.

She waited patiently, standing as straight as she could to stretch out her back. It had ached for a rest stop near Columbia, but she'd insisted on pushing through, driving the four hours to St. Louis without stopping until she pulled into the hospital parking lot.

Jean had never been a fan of road trips, and she and

Wayne had felt like they were in the way the few times they'd invited themselves to Laura and Curt's house (Laura had extended the invitation only twice), so she was not used to the drive. And she was especially unused to the drive alone, without Wayne behind the wheel cracking jokes and singing that infernal Willie Nelson song. Her unfamiliarity, combined with her worried and hurried pace and her refusal to stop, had set her back to aching something fierce. She was far too old for tests of endurance.

Curt came back a few seconds later, stuffing his phone into his pants pocket.

"She's sleeping it off now," he said, gesturing over his shoulder at the room behind him. "She's been out for a while. Bailey's on her way. Neighbor's bringing her, even though I told her to have Bailey call instead. The last thing she needs is to be a part of this."

"What should I do?" Jean asked. The sterile scent and faint beeping emanating from somewhere unidentifiable on the ward threatened to tug her memory back to an awful place of unsuccessful treatments, shed tears, and eventual surrender to the inevitable. She had not been in a hospital since they had decided to take Wayne home to fight his final losing battle. She did not miss the depressing corridors, the grim-faced people. "Can I see her? Where is she?"

He turned in a slow circle, as if looking for someone to answer her questions, then scratched the back of his neck and cocked his head at her. "Listen, Jean. There's something you may not know," he said. "Laura is an alcoholic. I need you to understand that."

Jean tried to give a reassuring smile, tried to nod as if this were something she had a firm grasp on, but she was still reeling from the short rundown he'd given her on the phone. Her daughter was in the hospital with alcohol poisoning. On a Tuesday afternoon. She'd gone to work—which was what her daughter did best, work—and had proceeded to cause some sort of scene. They'd threatened to call the police if she didn't vacate the premises and, hours later, during which time Laura had been God-knew-where doing God-knew-what, her friend found her, sprawled facedown on the front lawn, car keys still clutched in her hand. What in God's name was understandable about that?

"You told me on the phone she was drunk," Jean answered, as if this settled everything.

He shook his head. "Drunk and then some. But today . . . this . . . This is nothing unusual. Your daughter has a drinking problem. It's gotten worse since we split, but it's been going on for—"

"What do you mean, since you split?"

He pulled his cell phone out of his pocket nervously, glanced at it as if he didn't know how it had gotten into his hand, and then shoved it back into his pocket. "She didn't tell you," he said. A statement, not a question. Jean shook her head. "Of course not," he mumbled, then took a deep breath and let it out through pursed lips. "I left her about a month ago. I couldn't take the drinking anymore. It got to be too much. And Bailey's just been impossible to deal with." He shook his head, wiped his hand up and down over his face a few times, and sighed; then he took another deep breath. "Laura's going to have to go to rehab. There's just no way around it. She's been telling me for a year that she'll quit when she's ready, but she's too far in to do it on her own now. She'll never be ready. She's going to kill herself. Or someone else."

Jean blinked. "For a year," she said, trying to maintain a sense of poise, to not look like she'd been made a fool of by her daughter all this time. After Laura landed that big job of hers five or six years ago, she hardly spoke to her family at all. Kenneth never heard from his sister. Wayne and Jean received only the rare phone call, and they saw Bailey only intermittently. Laura always seemed to have an excuse for why they couldn't come home for Christmas. *Things are crazy at work, Mom. I'm barely going to get time for Christmas here with Bailey and Curt. I can't possibly get to Kansas City. We'll just have to ship gifts again,* she would say. To hear Laura talk about it, Bailey hadn't had a birthday party since she was ten. Wayne's funeral was the first time Jean had seen Laura in well over a year, and here it had been another two years, and she hadn't seen her since. But to not know her daughter well enough to know that she was struggling with booze so much so as to have ended up in the hospital felt like a failing somehow. She should have visited without invitation. She should have invited Laura and her family more often. She should have called more often. She was ashamed.

"And Bailey will be with you?" she asked. "While Laura's . . . away?"

He rolled his eyes. "She won't want to, but yes. She'll have no choice. I'll write down my apartment address for you. And I'll let you know where we decide to put Laura."

"Put Laura," Jean said, realizing she was only repeating again. It was just that she felt so very knocked down by this news, so very confused and unsure of how things could have gotten this out of control without her even knowing about it. "Like a dog needing a home." The words were out of her mouth, sounding sharp in the hallway, before she'd barely formed the thought in her head.

He held out a hand. "I didn't mean it like . . . I just meant I'd let you know what rehab she'd be staying in. This is hard, Jean. I want you to know that. This isn't easy for me at all. I love . . ." He paused, swallowed, his eyes suddenly looking very bloodshot and swimmy. "I love them both. But I can't say I love my family, because for the longest time I've had no family. Maybe it's my fault too—I don't know."

"Well, she had a reason to drink, I would imagine," Jean said, trying to offer sympathy, but also hoping for an explanation. She realized her words might have come off as blame, and maybe that was what she was looking for. If Curt had done something to cause this, then maybe she hadn't done it. "Something must have been wrong."

He looked up at her sharply, and though she didn't know Curt well enough to guess what anger looked like on him, she thought maybe that was what she was seeing in the pinched creases on his temples. She pulled herself up taller, scrunched her purse tighter into her stomach, and lifted her chin. She certainly didn't feel as strong as she used to be, but she wasn't one to back down when cornered, either.

"There was a lot wrong," Curt answered. "But if you're asking if I did something to her, like cheat on her or hurt her in some way, the answer is no. I've been devoted to her. Longer than most men would be. Longer than she's been devoted to me."

"I wasn't asking that," Jean said, though, of course, she had been.

"Most of what was wrong was she was so married to her job and her booze and her projects, she didn't have time to be married to me," he said. He stared at his shoes for a moment, then suddenly stood up straight and gestured toward the room, stepping aside. "You might as well go in. But don't expect to have a conversation with her or anything. Already tried. Didn't go well."

Jean took a couple of steps forward, suddenly feeling very sorry for her son-in-law with his stooped shoulders and the way his pants seemed to hang on his hips as if he'd recently lost a significant amount of weight. Sadness and regret seemed to envelop him. She couldn't help but call to mind his and Laura's wedding day, the way he followed

Laura around, skimming her lower back with his fingertips or clutching her hand like a dazed child, laughing at all her jokes, brushing his knuckles along her chin adoringly. He was so utterly bulldozed by Laura, Jean was sure if she looked closely, she'd see hearts in his eyes. He might have followed the girl anywhere; he just must have never expected to have to follow her here.

Jean put her hand on his arm, very lightly. "I'm sorry," she said, though she wasn't sure if she was simply expressing sympathy, or if maybe she was apologizing too.

The curtains in Laura's room were pulled shut—surely to ward off the immense hangover that she would be likely to wake up with—and the room was dim, gray. From the doorway, Jean barely recognized the form in the bed as her daughter. She, like Curt, had also lost weight—a lot of it, from the look of things. She was skeletal. But as Jean stepped closer to the bed, she could see that her daughter's face had a certain puffy, doughy quality to it, as if she were a Christmas roll ready to be popped into the oven. She was strapped to a monitor, which, from what Jean could tell, the hospital put everyone on, whether they were there for a heart attack or an ingrown toenail, and an IV snaked into the back of one hand. The other hand, wrapped in a cloth bandage, was resting across her chest.

Jean stood next to the bed and simply stared down at her daughter. Alcohol poisoning. It still didn't make sense. And now separation too? What on earth had happened? And why hadn't Laura told her?

Laura had been such a pretty child. Everyone commented on it, how pretty she was. Her features were striking, and she had a way about her that was so easily flawless. Dainty. She'd been Jean's "moon child"—always orbiting around Jean's legs as she tried to vacuum or shop or cook dinner. She had rarely been more than a few steps away. While Kenny had taken every chance to bolt and explore the world in his bold, fearless way, Laura was more careful, more prone to worries and fears. And she seemed to take everything so personally.

She could do things. Schoolwork was easy for her. So was making friends. She could sing reasonably well, and she was artistic when she wanted to be. She was incredibly organized, even from a very young age—she had a tendency to stack and line up her toys just so—and she seemed only to get smarter, better with age.

She was pretty. She was talented. And she was a perfectionist like Jean had never seen before. She was the kind of child you didn't worry about. The kind of child who had it all together. Who grew up to have a romantic marriage and a beautiful baby and a high-pressure executive job that she loved—loved!—with everything she had. The kind of child who grew up to be the woman who had it all. And had it all together. The kind of child who allowed you to sit back and be proud of a job well done.

Only now she was lying in a hospital bed. And as Jean looked down into that puffy face, she could still see the shades of her "moon child." She could still see that pretty little girl beneath.

A nurse bustled into the room, interrupting Jean's thoughts. "She probably should get some sleep. She'll have to have that wrist X-rayed when the doctor comes in."

Jean's hand wrapped around her own wrist involuntarily. "What happened to it?"

The nurse shrugged. "Nobody knows. Probably never will. That occurs pretty frequently in cases like these. People get drunk, they injure themselves, they black out or pass out, and then the next morning are wondering how their wrist got broken. It's all a mystery to everyone."

The nurse left the room, and with her gone and Curt gone and Laura snoozing, the room once again seemed bleak and gray and filled with a sweat-soaked stranger who might have had a passing resemblance to Jean's daughter. Jean felt a sense of surrealism—maybe she was actually still at home and Dorothy was telling one of her long, complicated stories about her son's legal troubles, and Jean had simply zoned out. She was imagining this, and would soon snap to, only to find that, frustratingly, she'd dropped a cheese-coated roasted red pepper into her lap. But the longer she stood there, listening to that infernal faint beeping, the more real it became.

Her daughter was in trouble.

Softly she crept forward until her knees brushed the crinkly mattress. Laura's skin was pale and glossy, and each time she breathed, Jean got a new whiff of acrid alcohol-laced breath. She brushed Laura's bangs off her forehead with one finger and was transported back in time. It seemed every memory she had of her child was one of achievement—graduations, weddings, brunches to celebrate new jobs, new promotions. But how deceiving had those appearances been? Had Laura gone out after those graduations, gotten smashed on cheap cocktails, and ended up sobbing in someone's backseat about how bleak her life really was? Had she been an inattentive mother, unable to handle the imperfection, the mistakes that every mother must face over and over again? Why did she need to do this to herself?

To hear Curt talk, it certainly sounded as if there were imperfections with Bailey. That sweet child with the long hair that curled up in little wispy waves at the very ends. The one who sucked on her index and middle fingers so much that she talked with a lisp until she was eight. So adorable, with those big brown eyes and the freckles across her nose. So deep, those eyes. Jean had always felt as if another child were lurking somewhere beneath—another child that nobody would ever truly understand or know.

"What happened, Laura?" Jean whispered, and at the sound of her voice, Laura stirred, chewing out a garbled sentence that made Jean worry that she'd awakened her. She backed away from the bed and left the room, unsure of what to do next. Stay here? Go find a hotel? Turn around and go home? Curt hadn't made it exactly clear what he'd brought her here for.

She walked a ways down the hall and happened upon a small cut-in that housed half a dozen chairs and a silent but running TV. Curt was slouched in one, a bottle of water in one hand, his other hand holding his forehead. His elbow was propped on the arm of the chair so his face was tipped downward. A man in a pastel pink sweater and khakis sat in a chair across from Curt, leaning over so that his elbows rested on his knees. He was saying something in a low voice, and Curt was nodding. When Jean paused in the doorway, the man stopped talking and looked up at her.

"Oh, excuse me," Jean said, feeling as if she'd interrupted something important.

Curt looked up. "No, it's okay. This is Will. He's our pastor. Or . . . used to be. We . . . stopped going to church a while back."

The man in the sweater stood up and offered Jean his hand. She shook it and stepped in just far enough to perch on the very edge of the chair closest to the door, even though it had a stain on it that would have normally made her choose somewhere else. "I'm Jean," she said. "Laura's mother."

"Wonderful to meet you," the man said, his voice gentle and kind with an undercurrent of cheer that Jean found somewhat off-putting in the hospital surroundings. A pastor in the hospital, to Jean, inspired gravity.

"He was just telling me about a program over at Blue Serenity," Curt said between gulps of his water.

"I've had a couple of parishioners get good results there," Pastor Will added, as if he were talking about a used car dealership or a tanning salon. "We're confident we can get Laura back on the right path. A little detox, a lot of prayer."

Jean nodded, but directed her attention to Curt. "Her wrist. You have no idea?"

"Nope. Two months ago it was four stitches on her forehead, another time a sprained ankle. I'm almost afraid to leave her alone with her doing this, getting so drunk she's falling and hurting herself and not remembering anything."

"And you say Bailey is misbehaving," she said. "Is it because of this? Is it because of what's going on with Laura?"

Curt shrugged. "Who knows why Bailey does anything she does? She never speaks, and when she does speak, it's lies. When she gets off the couch, it's to do something unbelievable. Shoplifting ridiculous things like wrenches and shoe polish, shit she doesn't need—sorry, Will."

"I understand."

"Breaking stuff, sneaking out at night, smoking cigars of all things, and then burning holes in my suit coats with them. Just bizarre stuff. I can't get through to her. I don't think anyone can. The girl has no friends. Her teachers see her as a problem in the classroom. She's just a mess. I predict jail." He took another drink, swallowed. "Soon, if this keeps up."

Jean's heart was half-broken, half-frightened. She hated the idea of her granddaughter struggling, her daughter suffering, but dealing with the flailing had never been her strength. She'd barely survived Wayne's demise. She was just getting her control back. She was just getting to normal again. Even before, she'd never been good at showing emotion. She didn't know how to fix a broken person. She liked life steady, stable, predictable.

"Is there something I can do?" she practically whispered. "With Bailey?"

Curt seemed to consider this, then shook his head. "She's such a handful right now. I don't know what you could do. I don't know what I'm going to do. I'll figure out something."

"Should I go with Laura? To this Serenity place?"

"She won't be going tonight, I'm afraid," Pastor Will said. "They've got to X-ray her wrist, and they're going to keep her for observation since she was unresponsive when her neighbor brought her here. And the vomiting. They'll want to keep her on an IV at least for a little while, keep her from getting dehydrated. You should go home."

Jean fiddled with her purse handles. She hated to admit it, but she was somewhat relieved. She ached to get to a hotel, to her quiet sanctuary. She needed to rest her back. And process everything she'd learned—somehow make the pieces fit. She could visit Laura in the morning. Could follow her to the rehab center. Could see if she could get some answers then. She glanced to Curt for confirmation. He nodded.

"I'll call you in the morning," he said.

"I'll just come by," she offered. "I don't know where I'm staying yet."

"Okay, that's fine. Thanks for coming. She won't know you were here, but I'm sure she'd have appreciated it. She always said she wished you two had a closer relationship."

The sentence struck Jean cold. If Laura had wished it, why hadn't she ever tried?

Jean felt herself nodding and shaking hands with Pastor Will again and felt her mouth move around niceties, but as she walked down the corridor toward the big sliding double doors, her movement felt more like escape than anything. She didn't even notice the chubby girl in the black ripped pants plowing past her, coming in the doors as she went out.

THREE

Jean didn't sleep at all that night. Not that she'd been sleeping exceptionally well since Wayne died, anyway. She was not the same woman who had once slept easily. She was the woman who had stayed up into the night feeding her husband ice chips, had moistened his lips for him when he was too weak to even lick them, had pressed a cold cloth to his sweating forehead, had held his hand when he wept with pain. That woman feared she would never sleep well again.

Sometimes it was hard for Jean to believe these things had ever happened to her, that she'd lost the love of her life in just a few, awful, short months. There had been no time to plan or prepare or take that trip to Yellowstone that they'd talked about since before they ever got married.

God. How was that possible? How was it possible that they'd lived an entire lifetime together and had never gotten around to jotting up to Wyoming for a long weekend? What had they been doing with that time instead? Nothing important; Jean was certain of that. As she'd sat there and smelled the foul odor of approaching death radiate off her husband, always smiling that ridiculous don't-be-afraid-everything's-going-to-be-fine smile down at him, even though she herself was so terrified, her insides feeling like they were liquefying, she thought about all the things they'd done instead. Pointless chores, or weekends spent in silence over some silly disagreement or running the children to birthday parties of kids they didn't even know. Why did they choose those things? Why did they construct a life of tedium, always putting off wishes and dreams for another day that ultimately would not come?

These were the things Jean turned around in her mind endlessly, when she should have been sleeping. These were the things she thought about. She'd remember reading books aloud with Wayne, each of them sipping a glass of merlot, their legs intertwined on the couch or his head in her lap, his voice racing up and down the words like a bus on a hilly highway. She'd think about the last book they'd read together—the one she read to him at his bedside—the one they didn't finish. She'd recall the last sentence she'd read to him—*Adele came to him in his sleep that night*—and how she'd so often wished that she had kept on reading that night, pressing on until the story was finished. Mostly she'd think just that. *Our story was not yet done. In so many ways.*

But something about the hotel room made it particularly difficult to sleep. Maybe it was the way his empty half of the bed made her feel sunken into her half, her aliveness shrieking at her every second of the night. They'd rented a bed for Wayne at the very end, had placed it in the unused dining room just off the kitchen. Jean could then tend to him without schlepping up and down the stairs, and she could be close enough to spot the end when it came near (which she did, falsely, about a million times over those last couple of months, always feeling like a grim specter of doom lurking in the doorway, tissues at the ready). But, most important, and Jean knew this but didn't really know it, didn't face it baldly—moving Wayne to the dining room meant that he wouldn't bring death to their bed. They'd loved there. They'd *made* love there. It was a sacred place, a place where their relationship came alive.

True, he never laid his cancer down in their bed, but his absence was a cancer, one that made Jean toss and turn and wish for morning, even though she knew she'd perpetually face it with swollen eyes and tired limbs.

But she slept in the bed at home immeasurably better than she did in the hotel bed. It wasn't just the bed, which, true enough, felt like a medieval back-straightening device, or the pillow, which sank all the way to the hard mattress if she so much as put a breath's worth of weight against it, but it was the realization that this was the first time she'd ever been in a hotel room alone.

At first she'd tried pretending Wayne was in the bathroom, heat light glaring down on him as he took one of his long "vacation showers." She even got up and turned on the bathroom light, then shut the door, just for the strip of light stretching from under the door across the floor. How many times had she fallen asleep to that light? Colorado, Omaha, Branson, even right here in St. Louis (but not Yellowstone—never Yellowstone). The kids would be snoring softly in their shared bed next to her, the scent of hotel pool chlorine lingering in the room, the window air-conditioning unit rumbling like a jet through the darkness, anticipation of the next day's adventures heavy in the air. They'd shared so many great times on those vacations. The kids were always too excited to argue, having too much fun to throw fits. And on every vacation, up until Laura went off to college, Jean had always made it a point to do something "girly" with her—get a manicure or visit a doll museum or just go shopping without the boys. It had been such fun. Laura had been such a fun child, even in her precise way.

Jean tossed and turned, the light not helping, and ultimately decided to call Loretta, though it was decidedly past Chuck's bedtime (Chuck used the "bed" in "bedtime" loosely—most nights he sacked out in his worn recliner, leaving poor Loretta with a stack of inspirational but unrequited Flavian Munney romance novels by her bedside). Loretta answered on the second ring.

"Well, I'd started to think I was going to have to check the ditches on I-70. You got ketchup packets in your glove box?"

Jean laughed. Her friend never could just answer with a simple hello. "Ketchup packets?"

"To survive on in case you're trapped for days in a tree."

"How would my car end up in a tree? It's not a hovercraft."

"Exactly. No one would think to look for you up there. How is she?"

Jean sighed, closing her eyes to keep from staring at that strip of light coming from out from under the bathroom door. Had she really thought she'd fool herself with that tactic? "Awful. Just awful. I'm just glad her father wasn't there. But I don't want to talk about it. I already can't sleep. I just wanted to see how the group went."

"Ah. Well. Nobody found hair in May's cheesecake bites. Which of course made everyone worry that they'd gone and swallowed it. I swear we all looked like a bunch of cats about to urp on the carpet. I saved you one, by the way. Maybe yours is the lucky one. Sort of like a king cake. I put it in your fridge."

"Thanks. I'm afraid I'm not much in the cheesecake mood right now, though."

"Are you kidding? You would not believe the amount of restraint it took for me not to inhale it. Especially once Mitzi got rolling with her 'die-hard' this and her 'bleeding-heart liberal' that. Someone needs to tell her those phrases are oh-so-1990s. And then Dorothy got a phone call from Elan, and it seems one of her boys apparently set a recycling bin on fire at the elementary school, so we decided to just go ahead and call it a day. Seemed like the right thing to do at that point. You are eating this cake."

"That's it? You didn't talk about our next book at all?"

"Nope. Just didn't feel right without you. We thought we might meet again in two Tuesdays. Kind of an abbreviated do-over meeting. What do you think? We can do it here if you're not up for it. The girls are worried, of course. About you, and about Laura."

Jean made some noncommittal noises. Loretta yawned, and soon Jean was sure that if she didn't get up and turn off the bathroom light, she would be sick. She cut the conversation short, promising to call the next day to let her know how long she'd be in St. Louis, and hung up, practically diving for the bathroom switch and twisting up the knob on the air conditioner so far it rumbled as if it were going to launch itself into the parking lot. The back of her neck was sweaty. But she was tired. So tired. Tired as though she hadn't slept in years. Surely she would sleep now.

But she never did. She flopped around on the bed so much she had to stand up and untwist her pajamas three times. She was too hot. She was too cold. She was hungry. She was weary, so very weary, and scared and wracked with guilt over all the times that Laura wanted or needed something from her and didn't get it. All the times she'd made a mistake as a mother, the memories of each and every one vivid in her mind. Why did mothers do that? she wondered. Why did they carry their guilt around like a banner?

Jean sorely wished she could offer a hug or a kiss and make Laura all better now. But mostly she longed for just one more girls-only vacation outing with her daughter.

By the time Jean arrived at the hospital in the morning, her head so foggy with sleep deprivation she worried that she might nod off in the car on the drive from the hospital to the rehab center, the nurses had long since awakened Laura. Her wrist was set in a cast, and she was wearing her work clothes from the day before. Jean noticed grass stains pressed into the elbows of her tan blazer and some other unidentifiable smudges across the front of her blouse, which also appeared to be missing the top button. Laura hadn't showered, and the places where her cheeks met the undersides of her eyes were deep and bruised-looking. Her hair was pulled back in a loose ponytail, but it looked greasy and stiff. She saw Jean and let out a puff of air.

"Don't tell me Curt called you."

Jean stepped into the room, careful not to get in the way of the nurse who was removing Laura's IV. "He did," she said.

Again with the puff of air, followed by a wince as the nurse pulled out the needle. "Of course he did," she said. "He shouldn't have. It was unnecessary."

Jean wasn't sure what Laura meant by that. He shouldn't have because Laura didn't want her mother to be inconvenienced? Or he shouldn't have because Laura didn't want Jean there at all? Suddenly Jean felt big and unwieldy, taking too much space in the small room.

"I want to know when you're . . . sick," Jean said defensively. "I'm your mother."

The nurse bandaged the back of Laura's hand and gathered up her trash. "I'll be back with instructions," she said, and squeaked out of the room.

"Yes, but you live four hours away. And I'm not sick. I had too many Bloody Marys," Laura said, rubbing the back of her hand. "He's always making such a big deal out of nothing."

"But it wasn't nothing," Jean said. "You were . . . passed out and . . . your wrist is hurt . . . and you didn't tell me that you two split up." Jean realized she was sputtering and not making much sense at all, and once again she wished for Wayne. She always felt calmer when he was nearby, as if he were her voice of reason. He wouldn't have felt awkward. He would have had no problem making his opinions known. And despite their frequent fights and the cavalier way Laura had treated his death, Laura would have wanted Wayne there; Jean felt sure of it. She would have gathered some strength from him.

Laura frowned and waved her off, then reached up and felt her hair, gingerly, as if to not mess it up further, if that were even possible. "Come on, Mom—I'm not the first person to drink too much vodka. Curt's just being a drama queen as usual. I suppose he had Bailey here too."

"I never saw her," Jean said.

"Oh, trust me, she was here, leaving a path of destruction like always," Curt said, and Jean and Laura both turned toward the doorway. Laura immediately rolled her eyes and stood up, as if readying for battle.

"Let's just go," she said, bending to retrieve her purse from the chair next to her bed. "I can't handle being in the same room with ⌐ ⌐ n right now."

"But you haven't gotten your release papers yet," Jean said.

Again Laura waved her off. "I don't need someone telling me how to take care of myself. I've been doing fine for forty years, and I'll do fine now."

Jean tried not to let the "forty years" part of that comment sting. Did Laura really feel as though she'd always been the one caring for herself? Did she discount everything Jean had ever done? Maybe Jean really hadn't done enough. Maybe that was part of the problem. Maybe it was all of the problem. Suddenly she wanted to cry—to curl up in Laura's hospital bed and wrap around a pillow and cry herself to sleep.

"What about rehab?" Jean asked, and Laura stopped, halfway toward the door, and let her arms droop loose.

Her eyes flicked from Jean to Curt and back again. "Look. I drank too much on a weekday. It was wrong, I get that. I messed up. Royally. I probably got myself fired. But don't either of you two act like you've never had too much to drink on a Tuesday afternoon. People make lapses in judgment, and that was mine. I'll fix it. I'm not some street drunk. I'm hardly pissing myself and hallucinating. I don't need rehab."

"Yes, you do," said a voice from behind Curt, and Jean's stomach flipped at the sound of it, her weariness and doubt chased away immediately. Curt took a step to the side and there, standing in the corridor right behind him, was a girl Jean instantly recognized as her granddaughter, Bailey.

"Great," Laura hissed to the floor.

"You were supposed to stay in the car," Curt said.

"But she does need rehab," the girl said, her voice ratcheting up a notch.

Jean gazed at her granddaughter for the first time in years. Thick in the middle, with big bones and fleshy features, a washed-out look as if she too needed sleep, her hair dyed so black it shone blue under the fluorescent hospital lights and cut in blunt, choppy layers. Her jeans were filthy to the point of being crusty, and a rock band T-shirt, black faded to gray, clung to her belly uncomfortably. But underneath it all was the voice, the voice that Jean remembered from the last time she'd seen her. The voice, clear and angelic, was far too young to be saying the things it was saying, and for its owner to be worrying about the things she was worrying about. Jean felt as if her heart split in two as she remembered the sweet little girl who used to climb up into her lap, thrusting books at her with wide, eager eyes, and she tried to pair the image with this strange child who wore her hurt and anger on the outside like a coat.

"Oh, how very melodramatic of you," Laura said. "You must be so proud, Curt, turning her against me like this."

Curt's hands flew up to his shoulders innocently. "I didn't turn anyone against you, Laura. You've done that all by yourself. But she's right. You're an alcoholic and you need rehab. This isn't the first time I've said that to you. Not by a long stretch. Maybe you'll listen if it comes from Bailey."

"And a sixteen-year-old kid would know so much about alcoholism because of why again?" Laura asked.

"Is that a serious question?" Curt answered. "I'll spell it out for you. She knows so much about alcoholism because her mother"—he pointed at Laura—"that's you, is an alcoholic."

"Oh, ho-ho, is that so, Mr. Perfect? Well, let me tell you something about what's wrong with me, then. It isn't the booze. It's not having a husband to rely on. How convenient that you left me right when the parenting got tough. For better or for worse, remember?"

"It's been worse for a long time."

She leveled hard eyes at him, making Jean feel uncomfortable and in the way. "Boy, don't I know it."

They continued bickering, and Jean watched Bailey, who stood behind her father, her eyes moving back and forth between the two of them, as if she were watching them physically duel, but her face was turned down, her hair obscuring it like a veil, and Jean's heart just kept breaking into pieces and more pieces because she could see it. Even if they couldn't see it, she could see it—her daughter and her son-in-law were ruining this little girl.

Jean took a step forward so that she was between them. "You two need to stop doing this in front of Bailey." She sensed Bailey's head tilt up just the slightest at the sound of her name.

"No offense, Mom, but you shouldn't even be here. I appreciate your concern, but this isn't your business," Laura responded. "It's him. If he'd just leave me alone like divorced people do . . ."

"We're not divorced. I'd like to save the marriage, in case you forgot."

"Why? So you can live off my paycheck while you hang out with your buddies all the time and then come home and belittle me for finding a life while you were gone?"

"What the hell is that supposed to mean?"

Jean didn't know what to say. As impossible as marital fights were—and she and Wayne had had their share of them—inserting oneself into someone else's marital fight was even more futile. Her gaze roamed back to her granddaughter, who happened to be looking right at her, a smirk on her face. But it was an unkind smirk, as if she was daring Jean to say her name again—challenging Jean to bring her back into this nonsense.

Jean looked away, uncomfortable under that gaze. "Laura, I think maybe just a couple days to recover might not be such a bad idea," she said.

"So is this an intervention now?" When Jean didn't answer her, Laura shook her head and stared at the tiles for a few moments. "Fine," she said. "Fine. You all want to lock me away in some rehab program? Fine. I'll go. I could use some time off. But when your lives are still shit while I'm gone, you'll see that I'm the one holding it all together. Not you." She pointed at Curt, and then at Bailey and Jean. "Not you. Not you. Just me." She shouldered her purse. "I'll take myself. Don't go with me."

"You don't have a car," Curt said.

"I'll take a cab." And with that, Laura left, pushing past Curt and Bailey and not even bothering to acknowledge Jean at all.

They all stood in silence, not looking at one another, Laura's absence filling up the room almost as much as her presence had. Jean could hear her daughter barking orders loudly at the nurse's station, then the sound fading as she stormed away.

"Should I follow her?" Jean asked.

Curt shook his head. "I'll go with her. Why don't you head over to the restaurant at your hotel and I'll meet you there in an hour?"

Jean nodded and started to say something to Bailey—though she wasn't sure what. Maybe she should ask her about school or tell her that her new hairstyle looked interesting, or just . . . something that a grandmother should say to a granddaughter. A way to show her granddaughter that she was interested, that she cared. And maybe to bring some normalcy to the teen's day, if that was even possible. How did you do normal when your mother was huffing off to a rehab center at that very moment?

But Jean never said anything, and by the time she looked up again, Bailey was gone as if through a magic trick.

FOUR

Dear Margaret Wise Brown:

*My name is Bailey and I am six years old.
My favorite book in the whole world is <u>Home
for a Bunny</u> by you. My mom reads it to me
every night. I love how fluffy the bunny is in
the pictures. I would like to pet him sometime.*

*I only have two questions for you: Why
didn't the bunny have a home? Where was his
mommy bunny?*

Love,
Bailey Age six

*P.S. My mom is writing this for me, because I
don't know how to make all my letters yet.
P.P.S. I also like it when my mommy says the
"Spring, spring, spring" part in her frog voice.
It's really funny.*

B ailey watched from the loft above the living room.
　　She was curled behind the rocking chair, hugging
her knees to her chest, her fingers rubbing against her stub-
bled ankles, digging harder and harder into the skin until she
felt soreness there. She pressed her cheek against her knees, a
tattered copy of *Anne of Green Gables* trapped between her
legs and stomach. It was a book that most of the kids from
school deemed "lame" and "old-fashioned," something they
were forced to read in eighth-grade English, but it had always
been one of Bailey's favorites—a story she returned to when
she felt like her life was slipping out of control. She couldn't
explain it. Not even to herself, really. All she knew was the
book was like an anchor tied around her feet, keeping her
tethered to the ground, where things were safe and pretty.

She would turn the pages, the words practically memorized by now, and picture herself as the imaginative and
determined Anne. She would run her fingers over the
text—*Marilla, isn't it wonderful to know that tomorrow is a new
day with no mistakes in it yet?*—and try to absorb them
through her skin, wishing real life were like that: that you
could show up on someone's doorstep, a mistake, and still
end up belonging. Most of the time she felt like she didn't
belong in her own family, if you could still call it a family.
Could you still call it a family when the dad was living
somewhere else and the mom was living in a bottle and
nobody seemed like your kindred spirit anymore? Most of
the time, she felt like she was the mistake, and every tomorrow was messed up before it even got there.

She'd been reading behind the rocking chair for hours, until her eyes got droopy, but now she was just watching. Just waiting for the world to blow up around her.

After her mother had stomped out of the hospital, and her father had brought Bailey home, she'd "taken off"— stormed out the front door, slammed it behind her angrily, shouted something about how not at all awesome it was that her mom was going to rehab and now she was stuck with *him*, and no, thanks, she'd rather live on the streets alone. It was one of those speeches that sounded good at the time, even though she knew while saying it that she in fact had nowhere else to go but with him.

In truth, she'd walked to the next-door neighbor's back porch and watched until, after way too long of a time for him to ever convince her that he really did care as much as he said he did, her dad barreled outside, calling her name, and then got into his car and squealed away. She'd quietly snuck back into the house, grabbed *Anne*, and hidden behind the rocker. Because, really, where else did she have to go? There were no mistake-free tomorrows for her anywhere.

Her father had blown through again about an hour later, shouting her name angrily. His suit coattails had flapped behind him, showing the little potbelly on which he'd been working so hard for all these years by sitting in front of the TV all alone with his beer and his cell phone, texting nobody, saying nothing, doing nothing, a ghost in the house. He'd gone from room to room, slamming doors and cussing.

He'd never looked up at the balcony.

Why would he? It wasn't like he really wanted to find her, anyway. She'd been right in front of him for so long, yet he'd never wanted to find her, not really. How long ago had she learned that if she wanted to disappear, all she needed to do was get in front of his face?

She'd tried. Oh, how she'd tried. Over the past year, it seemed like she did nothing but try to get her parents to notice her. But they'd been so wrapped up in their own stuff, it was as if she didn't exist, no matter what she did.

The day before, when she'd found out about her mom, she'd had her mom's friend Becky drive her to the hospital and drop her off there. She didn't know what she planned to do. She only knew that she felt like she needed to do something—something to show them that she existed in this too. That she was *there*.

After Becky had dropped her off, she'd stopped at the information desk and found out where her mom was, and five minutes later she was standing next to Laura's bed, watching her chest move up and down beneath the flimsy hospital gown. Even though she hated Laura Butler, Alcohol-Poisoned Hospital Patient, a part of her felt awash with relief that the woman wasn't dead. Not today.

She'd seen her dad out in the hallway, talking on his cell phone. It was sort of amazing that he'd bothered to show up at all. It was so totally unlike him—must have meant things were serious this time.

What he didn't know, and maybe what Laura herself

didn't even know, but what Bailey could totally see, was that her mother had been trekking slowly and steadily downhill since the moment he'd left them four weeks ago. And Bailey's dad had left her to deal with it. Who did that? Who left a sixteen-year-old to deal?

Dealing with it was scary. And it hurt. This was the same mother who'd read bedtime stories to her every night. The same mother who'd sewn a Native American princess costume for her for Halloween. How was that possible? How could the same life include both of those mothers? It wasn't fair. And the unfairness that used to pop up at unexpected times now seemed to rage inside Bailey all the time, which only scared her further.

Bailey had wandered the hospital room, pulling open drawers and rifling through the rolls of paper tape and stacks of gauze and tape measures and little wooden sticks.

She considered a glass jar filled with cotton balls sitting on the counter. She ran her finger along the smooth side of it, imagining herself picking it up and throwing it to the floor. Letting it crash.

She'd been swept over by these strange feelings a lot lately, this need to do something crazy, to be shocking. To make her parents sit up and notice her, even if it was only to complain or punish her once again. At least it was something—a punishment was preferable to being invisible.

She put both hands on the jar, picked it up, felt the heft of it. But her mom's blank face was right there, and the sight of it hurt Bailey's heart too much. She returned the jar and stepped away from the counter. She knew it was best to stop before she did something stupid. These days it seemed like she specialized in stupid. It seemed like her whole life specialized in stupid, and none of it made her feel any better.

She stood awkwardly between the counter and the bed, staring at her mom, willing her to open her eyes and be normal again. Willing her to stop this nonsense and care about things and be a mom. She stared so long, her eyes ached and tears streamed down her cheeks. But the longer she looked on, the more her mom slept, the more Bailey realized that this was real and her mom wouldn't change, not for a messed-up wrist and a little embarrassment of a hospital visit. It would take more.

She heard a shuffle in the hallway and a woman's voice. "Mr. Butler?"

"Hold on, Ted," she heard her dad say, and then, "Yes."

"I've got the phone number for the rehab center for you . . ."

Bailey looked up. Rehab? They were sending her mother to rehab? Nobody had said anything to her about that. What would happen to her if her mom was locked up? Would she have to go with . . . *him*—her dad? The deserter? No way. Never.

She wanted nothing more than to go home, grab her book, sink into the beautiful Prince Edward Island farmland where drunk moms and ghost dads and embarrassment didn't exist. She wanted nothing more than to escape this messed-up family, and the fact that she wanted to made the anger that had been percolating inside of her burst to a boil.

Bailey wiped her cheeks on the back of one arm and turned to the counter. In one swift motion she picked up the jar of cotton balls, held it high over her head, and threw it to the ground with an ear-shattering crash.

She'd dashed out of the room, out of the ward, laughing and crying until her belly hurt.

Her father hadn't been amused. Not in the least. And after they cleaned up the glass, he'd yelled at her for, like, a million hours, but somehow it had kind of been worth it. Even if her mother didn't remember any of it this morning.

And now her mother was in rehab, and her father was looking for Runaway Bailey, and she was behind the chair with a book—*There's such a lot of different Annes in me. I sometimes think that is why I'm such a troublesome person*—listening to the hum of the refrigerator and the whoosh of the air conditioner kicking on and off, and underneath all of that, a faint buzzing of flies in the kitchen. Or maybe she wasn't really hearing those. Maybe she only thought she was hearing them because she knew they were down there, swarming the trash.

Three times the phone rang. If she closed her eyes and imagined it, she could hear the pounding of her mom's feet toward the phone, the beep of the TALK button being pressed, her mom's voice starting low and steady and ending high and shrieky as she took on yet another battle. Who would it be this time? Work? The mortgage company? Maybe it was the phone company, and the ringing would at last be turned off for good. Peace. Peace would be good. She once knew peace. She once knew what it felt like to curl into her mom's chest, touch picture book illustrations, mouth memorized stories along with her mom. That was peace. But it was so long ago, it didn't even seem like a real memory anymore. Like that girl was a fictional character Bailey had once read about and loved.

She wondered where her dad was now, if he was still looking for her. Or maybe he'd gone off to the rehab to make sure her mother didn't detour into some bar along the way. Had it really gotten that far? Was her mother frequenting bars now, begging for brews, belching and tipping sideways off barstools, only to fall into the waiting arms of some trench-mouthed troll? She doubted it. Laura Butler was a lot of things, but tacky wasn't one of them. Laura Butler would rather be dead than be tacky.

Still, her mother hadn't exactly been excited about going to rehab—was anyone, ever?—and he probably was rushing to her, rushing to make sure she got checked in, to exert his will on her or maybe to fight with her some more or to do . . . God knew what.

But whatever it was he was so hot to do, it was not to find Bailey. Not really. Because she'd been just above him the whole time and he'd never bothered to look up.

She'd stayed after he'd left. Had wrapped herself up

into a tighter ball and watched the dust motes swing around on the air. After a while, her mind wandered and she saw herself get up and climb onto the rocking chair, then step over the loft rail and just float there in the sun with the dust. Just twist and turn and ride the invisible breezes of life shifting around her. Weightless. Beautiful. In her daydream, her hair even turned red and floated out behind her in plaits.

She was snapped out of her daydream by the front door opening a second time. She blinked, rubbed her eyes (had she fallen asleep?). She'd lost track of the time, but from the way the shadows had shifted—the swimming dust particles were no longer in her direct line of sight—and the stiffness in her legs, she guessed it had been hours. Her knees now ached from being pulled up against her; her cheek felt hot and bruised from resting against the denim of her jeans; her book had fallen out of her lap and lay beside her now.

The door pushed open farther and her father stepped in again, but then stood to the side and waited, letting her grandmother in after him.

She couldn't even really remember her grandmother. Their visits had been few and far between. They'd almost never driven to Kansas City to see them (her mother called it "That Godforsaken Town"), and her grandparents had only slightly more often come to St. Louis to visit. Her mother had gone to her grandfather's funeral alone. Until this morning at the hospital, she hadn't seen her grandmother in what seemed like forever. She looked smaller than she remembered. And older.

So what was she doing here now? Was this curiosity? Voyeurism? Some misplaced sense of needing to take care of Laura after all these years? Was that what she had waiting for her in the future—a life so messed up, her mother might finally take an interest in it?

Her grandmother stepped in and made a face, and she could see the woman making an effort to not cover her nose.

"It's trash," her father mumbled, leading the way into the living room and reaching over to snap on the light. "I guess she stopped paying the bill. There's loads of it stacked in the garage too. As bad as it is in here, it smells even worse in there."

The grandmother looked dazed, following him at a gait that didn't seem entirely even.

"Besides, there are dishes. Piled up to my chest. Stuff caked on them for weeks. I don't know what . . . Usually Bailey is really good at doing those," her father added.

Usually Bailey is really good at doing everything, she wanted to correct him. *If Bailey doesn't do it, usually it doesn't get done.*

"I had no idea," the grandmother said. "I wouldn't have guessed Laura would let her house go like this."

Trust me, Sober Laura wouldn't, Bailey wanted to cry. *Sober Laura would die if she knew there was somebody in this disgusting house right now. But Sober Laura left the building a long time ago. Gosh, could it have been the night that Ghost Curt suddenly discovered he wanted nothing to do with this life anymore? Why, yes, yes, I think it was.*

And would that also be the night that they had the not-so-sober knock-down-drag-out about who had to take Bailey in this mess?

Why, yes. It was that night too.

Her eyes burned and she blinked hard, savoring the pain beneath her eyelids as they moistened her eyes.

"So let me just get a few of Laura's things, so I can take them over to the clinic," her father said, heading toward the bedroom. His voiced trailed down the hall as he moved. "Make yourself at home."

"Okay," her grandmother said, meekly, and Bailey watched as she moved to the middle of the living room and turned in slow circles. She could hear the grind and thud of her mother's dresser drawers opening and closing, the thunk of the suitcase being dragged out of their closet, the whine of a zipper being drawn back. Usually, the whine of that zipper heralded the beginning of a mirthless vacation to a trendy destination, everyone squinting balefully into the sun until Laura found the mini bar, Curt found the right cable channels, and Bailey found herself curled around a paperback, lonely.

The grandmother stood, arms crossed, for a few more minutes, then leaned over and began stacking papers on the coffee table. As if that would do any good. She picked up a handful of empty soda cans and carried them into the kitchen. After a moment, there came the loud rattle of them dropping into the recycle bin. She came back, brushing her hands, and bent to pick up something in front of the couch. And then something else. And a third thing. She straightened, setting them all on the couch, then shrugged out of her cardigan and balled it up in one hand, used it to edge some dust off the table, and then the fireplace mantel.

Finally, with a shrug, the grandmother sat down on the couch, crossing and then uncrossing her arms uncomfortably, taking it all in, the disaster that the house had become.

And that was when her gaze drifted upward.

They locked eyes.

Bailey jolted, hugged her screaming knees tighter, lifted her head up straight, pushed her back harder against the wall. But there was no hiding up here, not where she was sitting. And that had been what she'd wanted, hadn't it? To be so easily found, if only someone had been interested enough to look?

Neither of them spoke. For what seemed like ages, they just stared, each daring the other to be the first to say or do something, anything. Her breathing seemed loud in her ears. Her heart beat like drums in her chest. But she felt still, so very, very still.

Finally, noises tumbled down the hallway as her father came back, carrying a stuffed suitcase in one hand and a canvas bag in the other.

"I think I got it all," he said. "Whatever's not in here,

she'll just have to do without until she's sober. Not like she's going to any formals or anything."

The grandmother stood. She grabbed her wadded-up, filthy cardigan, and faced him.

Bailey waited for it.

Waited for her grandmother to out her.

Squinched her eyes shut for the firestorm that would erupt from her father. Her fingers wrapped themselves around her book, a talisman against the storm.

"I picked up a bit," was all the grandmother said, though. "It needs some real cleaning, but I didn't think I'd have time to run the vacuum or anything like that. I can stay on a day . . ."

Her father shook his head. "What? Oh, that. No, no. I'll take care of it. Soon as everyone gets settled."

"If you're sure."

"I'm sure. You ready?"

Again, Bailey braced herself, and again there was nothing. The grandmother nodded her consent, and the two of them headed back out the front door, her father going out first in his typical chivalrous manner.

But aside from another quick glance up just before pulling the door closed behind her, the grandmother again did nothing.

Which was confusing.

And maddening.

She finally gets someone to notice her, and they don't bother to say a word.

Why? Why was she so difficult to notice? Why couldn't she be seen? Why did she have to resort to ridiculous tantrums? Why did she care so much?

Bailey turned and scooted backward on her butt, edging out from behind the rocker, straightening her legs out toward the loft rail. Her knees crackled as she straightened them, and she winced.

And then she scooted forward until her legs were bent, and with a rush of breath, kicked her feet forward with all her might. All too easily, a spindle cracked in half, the bottom of it coming loose from its nails and plunging to the coffee table below.

She grinned, scooted down to the other side of the rocking chair, and did it again. And again. And again. Until all the spindles were trashed.

She could hear him, her father, in her head, ranting and raving, practically foaming at the mouth. *Why in God's name, Bailey, would you do this?*

"Because," she said aloud, breathing heavily as she gazed down at the splintered mess below. She dropped her worn paperback, which fluttered to a landing on top of it. "Because you never looked up."

FIVE

"**K**nock, knock!" Jean heard from the entryway just as she pulled a bubbling rosemary chicken potpie out of the oven.

"In the kitchen," she called, shutting the oven door with her knee. She carried the potpie to the counter, which she'd already arranged for the book club meeting. There were potholders scattered about, serving spoons laid out, even a set of salad tongs, just in case. She knew it was supposed to be a quickie do-over meeting, to replace the one she'd cut short when Curt had called. But she also knew the ladies well enough to know that "do-over" did not mean to skimp on the cuisine. She set the pie on a potholder.

"What do I smell?" Loretta said, scuffing through the kitchen in her house shoes, her arms full of a cheese tray. "My nose is doing backflips."

"Cheese?" Jean said, incredulous. "You know Mitzi's going to say it's cheating to just cut up a block of cheese."

"Well, Mitzi can just keep her man hands off it, then."

Jean chuckled, waved at Loretta with a towel. "Stop it. She does not have man hands."

"And cheese is not cheating. See? We're both right." Loretta leaned over the potpie and took a deep breath. "I do believe you are becoming quite the chef, Miss Jeanie. This smells amazing. I can't wait to get my man hands on it."

"Thank you, I'm proud of it," Jean said. "If it tastes as good as it smells, anyway. Did you bring the books?"

"Chuck is pulling 'em over in Wendy's old red wagon as we speak. I told him to leave them on the porch, and everyone can pick one up as they come in. I'm excited to read it. I hear it's causing quite a stir."

Jean picked at the crust, nibbled it. "Doesn't Thackeray always? I thought that's why we read him."

Loretta stole a cheese cube from the tray and popped it in her mouth. "Maybe that's why you read him. I read him because I think he's sexy. Where's the wine?"

"At the table, breathing." Jean sauntered toward the dining room, Loretta following close behind and palming another cheese cube on the way. Jean didn't know any more about wine than she did about cooking, but she thought *letting the wine breathe* was something wine-knowledgeable people did. Sort of the oenophilic equivalent of stirring roasted red peppers into macaroni and cheese. "Sexy? Really? He's kind of . . . loose skinned, don't you think?"

"Oh, honey, at our age who isn't? Loose skin is the new black—haven't you heard?" Loretta saw the bottle, made a noise. "Pour it, Jeanie. It's not the wine that should be breathing. It's me. I should be inhaling a glass right now. Maybe if I drink enough, Chuck will get some ideas."

Poor Loretta. Her marriage to Chuck had once been vibrant and exciting. They were one of those couples everyone envied—a couple with such chemistry, it radiated off them. But after Chuck retired, things changed. He bought a new recliner, and that chair became his mistress. Loretta could barely get him out of it to come to the Sunday dinner table, much less the bedroom. Jean knew Loretta was all talk when it came to men like Thackeray—she loved Chuck dearly and would never lay a hand on anyone but him. But that was the problem—Chuck wasn't laying his hands on anything but the remote, and it drove Loretta crazy. Loretta's way of dealing with it was sexy novels, inappropriate crushes, wine, and lots and lots of jokes.

Jean poured Loretta's wine, and they sat next to each other. "You're full of it today," she said, tipping her glass to clink against Loretta's.

"Aw, what the hell, I'm full of it every day. You're just noticing it today."

"Oh, trust me, I notice it every day," Jean said.

The doorbell rang, followed by the sound of footsteps on the entryway tile. As always, Mitzi and Dorothy arrived together, Dorothy complaining about her sons and Mitzi offering tough-love advice that would make most people wince.

"Hello," Jean called out, moving into the kitchen to help them unload their food.

"You're back," Dorothy exclaimed, wrapping Jean in a quick hug. "How is she?"

Jean shrugged. "I haven't heard a thing. I can only guess no news is good news."

"How odd," Mitzi said, leaning against the counter and eating a piece of cheese. Loretta had been right—not a word about cheating. "Laura of all people. I never would have guessed. She always seemed to have it all together."

Jean nodded. "I never would have guessed it, either." Jean hadn't told them about Curt's leaving Laura, or about Bailey's misbehaving. She'd wanted to let Laura have some semblance of dignity. Or had she been too embarrassed herself? Was she that shallow, that she wouldn't tell her friends about her own troubles, while they told about theirs? No, surely not. It was just about privacy.

As they unpacked, the house began to warm up with heavenly smells—a rich tomato basil bisque, steaming in a Crock-Pot, something sweet and cinnamony in a foil-covered dish by the sink. May, and then Janet, arrived, each clutching a casserole dish in one hand and a book in the other.

"Santa left us goodies on the doorstep, I see," May said, setting down her cheesecakes and waving around the new book. She turned it over and read a blurb from the back. *"Provocative and timely . . . you will never look at your mother the same again.* Oooh, sounds . . ."

"Provocative," Loretta supplied, holding her wineglass in the air.

"And timely," Mitzi added, and she and Loretta giggled.

Dorothy leaned over May's shoulder to read more. *"Thackeray pulls the rug out from under the outdated American family model of Mother Knows Best.* Ugh, who wrote that?" she said.

"My mother would die if she knew I was reading a Thackeray book," Mitzi said. "He's such a liberal, always saving this or that downtrodden somebody or other and going on about war. He's gay too, isn't he?"

"Well, I don't see why that should matter," Dorothy said.

"It doesn't," Mitzi said, a little too defensively to sound completely honest. "I'm just saying if my mother knows best, we wouldn't be reading this guy's book at all."

"We voted," Jean reminded her, knowing Mitzi's democratic convictions would outweigh her concerns about Thackeray. "You voted affirmative, from what I understand."

"Of course I did," Mitzi said, popping a raw carrot into her mouth and moving toward the dining room with a mischievous grin. "I never did anything my mother told me to. Why would I start now?"

"Starting with marrying Blake," Dorothy added, picking up a carrot of her own and following her friend, her Keds looking very white against Jean's hardwood floor.

"Oh, yes, Mother did have a thing against Blake," Mitzi said, pouring herself a glass of wine. She took a sip as Jean opened a second bottle and passed it down the table. "She thought he was—how did she put it?—horny as a dog with a brand-new humpin' pillow. And worse, a Catholic."

The ladies burst out laughing. "Speaking of," Loretta said, pulling Dorothy's book toward her and opening it to the About the Author page, then turning the book out for everyone to see. A photo of Thackeray, sitting in an antique maroon chair, a cigar dangling between the fingers of one hand, his hair brushed straight back in a way that looked wet and overly coiffed, took up half the flap. "Am I the only one who thinks he's sexy?"

"Ew," May said, sauntering in with a glass of ice water. "Yes, you are the only one."

Mitzi picked up the wine bottle and waggled it at May. "What's with the water?"

May looked down at her glass, a hint of disappointment on her face. "Too many calories for a Tuesday. I'm on a diet."

"Lady, you are always on a diet," Loretta said. "And you know what? Gravity takes it all in the end anyway. If I were thirty again, I would strike the word *diet* from my vocabulary. I'd let it all loose like a house made of Jell-O."

"Whatever," May said. "You're fabulous. And I've seen pictures of you and Chuck. You were a rail."

"I think you're beautiful just the way you are, May," Jean said from the kitchen.

May glanced in that direction, blanched, embarrassed, and then gathered herself. She pointed at the photo of Thackeray. "He looks like a sharpei. You can't even see his eyeballs."

"Pshaw," Loretta said. "What do you know? You dated that guy with the out-of-control mole situation."

"Oh, that reminds me," Mitzi said, turning to May. She patted a space at the table, inviting May to sit. "How'd your date go last night?"

May blushed, as she always did when the ladies asked about her love life. Never married and with no kids, she was something of a curiosity for the group. Loretta once claimed that her culinary talents were wasted on having no man to share them with, but Mitzi accused Loretta of being sexist, and a loud debate on the merits of feminism had ensued. Jean had sat back and listened, sipping her wine and thinking that Wayne would have loved to have been a part of it, especially when it ended with everyone eating May's cheesecake bites and drinking the pear wine Mitzi had brought and agreeing that one thing was right— nobody could cook like their curly-haired singleton. Later that same day, after everyone else had left, May had stuck around to help with dishes.

"I have a confession," she had said, twisting a sudsy

washcloth around the rim of a wineglass. "All those guys I've been talking about?"

Jean, who was busy covering leftovers, glanced at her. Even at the end of the day, May's hair was beautiful, effortlessly curly. "Yeah?"

May pressed her lips together, ducked her chin down a bit into the neck of her turtleneck. For someone so young and pretty, May always dressed so buttoned-up and conservative. Or, as Loretta put it, *A sexy librarian horn beast is lurking under there somewhere, but it's trapped by all those buttons and snaps and embroidered appliqués.* "Made up. All of them. Fiction. Even the guy with the moles."

Jean glanced at her again, then a third time. "What?"

"I just . . ." May dipped the glass in the water, held it up to the light. "I gave up. On men. And dating. I never liked it. I don't want to get married. I don't want kids. I like being by myself. But nobody ever understands that. They think that if you're alone, you must be lonely, and I'm not lonely. I mean, look at today, right?" She rinsed the glass and set it, upside down, in the dish rack. "If I were married with kids, I'd probably be way too busy to join a book club. I wouldn't even know you guys."

"But you're only with us once a month. That's hardly the same," Jean said.

"But it's all I need," May said.

She picked up another glass and dunked it in the sink. "I don't know. It's just . . . It's such a scary world. I'm afraid to bring more people into it. Half the time these guys . . .

They ick me out. They're either gross or they're over-grown babies. They're divorced because they cheated or they have no job and . . . God, to think about bringing a daughter into this world to face all that . . . I just . . . can't."

"I can see that," Jean said. More than May even knew, probably.

May let the glass float, and made a face at Jean over her shoulder. "I make up fake disastrous dates so I can stay home with my cat and eat takeout in my pajamas. That's not normal, is it?"

Jean and May gazed at each other for a moment; then both burst out laughing. "No, I suppose it's not," Jean said. "But whatever works for you is what is normal, right?"

"Right," May said, going back to the dishes. "And I don't make them up for me. It's just that . . . the ladies, they all want to know how it's going. It's like they need proof that I'm at least trying to find myself a husband. So I just give them what they want, you know? And I make them all crazy bad dates so I won't look weird for not wanting to go on another one. I figure they're little white lies, so what does it matter? This way I don't get judged. There's probably something wrong with me. Do you think?" She went back to washing her glass.

"Of course not," Jean had replied. "Nobody's required to do it a certain way. If you're happy, you're happy. It's possible to be happy alone. Look at me." She'd meant to finish the sentence with something hopeful like, *Look at me! I'm alone and I'm happy!* but she couldn't make herself say the words. She was alone. But, unlike May, she cared. She still longed for him every day, like a silly fairy-tale princess. And not for *a man*. She longed for one specific man: Wayne.

"Mitzi would think there's something wrong with me," May had said.

"Mitzi thinks there's something wrong with everyone," Jean had answered, and they'd laughed.

She'd never told anyone about her conversation with May that day, not even Loretta, with whom Jean shared everything. Had Wayne been alive, she might have told him, but otherwise, she'd seen May's doubts and fears as their secret, and she'd stopped jumping on the when-are-you-getting-married bandwagon whenever the others brought it up. Which they always did. And today was no different.

"Yeah, tell us about the date," Dorothy urged. "Was it love at first sight?" Jean waited for the lie.

May shrugged, stroking the Thackeray cover. "He was bald. Well, not bald-bald, but balding, so he's still in denial about it."

"Uh-oh, comb-over city," Mitzi said in a low voice.

"Exactly. And he wore a lot of brown."

"What's wrong with brown? I like brown," Jean said. Of course, she was wearing a brown plaid flannel shirt with a brown turtleneck underneath it, which May took one look at and cracked up.

"What? Brown is fine," Jean insisted.

"But brown and balding on a first date is not," Mitzi finished. She lifted her wineglass and clinked it against May's water glass. "I'm with you on that one, sister. Kick him to the curb before he brings out the white socks and black shoes."

"Can we get back to the dog humping a pillow?" Loretta said, turning the book around again and tapping it on the table. "I do not see sharpei."

"I think he's kind of handsome," Janet said, and everyone turned at once, suddenly reminded that she was in the room with them. This happened often. Janet would finally get the courage to squeak out something, and everyone would stop what they were doing and stare at her. It couldn't have made her shyness any better. She sipped on her water and swallowed much harder than she needed to. Redness crept up her neck.

"Well, finally!" Loretta said, a little too late to be seamless. She set the book down and gestured toward Janet. "Someone who knows sexy. The rest of you have no taste."

"Oh! Speaking of no taste," Dorothy said, gulping down the last of her wine. "I heard the ex's skank got a job at Lookie Lou's."

"Before we get off task," Jean began, but it was already too late. You didn't bring up an establishment like Lookie Lou's and not get a reaction. Not in this group, anyway.

"No way!" May gasped. "The stripper place?"

Dorothy nodded. "That was my reaction too. Who wants to see that old broad take her clothes off?"

"You mean other than Elan," Loretta pointed out.

"Well, Elan's standards plummeted the moment he turned fifty and bought that dumb motorcycle of his," Dorothy said.

Loretta rolled her eyes. "That thing's not a motorcycle. It's a glorified bicycle. All it needs is tassels on the handlebars."

"I'm pretty sure the tassels are on his girlfriend, if you know what I mean," Mitzi said.

"How'd you find out?" May asked.

Dorothy made a face. "You'd rather not know."

Which, of course, made everyone want to know.

"Justin saw her there," Mitzi finally volunteered. "Can you imagine? Busting into a strip club with your fake ID, all ready to get your excitement, and there's your dad's girlfriend? Hi, Stepmom! When's dinner?" She cackled and upended her drink.

"For real?"

Dorothy nodded miserably, then turned to Jean. "We gonna eat soon? This conversation is going to turn my stomach."

"Of course," Jean said, jumping up from her chair and herding everyone back into the kitchen. "Before everything gets cold." Not that Jean cared too much about cold these days. Lately she'd taken to eating cold soup out of the can while standing over the kitchen sink. What was the point of dirtying a bunch of dishes for one person? Although, on the inside, she supposed she knew that was hardly healthy behavior.

Truth was, she wasn't really in the mood for food right now, either. She'd been too into everyone's stories. The dating, the ex-husband, the mother, even Loretta's creepy adoration of R. Sebastian Thackeray. Keeping tabs on her friends' lives helped her feel connected. And helped keep her mind off Laura.

"So, Jean, how is Laura, really?" Mitzi finally asked as they all sat down around their plates.

"I haven't talked to her since the hospital," Jean said. "And Curt hasn't called me in two weeks. I'm assuming everything is status quo."

"Is she still in there?"

Jean shrugged. "Who knows? They don't exactly keep me in the loop. And I hate to bother them. Curt seems . . . frazzled, I guess."

"Who'd blame him?" May said. "Sounds like his life is a shambles right now. I think I'd be frazzled."

"Both of their lives," Jean said. "My granddaughter, Bailey, is apparently acting out too. Being a real problem, from the sound of it."

"Aw," Mitzi said, and clucked her tongue. "Poor thing. Probably doesn't know what hit her."

Jean shrugged, remembering the sadness she saw in her

granddaughter's eyes that day she'd spotted her up in the loft. There was something about those eyes that begged for help, yet at the same time seemed to also threaten. In the end, Jean couldn't bring herself to tell Curt he'd seen her up there. She felt as if it wasn't her battle, and Bailey wanted it that way. She couldn't pretend to know what was going through Bailey's mind, or what the girl was thinking and feeling. Surely she felt lost and alone. Surely she missed her mother. But Jean couldn't shake the nagging feeling of guilt for not reaching out to her when she could have. She wasn't sure she'd done the right thing. "I'll call them again tonight, see if I can find out what's going on," she said.

"It's all you can do," Loretta agreed.

"Maybe you haven't heard anything because it went so well she's already out and back at home," May added.

"Hopefully so," Jean said, but deep down inside she knew it meant anything but that.

After lunch, they convened in the living room, where everyone sprawled back against the thick cushions, complaining about how full they were, followed by how amazing Mitzi's egg rolls had been, and flavorful Dorothy's sliders, and as always they joke-guessed about who was going to get May's "extra protein" in their cheesecake bite.

"I'm wearing a bandanna when I cook now, you guys. I told you," May said, but everyone continued to giggle anyway.

And then, since Jean's emergency trip to St. Louis had derailed their last meeting and they had no book to critique, they all agreed on reading the first few chapters of *Blame* aloud, Mitzi starting, followed by Dorothy, and rounded up by Loretta, who made everyone laugh with her sultry, deep Thackeray voice.

"Gross, you sound like Count Chocula trying to get it on with Franken Berry," Mitzi said, which elicited more giggles, especially after Loretta retaliated by smacking Mitzi's arm playfully with her book.

Too quickly, the meeting was over. The dishes were washed and put away, and Jean was too full to eat dinner, too tired to watch TV, too wired to read.

She ended up taking an early shower to wind down, and then wrapping herself in her fluffiest terry-cloth robe and bunny slippers. She turned on the television and held the Thackeray book in her lap while watching the evening news, her wet head still wrapped in a towel.

"Well, Wayne, we've got a doozy this month," she said aloud, and held up the book as if to show it to someone in the room. She opened it and began reading. *"Johnna Bland's life was a travesty. She'd been hooking since she was thirteen, stuffing her grand, vellicating thighs into clothes three times too small, counting on her meth addiction to keep her thin, to keep her pretty, too blind to realize how not thin and not pretty she already was. Not even to her daughter, Blanche, whose grandest hope was to hook half as well as her mother someday, to gather up a little cash and have a little fun before unceremoniously killing herself on a subway track.*" She frowned at the page. "Dear God," she said, then looked upward toward the ceiling again. "We're in for a long one, I'm afraid," she said. She let out a long sigh. "I sure wish you were here to read it with me."

The day Wayne died wasn't the day Jean felt her life spin out of control. That actually happened on the day he was diagnosed.

She would never forget the silent car ride home from the hospital. She'd driven to the appointment, because Wayne hadn't been feeling well and wanted to push his seat back and recline, maybe grab a quick nap while she traversed cross-town traffic. But on the way home from the hospital, he'd snapped his seat back into its upright position and had simply stared out the window, the only sounds being the rushing of the heater and the muted noises of the cars around them—a thumping bass here, a honk there. He was thinking. Jean knew the set of her husband's jaw when he was ruminating. But she didn't ask him what he was thinking about. She already knew.

She couldn't remember blinking once on the way home.

They'd sat that way all night—side by side at the dinner table, on the couch watching a movie, in bed reading paper-backs. All in total silence, as if neither of them knew what to say to the other. *It'll be all right* would be a lie. *I'm scared* would be too honest for either of them to handle. *Maybe it's a mistake* would be so optimistic as to be idiotic. It wasn't a mistake, and it wouldn't be all right ever again, and they were both frightened as hell, and to admit any of those things aloud would be to say a truth that neither was ready, or prepared, to face.

"We need to tell the kids," Jean finally said after Wayne had flipped the switch on the bedside lamp and they'd both lain in the dark, silent, side by side, eyes wide-open and staring at the ceiling.

"I know," he'd responded. "Can we wait?"

"The doctor said it could be just months." Jean almost choked on the word *months*, her voice wavering at the end of it. "We want to give them time. To say . . ." *Good-bye. Give them time to say good-bye.* But her throat wouldn't let the word out.

"But I don't want it to be just months, Jeanie," Wayne had said, and he'd sounded almost like a little boy rather than the fearless man she'd known and loved for decades. She'd reached out under the covers and touched his hand.

"I know," she said. "Neither do I." And she'd swallowed and swallowed because she didn't want to cry in front of him. She didn't want his fears confirmed, that he would leave her broken and alone. She'd wanted him to feel she could take his death. That she could handle it and be okay. She wanted to gift him that peace.

They'd called both kids the next evening on the speakerphone. Wayne had told them himself, breaking down halfway through the sentence each time. Kenneth had cried like a baby, had blubbered on about how his dad was a fighter and he could beat this. Laura had sounded distant, distracted, as if not really taking in the news.

"Whoa, that's rough," she'd said. "How long?"

Wayne had squeezed his eyes shut. "They're saying not very, I'm afraid. I'd like to see Bailey soon."

"Sure, yeah," she'd said, but in a very *yes, dear* sort of way. "Wow. Cancer. You're what, sixty-seven?"

"Yes," Wayne had answered.

"A hundred years ago, you would've been thought of as an extremely old man," she'd said. "For what it's worth."

Wayne had glanced at Jean and then frowned, a perplexed crease between his eyebrows. "I suppose you're right," was all he'd said.

That's Laura, Jean had told Wayne when they hung up. *That's her way of dealing with hard stuff. You know how she is. If she can't solve it, she doesn't know what to do with it.*

But given events of the past couple of weeks, Jean couldn't help but wonder if maybe Laura had been drunk that night too.

And now look at her. Sitting in a rehab center out in a St. Louis suburb somewhere, fighting with her husband, fighting with her daughter, fighting with bill collectors, fighting to keep her job. So much fighting.

Jean wondered now if Laura was feeling like she had felt back when Wayne was diagnosed, back when he first got sick. She wondered if Laura felt like she was swimming and swimming, taking in water with each choking breath, but never getting anywhere. She wondered if she felt jellyfish stinging her gut and sharks nipping at her heels, prodding her to go on, to hurry up, to get on top of things. She wondered if that was why Laura had gotten to where she was right now—just trying to get out of the damn ocean. Just trying to get to the beach where she could dry off and get her wits about her.

Not that it mattered. You could lose control, but that didn't mean you got to check out of your life. It didn't mean you let your teen daughter drown because you couldn't hack the temperature of the water.

Jean decided not to read any more aloud after all. She laid the book in her lap and leaned her head back against the sofa cushion, closed her eyes, imagined what Wayne's reaction to the Thackeray book would have been. *Jeanie,* she could hear him say, *I'm trying to find a greater truth here. There has to be a life truth he's trying to reflect back at us with this.* How Wayne had always done that—tried to find more in the books they read than was actually there. He'd felt so strongly about not only reading them, but also learning from them. She'd once joked that he could find a greater life truth in a Dr. Seuss book, so what had he done? Come home from the library with a Dr. Seuss book and dissected it for her, page after silly page. *You see, Jeanie, this book is, at its core, about courage in the face of adversity,* he'd said. *It's actually very sophisticated.* And then he'd started the book over, reading in the voice of a Shakespearean actor. He'd had her laughing so hard by the end of it that pain stabbed her sides, but she'd also been in awe of him. Of what he could do. Surely that was a gift. It felt like a gift to her, anyway.

The phone rang, jarring her out of her thoughts.

She got up, absentmindedly carrying the book with her, and set it on the table next to the phone.

"Hello?"

"Jean, it's Curt again."

Her heart sank. The last time Curt had called, it had been bad news. And he didn't sound any better this time. "Yes?" she asked timidly.

"It's Bailey."

"Bailey?" This took Jean aback. She was expecting it to be about Laura. "What happened? Is she okay?"

A pause, a deep breath. "Depends on what you mean by okay. Physically, she's fine, yes."

Jean waited for more, but he didn't elaborate. What did that mean, *physically, she's fine*? "Good," she said, unsure what else to say. Unsure what else would make him keep talking, or even if she wanted him to. Seemed like the only time Curt talked to her these days he was saying something that almost hurt her to hear.

"She's a pain in the ass," he finally added. "Out of control. I don't know what to do with her, and I can't . . . I just can't handle her anymore. She needs her mother, but we all know what happened there."

Jean sank into the chair next to the phone. Wayne had called it her "necessary chair," after the argument they'd had over whether to buy it. *Where in Sam Hill's name are you going to put it?* he'd asked. *In the telephone nook,* she'd responded, proud of herself for naming the little alcove in the hallway where the telephone jack was. *What the heck for?* he'd pressed. *To sit on while using the phone,* she'd replied as if he were dumb. *If you're going to have a telephone nook, it's necessary to have a chair to sit on.* Of course, not once had anyone ever sat on it. They'd simply carried the phone to whatever chair or bed or bench in the house they wanted to sit on. Now, finally, Jean was sitting in the necessary chair, and no one was there to notice it.

"Have you taken her to see someone?"

"See someone? No, listen, that's not why I'm calling."

"Okay?"

"I'm calling because I need to ask a favor."

"Okay?" she repeated.

"I need you to take her."

"Take who?"

"Bailey."

"Take her where?"

His voice grew impatient. "To your house. I need her to stay with you for a while. I can't control her, and it's starting to interfere with my work and just until Laura is back up on her feet and we can figure out what to do, can you take her? Can she live with you?"

Jean's mind swam. Take Bailey? Here? She hadn't had a child in this house in so long. She glanced across the alcove at the flower oil painting Wayne had bought at an estate sale years ago. It was all browns and deep reds and ochre, and it was lumpy and ugly. Something that screamed, *Old person lives here.*

"Well . . . maybe you should take her to a therapist of some kind," she stammered. "I'm not sure what I can . . ."

"I can take her to a therapist, but I can't be here twenty-four-seven to make sure she's not destroying my house. I have to work sometime or I'll lose my job, and then where will she be? A therapist can't help you if you're starving."

"Destroying your house . . . ?" Again, Jean glanced around her house, getting up from the necessary chair and walking into the kitchen, feeling like she was floating. Most things in her house hadn't been moved in years, except to dust under. Her kitchen was country themed with gingham and rattan and dark wood. Her dining room table could seat fourteen and was flanked by perfectly placed porcelain trinkets—her Made in Occupied Japan collection. Wayne's bar . . . She had never touched any of the aged bourbons or the crystal decanters. He'd been so proud of his bar. He'd loved playing bartender during their gatherings. They were dusty and fragile now.

Curt breathed hard into the phone. "She dumped a gallon of milk on my hardwood floor and left the house for the day. An entire gallon. Ruined the wood. She carved the words *no peace* in the bathroom door with nail clippers. She . . . She just does the most bizarre stuff, and I think it's me. If I tell her to stay in, she sneaks out. If I tell her to leave the house, she locks herself in her bedroom. Once, I told her to do her homework, and she ate it. Balled it up and stuck it in her mouth and ate it. Then barked at me. And she wouldn't stop. Just barked and barked and barked until I finally left the room. I can't ground her. I can't do anything with her. You punish her, and she either ignores you completely or just doesn't care. She's so willful and she hates me." He let out a flat chuckle. "Her mother is the one putting this family through hell, and it's me Bailey hates."

Jean had left the bar and had gone down to the living room. She sank into the couch, her fingers automatically drifting over to Wayne's glasses on the end table and running along the cold metal frame.

"It sounds like she needs help," she said. "She probably has a lot of anger."

"Yes, she does," he said. "She does need help. And we'll get her that help as soon as Laura gets out and everything is back to normal, I swear. Until then . . . I'm the one who needs your help, Jean. Please. I need you."

Jean felt dizzy and confused. It seemed there were so many questions that weren't being answered here. So many questions that weren't even being asked. She was certain there were more, but her mind kept coming up blank. "Laura's getting out soon? You've heard from her?"

"Well, there's not a definite date yet, no. But she'll want out of there as quickly as possible. She's smart. And she'll be motivated."

"But she doesn't know about Bailey."

"She's actually the one who suggested I call you. She

definitely would rather Bailey be with you than my parents."

"Wouldn't she prefer Bailey stay with you than go anywhere?"

He paused. "Jean. I need you. *We* need you. All of us. Please."

Jean took one last glance around the room, then squinched her eyes shut. This house didn't know chaos. She didn't know this child at all—this problem child.

But Bailey was her granddaughter.

Her only granddaughter.

And Wayne would have done it. He wouldn't have hesitated for a second.

"Okay," she said. "When are you bringing her?"

SIX

Dear Beverly Cleary,
Hi. I am Bailey. I like to read. My mom gav
me one of your books one day when she was
cleening out the groj. I don't rember wich one it
was but I think it was ramona the pest. I thot it
was going to be boring becos it was wrote a long
time ago. But I loved it and I started reading all
of your books. I am sometimes a pesk like
ramona. I am going to ask for mor books for
Crismas. Do you have any sujeshions?
                    Bailey Butler
                    Age 7

Bailey had been in Kansas City exactly twice in her life. Both times were to visit her grandparents at their house. They kept Lysol on the tops of their toilet tanks.

Her mom and dad had made fun of it. Lysol, as decor. Nice.

Now she was going to be living there? Had the man lost his mind?

She'd tried screaming, raging. It didn't work. He'd only continued cramming her things into suitcases—putting his dad hands all over her underwear. Gross. Like he knew what items were important to her. He packed about a thousand pairs of socks, as if she could care, but not one of her books. Left her bookshelf completely alone. Did he really not ever notice that she always had a book in her hand? Did he really think she'd need her snow boots in June, but not one paperback?

She threw things. She broke the few items in his depressing apartment that looked like they could maybe be considered important. He didn't care.

You won't listen to my rules; maybe you'll listen to your grandmother's, he'd said.

Why? Why would she listen to anyone? Nobody ever listened to her. Not ever.

Here's a rule for you: Don't drink and drive.

Here's another: Don't abandon your daughter and leave her to live with someone who doesn't have the first clue about rule #1.

Oh, and here's a good one: If you do, don't expect her to think you're the World's Greatest Dad or anything.

Eventually, she gave up. He was shipping her off, and if nothing else, at least now she didn't have to keep pretending she was "doing something productive"—her dad's newest catchphrase. And it wasn't like her grandmother was going to be too hard to fool. The woman sat in the same room with her for, like, thirty minutes before she ever looked up.

Although. She was the only one who ever did look up. There was at least that.

But she didn't say anything about seeing her. Bailey was still trying to figure that one out.

He left. Said he was just running out real quick to get some supplies for the road trip to Kansas City. But it was good for him to be gone, even for that amount of time. She wanted him away from her. She was so angry with him, her eyeballs hurt.

She lay back on his bed, as she'd done many afternoons when she'd skipped school to come home and nap. He'd spared no expense in buying his new bachelor pad duds, and the bed was ten times fluffier and more comfortable than the one she had at home, or the garage sale furniture he had for her here.

She clutched her rescued, but beat-up, *Anne of Green Gables* to her chest, flipping one corner of the pages over and over again for the satisfying *brrr* sound, and stared at the ceiling fan until she could swear it began to move on its own accord under her watery gaze. What did it matter, anyway? What was there for her here? What was left of her life? Where had those days gone, the ones where her mom would make peppermint cookies and play music on the stereo, and they would dance around, laughing, maybe dusting or vacuuming, making the house smell good and fresh? Where were those nights snuggled up to her mom's chest, listening to that story about the bunny who needed a home? God, she had made her mom read that book so many times. She was in love with the story, but she was more in love with the moment. The tenor of her mom's voice, the smell of her perfume, the way her toes looked smushed up in her work panty hose—the memories hurt so much, but she couldn't stop thinking about them. She hadn't been able to stop thinking about them since her mom started being too drunk at night to take off her panty hose at all.

She dropped the paperback on the floor beside the bed, brought her hand up to her mouth, and poked a cigarette—filched from the gym teacher's desk drawer on the last day of school—between her lips. Then with a shaky hand, realizing that she was now embarking on a whole new level of messing with the system, she brought a lighter—stolen from the same desk—to the cigarette and thumbed it on.

The smoke burned a thousand times worse than she thought it would. She thought it would be like the wood smoke that drifted off her mom's fire pit on Sangria Sundays, but instead it felt like hot liquid pouring down into her lungs, and she coughed and wretched until she felt like her eyes would pop out, curling up onto one side and pressing her cheek against her dad's superfirm pillow, clutching her stomach with her free arm.

This. This was good. Physical pain to blot out the emotional pain. Bailey knew that was a dangerous game to play, but she couldn't help it. The pain made her feel alive, made her feel *there*. It had been so long since she'd been present, she sometimes wondered whether maybe she wasn't a figment of someone's imagination.

But the pain passed and then came the light-headedness; it felt so good to be weightless and out of contact with the world, so she pulled on the cigarette again and coughed again, but less. So she took another drag and another, perfecting various holds on it—perched between the first knuckles of her index and middle fingers, squeezing it between her thumb and index finger—and flipping ashes on the comforter, enjoying watching embers shrivel away the fabric into little holes. She tried to imagine herself as the smoking antagonist from one of her books, but, frustratingly, found that she couldn't think of any. Why didn't bad guys ever smoke? Finally, the butt was nearly down to the filter, and she wished more than anything that she'd taken the whole pack.

But there were always cigarettes to be found. Anything was easy to steal. For now, she'd just have to be happy with the relaxed dizziness that this one had given her.

There was a sound of metal clicking against the lock on the front door, and she knew her peaceful weightlessness was over. It was time to head out west. She needed to take some of those stupid socks out of her suitcase. She needed to find her bunny book. If she wasn't going to have a home, at least she'd have an old friend who'd been there, done that to help her along.

But first, she had a reputation to protect. She had to make the man feel justified in yet another abandonment. She was Bailey Butler, Pain in the Ass. Bailey Butler, Problem Child. Bailey Butler, Worthless Kid. She couldn't go without leaving him a little reminder that she had once been here. She sat up, giving her father's pillow one last appreciative pat, then drew back the comforter and snuffed out the cigarette right onto the pillow.

The scent of burned fabric was intoxicating.

SEVEN

Jean wasn't sure who was more nervous—she or her granddaughter.

Her *granddaughter*. It was so weird to say that word. Not that she didn't know she had one; of course she did. She just had always thought of the girl in generic terms. As "the Granddaughter," not as Bailey, the girl who would be showing up at her house any moment.

Cookies. In the end, she'd baked cookies. Not because she loved cookies, nor because she knew Bailey liked them, but because cookie baking seemed to her an undeniably grandmotherly thing to do.

So she'd baked them. Thick chocolate chip cookies, made with real butter and mixed by hand rather than by mixer, because she'd read that hand mixing them made them softer coming out of the oven. If nothing else, the house smelled like Christmas when Bailey arrived.

Jean put on her best smile when she opened the door. "Hello!" she'd cried out, probably far too loudly, far too welcomingly. Kids could sense fear—she knew this!—and if that was true, surely Bailey could sense terror coming off Jean. "Come in, come in!" She shuffled backward and gestured with her whole arm, realizing that she looked a bit like one of those game show models while she was doing it. *Show Bailey what's behind door number three, Jeanie! A new house!*

"Sorry we're late," Curt said, pushing past her, lugging a big, heavy-looking suitcase in each hand. "Someone decided to set fire to my bed right before we left."

"Fire?" Jean repeated, reaching out to help him with the luggage. He just kept walking, and again she was left with her arms waving around. "Is everything okay?"

Bailey stood on the front porch, clutching a pillow and blanket to her stomach. She rolled her eyes, which were ringed with massive amounts of makeup, and it was smudged and running, as if she'd been crying. She stood as if she'd grown roots, looking at the ground at Jean's feet.

"Come on in," Jean said again, brightly, but still the girl didn't move.

"Yes, everything's fine. Luckily," Curt said angrily. "Where do I put this?"

Jean jumped. "Oh, right. The guest bedroom is upstairs, first room on the right. You can just set your things in there and put it away in your own time." She directed the last sentence to Bailey, who still wasn't moving. "The comforter is a black bear pattern. I hope that's okay with you."

At the same time, Curt, who was trudging up the stairs, yelled over his shoulder. "Get in the goddamn house. You're letting the air-conditioning out."

Jean laughed uncomfortably. "I don't mind. It's okay, really. Take however long you nee—"

Slowly, hesitantly, Bailey entered the house, her hands still buried under cloth and pillow. Jean moved out of her way, and then shut the door behind her. Once Bailey was in, the atmosphere seemed very, very awkward, and Jean wasn't sure what to say.

Jean had never been particularly at ease around children, not even her own. When Kenneth and Laura were little, it had seemed that all of Jean's friends simply adored being mothers, that their lives were finally complete. But Jean had always felt clumsy and unsure. She loved her children with everything she had; she was just never sure how to turn that feeling into action. She felt continually judged—sized up other mothers, sized up by her children, especially Laura. She feared that she never quite hit the mark. Now, with Laura in rehab and Bailey standing ill at ease in her foyer, she wondered if she never did hit it. If she never would. She certainly had never predicted that she would be questioning her parenting skills in her sixties.

"I made cookies," she said, glad that she'd done it now, glad for the talking point.

Bailey swiveled her head slowly toward Jean and gave her a nonplussed look. "You do that for all your guests?"

she asked, and Jean was taken aback by how flat and cold and deep her granddaughter's voice sounded.

Jean blinked a few times. "I—I have some friends I cook for sometimes," she said. "And I suppose I've made cookies once or twice . . ."

Bailey made a sniffing noise and once again rolled her eyes. Jean had never seen someone roll her eyes so much, as if life itself were such a disappointment, such a lame attempt at everything, there was almost no point dealing with it.

"Would you like one?" Jean asked, heading for the kitchen and hoping Bailey would follow her there.

There was a long pause, and Jean noticed she was walking alone. But she kept going, kept moving forward, because that was what she did best ever since Wayne died, wasn't it? Kept going, never looking back, because what she might find back there might be even more frightening than what she saw ahead.

"She asked you a question," she heard Curt growl. There was a muffled thumping as he came down the carpeted stairs. Then he was in the kitchen, the opposite of his daughter: all pumping limbs and whipping, hard energy.

"No," Jean heard from the entryway.

"No, what?" Curt boomed, making Jean jump. He plucked a cookie off the cooling rack.

Bailey's voice came back, only this time sarcastic and squeaky-high. "No, thank you, dear Granny," she said, and Jean could feel her face flush, as if she were being made fun of, though she was pretty sure Bailey was actually mocking her father.

Curt shook his head. "You see?" he said around a mouthful of cookie. "You see what I'm dealing with? She didn't say one pleasant word the entire four hours it took to get here. She cussed me out for the first hour and a half. She locked herself in a gas station bathroom and took a nap. She ground candy into my floorboard with her feet. How her mother didn't see what was happening with this child . . ." He shook his head, shoved more cookie into his mouth, his jaw working around the bite angrily. Jean wondered if he could even taste what he was chewing. "Anyway, thank you for letting her stay here. It will do us all good, I think, to get away from one another for a while."

"Fly away, fly away, little ghostie," Jean heard muttered from the entryway. She leaned forward and craned her neck to see Bailey, still holding the pillow and blanket, turning in slow circles on the tile and gazing up at the chandelier as she did so. "It's what ghosts do best," Bailey continued, so softly Jean almost couldn't make out what she was saying.

"Is she . . . Does she . . . ?"

He held up one hand. "She's weird, but she's not as weird as she wants everyone to believe she is. It's an act. An attention tactic."

Maybe she needs some attention, then, Jean thought, though she didn't say it aloud. The truth was, she had no idea what this strange child needed. No idea at all.

"Okay. So she's got her laptop and her cell phone. She knows how to get ahold of me if she needs me. And you can call if you need anything. But hopefully you won't have any problems." He raised his voice for this last part, aiming it toward Bailey.

"Boo!" came the echoey return from the entryway.

He ignored the noise completely and dug his wallet out of his back pocket. "Here's her insurance card," he said, and handed a white card over to Jean. "And here's a couple hundred bucks to get us through the first few weeks. I can get you more next Tuesday if you need it."

Jean held the money in her palm as if she didn't know what to do with it, and realized that she really didn't. You couldn't take away the generic feel of a grandchild you didn't know by baking cookies, for God's sake. What did Bailey need? Did she need razor cartridges and shampoo and tampons? Did she like to eat Pizza Rolls? What did she want for breakfast, and did she remember to bring socks? Would she need a swimsuit? Jean almost felt dizzy under all the questions she'd forgotten to ask before agreeing to take Bailey in.

"And you have my phone number," Curt was saying, pressing along with his instructions, even though Jean feared she wasn't absorbing them. "She doesn't have her driver's license, so don't let her drive your car. She can't be trusted with a vehicle, anyway. I'll check in later this week, see if you need anything else, and . . ."

Jean closed her eyes and envisioned Wayne standing

next to her. The young, healthy Wayne. The Wayne whose blood cells were still marching along just fine in there, eating up the bad stuff. The Wayne who raised their two kids and who built the log fence around their backyard and who never put up with anybody's crap. She tried to channel him, to adopt his force of energy. *Please, Wayne,* she beseeched in her mind, *please help me deal with her. Please help me know how.*

Eventually, Curt finished talking, thanked her again, and announced that he had to get back to St. Louis, back to work. Jean bagged him up a couple of cookies to eat on the road and followed him to the door.

He stopped when he pulled up parallel to Bailey, but didn't make a move to reach out to her, though he looked like he wanted to, looked like he thought he should. "I'll call," he said, and Jean wondered if that was the best he could do, the closest he could get to being sentimental about leaving his only daughter behind. Again she was struck with a wonder, a fear, that this was exactly how she'd handled sentimentality with Laura, exactly how she'd handled it with Wayne and Kenneth too. Was it possible that Laura had grown up so accustomed to a lack of hearts and flowers that she attracted a man just like her? Was it possible that nobody ever told Bailey that they loved her?

"I'll be on pins and needles," Bailey responded, trying to sound tough, but coming off as only flat and hurt. Jean thought she saw the girl clutch the pillow and blanket closer to her stomach.

"Don't give your grandmother any trouble," he said. "Got that?"

At first it looked like Bailey wouldn't answer at all. She rocked herself side to side so minimally it was almost not there—Jean almost felt like she was the one who was swaying rather than her granddaughter. But then finally, "Sir, yes, sir," she said, in that same odd, flat voice.

And that was when things got really awkward. Jean almost felt as if she needed to leave them alone, but she was at the door—one hand on the doorknob—and Curt stood between her and the kitchen, Bailey between her and the stairs. She was trapped in their uncomfortable moment, unable to get out.

Curt raised his hand just a few inches, as if he thought he might put it on Bailey's shoulder, or maybe the top of her head, but then he changed his mind. But feeling the change in movement, Bailey immediately stopped rocking and stood still and tense, dipping her chin down into the pillow and blanket she held. And after a few moments that seemed to stretch into eternity, he finally just stepped forward and through the front door.

"I'll call," he said once again, and then jogged off the front porch steps and to his car.

After Jean shut the door, it was as if the uncomfortable moment had been transferred from Curt to her as he whisked past. Suddenly she didn't know what to do— whether she should talk or reach out or just leave well enough alone. Whether she should just go about her business and risk Bailey standing in the same spot in the entry-way for hours, or maybe even weeks, until Curt eventually came back to collect her. Or whether she should grab the child by the elbow and lead her to the cookies, which now seemed like the dumbest idea ever. Who bakes cookies for an event such as this?

"Do you need me to show you where the guest bed-room is?" she asked.

Bailey shook her head no.

"It has its own bathroom," Jean offered, "so you'll have all the privacy you need."

Bailey continued pressing her chin into the pillow.

"Are you hungry at all?"

Another head shake.

"Your room also has a TV. There's no satellite on that one. But you can watch satellite on the big TV anytime you want. I hardly ever use it. That's downstairs. Through the kitchen and dining room."

Nothing. Maybe no matter what she did, Bailey would just stand here. Maybe that was how it was going to end up regardless. The blanket that was looped over Bailey's arm shifted, and Jean saw what looked like the corner of a child's book peek out from underneath it. If she hadn't known better, she'd have thought it was a Little Golden Book, the kind she used to read to Laura and Kenny when they were small. Bailey followed Jean's eyes and tucked the book back into the blanket sheepishly.

"Okay, well . . ." Jean paused, wracked her brain for

something interesting or fantastic or profound or . . . anything that would make this child move, and found nothing. "Just let me know if you need something," she said.

She began walking back toward the kitchen, though admittedly she had no idea what she was going to do with herself once she got there. But just as she reached the doorway, she heard that low, melodic voice again.

"It wasn't a fire."

Jean turned. "I'm sorry?"

Bailey lowered the blanket, but still didn't raise her eyes. "I didn't set his bed on fire."

"Oh. I . . ."

"I put a cigarette out on his pillow. There's a difference."

"Okay," Jean said. "I see." Though she really didn't. "I don't smoke," she finally offered, and then felt stupid for not saying something more . . . soothing . . . more comforting. She wanted to say, *I believe you*, or, *What's between you and your father won't follow you here*, or, *I'm not worried*, or any number of things that might have expressed to Bailey that she'd come to a safe place, a place where she would be cared for and loved. But Jean couldn't decide which of those things to say, and the longer the silence stretched between them, the more absurd any of them would have felt coming out of her mouth. In the end, she didn't say anything. Just left it with *I don't smoke*.

Time seemed interminable as the two stood opposite

each other. Jean's mouth opened and closed, opened and closed, and it wasn't until finally the phone rang—it was Kenneth, wondering if Bailey had arrived, wanting to know how things were going, wanting to know if Jean needed help—that Jean could finally come up with a good segue to leave. By the time she got off the phone— mumbling cryptic answers to his questions as if she were FBI—Bailey had gone up to her room and shut the door. For a time, Jean stood outside the door, her hand splayed open on it as if she were reaching inside and touching Bailey, comforting her the way she couldn't do when they were face-to-face, her ears perked for any sign of move- ment, any sign of foul play.

What if her granddaughter did set her house on fire?

Would she? Was she that unpredictable?

After a while, Jean knocked.

"I need to go to the grocery store," she called. "Would you like to come?"

No answer.

"Bailey?" she called, her heart jumping. What if the child had done something stupid inside the room? What if she'd hurt herself or snuck out? There was a muffled sound. Jean tried the doorknob, but it wouldn't turn. She knocked again, a little more insistent this time. "Bailey?"

"I said I'm asleep!" came the annoyed response from the other side, screamed so loudly, Jean actually took two steps back from the door, her hand turning itself back into a fist. She stood in the hallway, unsure, then stepped back to the door.

"Oh. Okay. I'm . . . sorry I woke you."

She knew she should have felt afraid to leave Bailey home alone, but the truth was, the minute Jean was in her car, driving toward town, she felt so relieved, she almost tingled. Here, at the supermarket, there would be nothing unfamiliar. Here she could be in control.

She grabbed a cart from the corral next to her car and pushed it across the lot herself, liking the familiar jangle of the metal shaking and jarring over the potholed concrete parking lot. She liked the everyday whoosh of the automatic doors opening for her, the beeping sound of the cash registers permeating the air as if she'd just stepped into a heart monitor, the scuffle of shoppers, the clang of cart meeting cart, the music—Cyndi Lauper today—piping in over her head. All expected. All things she understood on every level. No surprises here.

She wheeled to the deli counter and began to order the usual—a half pound of kettle fried turkey breast and six slices of white American cheese—when she looked up to see Janet, her perpetually red-faced friend from the book club.

Jean barked out a surprised laugh, the one Laura had always called her "flaff." *It's a fake laugh, Mother,* she used to droll, rolling her eyes not too unlike her daughter had just been doing in the entryway earlier that day. *It makes you sound like some hoity-toity TV wife.* And then, of course, Laura had grown to be all about appearances, and Jean often wondered whether Laura flaffed now, and if it made her feel as ridiculous as it still made Jean feel when she did it.

"I didn't know you were working here," Jean said.

Janet shrugged, her nose going crimson. "Just started a couple weeks ago. It's killing me being away from the kids, but we needed the money, so . . ." She fidgeted with the hem of her apron.

"Totally understand," Jean said, and she flaffed again, which only made her feel even more awkward, and to Jean it began to feel as if this would be a whole day of awkwardness. "I've thought of applying here myself," she added, which wasn't true, and she had no idea what made her say it in the first place, especially since it only added to the discomfort, and she and Janet both shuffled their feet and looked down.

"I read *Blame*," Janet finally blurted. "The book? For our next meeting? I finished it last night after my shift."

"Oh! The book!" Jean said, relieved to have something to talk about while at the same time mortified that in all the strange goings-on of the past few days, she had neglected to read it herself. "Book club. Of course! Yes, yes. Quite the interesting book."

Janet's face turned so red on the forehead, it began to go white in the creases. She leaned forward over the counter, her gut with its narrow strip of apron pressing into the glass on the other side. "I thought it was—"

"Janet!" a voice barked, and Janet jumped, her hands flying up to her collarbone. A bald man, looking trussed-up in an apron that matched Janet's, was churning toward her. "I thought I told you to shave more sale ham."

"I was just about to," Janet said, her voice going tiny and the whites of her eyes turning bloodshot and glassy as she turned them toward the floor. "I've got a customer."

"Looks to me like you were standing around gossiping with your 'customer.'" He made air quotes with his fingers. "We don't pay you to chat with your friends," he said, pulling himself up tall and placing his hands on his narrow hips. "Get to work or give me your apron. There are a hundred people out there who would love to have this job."

"Yes, sir," she mumbled to her shoes, and Jean felt so embarrassed and guilty for her friend that she found herself growing warm.

The man stalked away, shaking his head and muttering something about "lazy cow" under his breath. Jean watched him go, her mouth hanging open. When he had gone and she'd refocused her attention on Janet, the poor thing was twisting the bottom of her apron between her hands and swallowing repeatedly, as if to swallow the whole episode inside herself so that no one else had to witness it.

"What a jerk," Jean started to say.

But Janet had finally swallowed enough to find her voice and at the same time said, "Can I get you anything? Because I need to, um . . ."

"Shave some ham," Jean finished for her. Janet nodded, fumbling with a box of latex gloves, and Jean decided that the best way to be Janet's friend in this moment was to let it go. She ordered her kettle fried turkey, took the bag of meat, and said good-bye. She forgot the cheese.

Besides, she had something much more pressing to worry about.

Something she hadn't realized until Janet mentioned *Blame.*

The book club.

It would be meeting again soon.

And Bailey, just as snarling and nasty as that man, would be there.

EIGHT

Even though Janet had reminded her that day at the supermarket, it was still days before Jean opened up her copy of *Blame* again. She'd stumbled across it on the coffee table and had been startled by the realization that she had still barely cracked it open. She'd gotten only about twenty pages into it, and had until the next meeting to read another six hundred of them. Thackeray was nothing if not prolific.

She plopped onto the couch and began reading, slipping over the words like an icy highway.

Blanche's daughter, Trina, was a disgusting mound of a thing, wrapped in a stereotypical fat-girl jolly shell. Blanche could scarcely look at the girl without wanting to overdose the pain of her failure away. Instead, she threw snack cakes at Trina like a zoo-keeper to a gorilla, and owned the blame for what she'd done to contribute to the death of expectations of humanity . . .

Truth be told, Jean hadn't finished the book because she hadn't really cared for it. It was offensive, difficult to swallow. How had it been getting so many rave reviews?

But it was not like Jean to abandon a book. She was not the type to give up entirely. She had a book club discussion to lead, and how could she lead a discussion without having read the book, no matter how disgusting it was?

She remained there until afternoon came and the sun bore down on her hard through the floor-to-ceiling windows and the shadows coming off the trees were long and dark.

She remembered reading her first Thackeray novel with Wayne. Kenneth had just left for college. She and Wayne were fresh empty nesters, and Jean had been gutted with loneliness. Even though she'd never been the "playing type" of mother, and she'd never quite felt in her own skin around her children, she'd enjoyed the noise and confusion of having them around. She'd worn her right to complain about children's craziness like a badge. In some ways, it was the only way she could relate to those other moms.

Right around the same time, Thackeray had written *Blood Boy*, a novel about a boy who went to college with stars in his eyes and the deeply felt convictions that only the young can truly hang on to with any real grasp, but had committed suicide by jumping from his third-floor dorm room. It was a mystery—not a whodunit, but a whydunit. Toward the end, the parents learned that their son had never had stars in his eyes but that they had only seen him that way. They'd missed all the warning signals; though he'd laid clues around like Easter eggs, they'd never picked them up, not a single one. By that point in the story, Jean was sobbing so hysterically, Wayne had to take over and read from there.

Jean would never forget Wayne's soothing voice intoning the last lines: *Of all the lessons Rita learned, the harshest, and sweetest, was that sometimes we see our children with the critical eye only, for who we want them to become, rather than who they actually are. But those are the children of our memories, the perfect ones, and she would rather live with a perfect lie than die with the terrifying truth on her tongue.* Wayne had closed the book with a soft whump and had laid it on the table. Jean had turned sideways on the couch, laid her head on his lap, and cried and cried, unsure which children she had sent out into her world—the perfect lies or the imperfect truths—but completely certain that they were both doomed regardless.

Wayne had stroked her hair.

And he had proclaimed Thackeray to be the greatest writer of all time. A real sage, he'd called him. A prophet. Someone with convictions to admire.

And an asshole of the highest order.

It had been a shocking enough proclamation to bring Jean to giggles. She still smiled at the memory of her writhing around on his lap, laughing until she was breathless, her face still slicked with tears as he poked into her sides, quoting Thackeray lines in a bored, uppity voice.

"Can I eat?" Jean heard, and nearly dropped her book, ripped out of her memory. In her haste to read, she'd forgotten all about Bailey, who now stood on the living room steps, her hair funky and frizzed out to one side, a handprint pressed into her cheek.

Jean nodded. "Of course you can. I . . . I totally forg . . ." She trailed off. Something told her it wouldn't be a good idea to tell Bailey that she'd been forgotten. "I lost track of time." She held up the book and grinned sheepishly. "Book club assignment and I haven't done my homework."

Bailey took a couple more steps down, scratching at one thigh absently. "You have a book club?"

"Yes, I started it when Wayne . . . when your grandfather . . . when . . ."

"When he croaked? You can say it around me. I'm not four. I get the whole circle of life thing. *Hakuna matata* and all that."

Jean pressed her lips together. When he croaked. She had never, not once, considered Wayne's death that way. Something about putting it so brashly felt like rocks pelting her skin. Frogs croaked. Bugs croaked. Great men . . . loves of lives . . . did not do something so trivial as croak.

"Anyway, we meet again soon," Jean said, trying to paste on a smile, knowing that today was not the best day to engage her granddaughter in a course of manners.

"Oh, great, so I'll have even less privacy than I already do. I can't wait," Bailey said.

"We won't invade. We'll be too busy talking about the book. It's called *Blame*, and it's about parenting, and honestly I'm kind of surprised by how he—"

"Yeah, I really just wanted some food," Bailey interrupted.

The girl turned on her heel and stomped back up the stairs, and soon Jean could hear her mumbling expletives to herself while rummaging through the pantry. Jean wasn't sure whether she should go up and help out or just let Bailey fend for herself. She wasn't used to this; neither of her kids had been so rude. At least . . . not that she knew of.

"Help yourself to anything you want," she called as cheerfully as she could. "I'll be . . . I'll be right back."

She replaced the bookmark and put the book on the end table, careful not to disturb Wayne's glasses, which still sat there after all this time, and walked outside through the back door.

It was only June, but the heat was already oppressive, and Jean found herself lunging for the long shadows of the trees, as she picked her way next door to Loretta's house. She let herself in without knocking, as she'd always done.

Chuck was snoozing in his recliner, so Jean tiptoed through the house, not calling out Loretta's name until she'd gotten upstairs.

"In the lounge," Loretta called back. "Just me and Flavian."

Jean knew exactly whom Loretta was talking about— Flavian Munney, the hunky main character in a long-standing series of steamy romance novels that Chuck and Wayne had jokingly called "librarian porn" way back when Loretta began reading them. Loretta used to joke back then that she was doing research, but since Chuck retired, she'd increasingly joked that it was more like reading a history book about events that she knew were true because they'd once happened in her lifetime, but were now as outdated as rotary dial telephones and *The Brady Bunch*.

After Chuck retired, and their only daughter, Wendy, moved to Rhode Island to live near her new husband's family, Loretta gutted Wendy's bedroom and made it into a room she liked to call La Ladies' Lounge. It was heavy on Pepto-Bismol pink and swoopy fabric, and was dominated by a crystal chandelier meant for a room three times its size. She even bought an antique lounge, the kind that does not collapse and looks like a 1950s starlet in feathered, high-heeled house slippers and a gauzy gown should be draped across it. She placed the lounge right next to the bay window, which overlooked the southwest corner of Jean's house and the wooded area beyond.

It was in this room that Loretta fed her love affair with a fictional character that she insisted looked like the guy who mixed the paint at Home Depot. Once every so often, Loretta would make the book club read a Flavian Munney book. Everyone—including Jean—complained loudly about it. The books were cheesy and predictable. But the Flavian Munney discussions were some of the best to be had. Hilarious and interesting, and sometimes, once the wine got flowing and confessions were made, shocking. It was during one of the Flavian Munney meetings that they learned that Loretta and Chuck hadn't had sex in two years and that Mitzi and her husband, Paul, once did it in a stairwell in a casino hotel. *You know there were cameras in there,* she'd hissed over her wineglass. *Thank God it wasn't my face they were looking at!* And they'd all burst into scandalized laughter, even Janet, whose hands shook around her wineglass afterward. It was at the same meeting that Dorothy told them about her impending divorce, and how, when she found out that her husband had been cheating on her, she'd gone to a bar and tried to go home with someone, but the only taker had terrible body odor. Since she couldn't make herself forgive her standards when it came to personal hygiene, she'd gone to a motel room alone and had cried herself to sleep. And then, just as the tone had gone sober as they all felt for poor Dorothy, May had spoken up: *Last weekend I totally went home with a guy who was missing his two front teeth,* and even Dorothy giggled, and so did Jean, although she knew it was a lie. It was a beautiful, sweet lie.

Jean could have used a Flavian Munney discussion right now.

"New one?" Jean asked, sitting on the white couch that took up most of the wall on the other side of La Lounge.

Loretta held up the cover, which featured a nearly naked man holding a belt between two hands, his biceps taught with strain. "*Whipped into Shape,*" she purred. "Flavian's hopped on the bondage bandwagon."

"Hmm, sounds frightening. Does Chuck know about this?"

"Who needs to handcuff Chuck? He doesn't move."

"How will Flavian hold his paint cans and that belt at the same time?" Jean asked, motioning toward the cover.

"You don't want to know," Loretta said, raising her eyebrows, and they chuckled. "I'm guessing you aren't here to talk about Flavian," she added after a beat. "How's the kid?"

Jean sighed, leaned her head back against the chair. "She's so . . . angry. My God, Loretta, I don't know what they've done to this kid, but she's just . . . I can't have the book club anymore. Not with her there."

Loretta swung her legs around front and sat up. "Of course you can. She's fifteen, not five."

"Sixteen."

"Even better. What's she gonna do, exactly?"

"That's the thing," Jean said. "I don't know. I don't know her. But to hear her dad talk, she could do just about anything. I don't want her to humiliate me in front of—"

"In front of who? Me? Not possible." She snapped the book closed and placed it, cover side down, on the end of the lounge. "You know that. Need I remind you of the thong incident of last December?"

"No, not in front of you, of course. In front of Mitzi," Jean said. Jean loved Mitzi—they all did—but sometimes they feared her more than befriended her. There was no-body in this world more fiercely loyal to her friends . . . and nobody more fiercely, and openly, judgmental of them. She claimed she judged out of love, and the most frustrating part was that they believed her. Sometimes it was both wonderful and horrible to have a friend love you so fiercely.

Loretta thought about it, nodded. "Okay, well, I could see that. But really, Mitzi's best friend is Dorothy, and there are no kids in this world worse than her kids. So Mitzi must be able to separate apples from trees, you know what I mean?"

"That's the thing," Jean said, smacking her leg. "I'm not her mother. And I don't know what has happened with her mother, but it can't be good, because this child is so pissed off. And I don't feel like I can mother her. Not right away. Who am I to tell her what to do? Last time I saw her, she was still wearing footie pajamas."

Loretta stood and held her hand out for Jean to take. "The hell you can't mother her. They didn't ship her to you for poops and giggles. They sent her here because she needs a kick in the ass. And you, my friend, are the kicker. You'll keep the book club, and that's all there is to it. You need that book club, and we both know it. If you're going to keep your sanity right now, you aren't going to keep it by holing yourself up with depressing memories and loneliness."

Jean wasn't surprised to hear Loretta defend the club's

existence so mightily. The book club had been Loretta's idea from the start. She'd nudged Jean into it just a few weeks after Wayne died.

"To hell with cookies and milk," Loretta had grumbled, shoving her way into Jean's cavernous kitchen where Jean had been busy packing up some of his belongings for donation. Loretta parked herself on a stool at the island. "You need something with a little testosterone. Glasses?"

Jean pulled two highball glasses down from the cabinet and rinsed the dust out of them. Loretta splashed a couple inches of brown liquid into each and held one up, toast-style. "He was a hell of a guy, Jeanie," she said somberly, and took a long sip from her glass.

Jean had immediately felt that inward melting feeling again. She didn't want to drink. She didn't want to do anything. She didn't even want to miss him. She just wanted him back. But Loretta gave the glass a small shove, and Jean picked it up and studied it.

"More than you know," she said. She tossed back some of the liquid and grimaced as it went down. "But he's gone now." She felt herself wanting to cry, but tamped it down by tipping the glass up again and having another drink. "These look great," she said, wiggling two fingers under the plastic wrap that covered the brownie plate.

"My insane aunt Helen's recipe," Loretta said, draining her glass. "You know, the one who always tries to show people her third nipple? Crazier than a loon, but, good Molly, can that woman cook."

"Maybe it's the nipple," Jean suggested as she handed Loretta a brownie.

"Could very well be."

The two of them bit in. They gobbled up one, and then another, and a third each, washing them down with more slugs of whiskey. Jean found herself feeling very loose—perilously so, as if she might bend in half or say something upsetting or go on a thinking spree that could be very dangerous. She sank onto a stool across from Loretta, crossed her arms on the counter, and laid her head on them.

"Kids made it home okay?" Loretta asked.

"Kenny got in last night. He called." Good old Kenny, Jean thought. God bless him. While her older child, Laura, had practically left skid marks in Jean's driveway, so eager to get back to St. Louis, to get back to work, Jean's younger child, Kenneth, had stayed on for weeks, working remotely on his laptop during the day, helping Jean sort out the paperwork and the lawn mowing and the grief by night. Jean had finally been forced by guilt and by an overwhelming desire for alone time to send him home, to get back to his wife, his job, his life. She'd needed time to think. To process. To cry without feeling on show. Kenny had called the minute his plane touched down in California. Laura hadn't even called to check in. For all Jean knew, her daughter never made it home at all. The more things changed, the more they stayed the same.

"They doing okay with everything?" Loretta had asked.

Jean turned her face down so that her nose hovered just above the counter. She could smell the whiskey on her breath when she spoke. "Kenny's had a bit of a hard time with it, but you know Laura." Loretta made a noise of affirmation, but neither of them finished the thought—Laura didn't have a hard time with much of anything, it seemed. Or maybe, Jean wondered, Laura had a hard time with so many things, this wasn't noticeable. Jean changed the subject. "Oh, Loretta, I hope Wayne knew how much I loved him," she muttered, her voice echoey to her own ears.

"Of course he did," Loretta responded. Loretta's hair was dyed as jet-black as an oil slick, her cheeks just as powdered and her lips just as red as the day she retired from the car dealership eleven years prior. Her hands showed more veins; the skin of her arms sagged a little. But otherwise she might have never aged a day since Jean met her. Loretta dropped another dollop of whiskey into Jean's glass and inched it toward her.

Jean wiped the corners of her eyes. "I'm just thinking about all the times we fought. Stupid fights that meant nothing. Now they seem so huge, and I hope he wasn't thinking of those things at the end. Because they're all that I can think about now. I can't help it."

Loretta patted Jean's hand. "That'll pass," she said. She bent to look Jean directly in the eyes. "It will."

They got up and moved into the living room, a room Jean had scarcely been able to force herself to enter. Wayne's eyeglasses still sat atop a folded newspaper on the end table next to his armchair, where he had had a habit of leaving them when he wasn't wearing them. Jean doubted she'd ever touch them. How could she move them? The date on the newspaper might grab her eye, startle her back to the day they'd learned about the cancer. Or worse, the first day he'd been too sick to put on his glasses.

Jean had eased herself onto the couch, on the opposite end of where Loretta was sitting. She felt like she was un-characteristically sprawling, and she was miserable, the chocolate slugging uncomfortably in her stomach as her eyes dragged toward the end table, and found a balled-up pair of black socks tucked underneath it. She'd missed those all this time. How had she missed them?

Loretta leaned forward and touched the spines of a couple of books stacked on the coffee table, pushing them around to read the titles. "Goodness, you read a lot. You ever been in a book club?" she asked.

"Not officially," she answered, though, of course, she was thinking of her nightly reading ritual with Wayne, and how that had felt like a club of sorts. They'd been doing it since the children were small—at first reading picture books aloud to Laura and Kenny, the whole family draped over one another in the living room, the kids' heads fresh-smelling with shampoo. But Jean and Wayne had continued it after the kids had outgrown bedtime sto-ries, choosing their own books, books that interested and expanded both of them. It became a private book club, just the two of them, holding their stories close to their hearts, reading and discussing with feeling, sometimes grieving together over endings or laughing so hard they had to stop reading to wipe their eyes. Wayne's favorites had always been the philosophical novels—Thomas Mann's *The Magic Mountain* being his all-time favorite. Jean had loved the quirky popular novels. They'd both chuckled over *Then We Came to the End* and had both cried over *The Heart Is a Lonely Hunter*. Jean had cherished those moments together. She missed them so much, the thought of cracking open a book without him left her a little panicky.

"You should start one. I'll be your first member," Loretta said.

"I don't have time . . . ," Jean started, but she trailed off because she and Loretta both knew now that Wayne was gone, she had nothing but time. Wayne had been where all her time went for so long.

"I understand," Loretta had said, picking up a Kazuo Ishiguro and leafing through it. "But if you ever decide you have time, I'd suggest a book club. It's a perfect fit for you. And triple nipple brownies and booze are a perfect fit for me."

Jean hadn't responded—really hadn't given Loretta's advice any more thought—and not long after, the whiskey had made them both sleepy. Jean had seen her friend out and had immediately climbed the stairs to the guest bedroom, had flopped, face-first, onto the bed, and had slept the sleep of the bone-exhausted.

When she'd gotten up again, she'd gone, as if pulled,

to the living room and had crouched next to the end table and plucked Wayne's socks out from underneath. She sat on the hardwood floor cross-legged and did what she'd been doing with his clothes since he'd gone—pressed them up to her nose. They didn't smell like dirty socks. They smelled leathery, and faintly of his cologne, as if he'd worn them on a special occasion. She wracked her brain to think of where they might have gone, but nothing came to mind. In that instant, it felt as if he'd been sick for such a long time, as if he'd been dying forever. Was it possible that she'd created a life around her husband's death? Was it possible that she'd not only lost him, but had lost a part of herself as well—the part that was Wife of a Dying Man?

Dear God, no.

She'd pressed the socks to her nose again and inhaled. Closed her eyes, saw Wayne's face, the fleshy, laughing face, the one that didn't know an army of monster cells was coursing through his body, defeating him from the inside out. The face that gazed at her, heavy-lidded behind the lenses of his glasses, his hands soft and relaxed around *The Three Musketeers* or *Blink* or Maya Angelou's *Celebrations*.

And she'd decided, right there on the darkened living room floor with her dead husband's dirty socks in her hand, that she would do it. She would start a book club. She would start living again.

Jean took Loretta's hand and let her friend pull her up out of her seat. She was being gently dismissed from La Lounge. "Let's have the meetings here," Jean tried. "Just while Bailey's . . . being difficult. We can move them back when she goes home."

"No way. You think the kid's embarrassing? Did you see the land whale that's currently rotting on my living room recliner? We can't give Mitzi this kind of ammunition. There are apples and trees, and then there's Chuck."

"Point taken."

"Besides, I can't be relied on to clean my house. You never know when Flavian is waiting for me. And I hate to keep those abs waiting."

"He's a fictional character. For all you know, he has Chuck's abs."

Loretta coughed out a laugh. "Cross yourself after such blasphemy. I love that old coot, but his abs are more of a . . . shelf. To set his beer on." She turned to Jean and patted her on the head, pushing her gently toward the door. "Now, go home and start putting together your recipe. And I'll let the ladies know that the club is on as scheduled."

"Okay, okay," Jean said, trudging out of the room. "But if Bailey blows up the meeting, I am going to blame you."

"Well, that's what the book is all about. Blame!" Loretta called, just before shutting La Lounge's door. "Way to get in the spirit!" Jean heard her call from behind the door.

Jean let herself out of Loretta's house and dawdled going back across the lawn. She gazed at the Knock Out roses that were just beginning to bloom along the side of the house. *Knock Out flowers for my little knockout,* Wayne used to say. He'd planted them for her. Jean plucked a hot pink flower off the stem and held it to her nose. It didn't have much of a smell, but something about the motion made her chest pound all the same. How Wayne had loved the roses. How he'd loved everything outdoors.

She dropped the rose to the ground. "I don't know what I'm doing, Wayne. You've gotta help me out a little here, okay?"

She waited, listening for a response that would never come, and then pivoted on the ball of her foot to head back inside, back to angry, expecting Bailey. She was completely clueless as to what would come next.

NINE

"Oh, don't even get me started," Mitzi bellowed as she plowed into the kitchen. She plunked down a plate of nachos, the solidifying cheese forming little grease beads on the tops of the chips. She slammed her copy of *Blame* on the counter. Jean noticed a forest of sticky notes poking out from the top. "What a class-A bunch of crapola this book was."

"Hold it for the meeting," Loretta called from the dining room table, where she was already two and a half glasses of wine and half an hour of basic bondage facts in. Jean now knew more than she ever wanted to know about collaring, age play, and the Gorean philosophy. *What's the problem?* Loretta had asked when Jean had scrunched up her nose. *It's literature-based. I'm just getting you into the right mind-set.*

"I don't know if I can hold it for the meeting. How can

you be so calm? How can you not want to find this jerk and just . . ." Mitzi trailed off, then growled, picked up the book, and headed into the dining room. "Pour me some of that. My blood pressure's through the roof."

"Where's Dorothy?" Jean asked, arranging a plate of beef and jalapeno empanadas, a perfect, and accidental, pairing with Mitzi's nachos.

Mitzi stood in the doorway between the kitchen and dining room, holding a glass of merlot to her chest. "Ugh, Chester's in jail. Arrested last night for DWI. She's trying to get him out. But I say she should leave his ungrateful bahookey in the clink. Those boys need to learn a lesson, and if their dad's not gonna be around to teach 'em, she's gonna have to get a whole lot tougher."

"Chester's hardly a boy anymore," Loretta said.

Jean considered this. "He's only sixteen, though, right?"

"Exactly," Loretta said. "Old enough to drive, old enough to suffer the consequences of being stupid, that's what I say."

May, who'd come in midconversation, set a box on the counter, then reached in and pulled out a beautiful cake. "Aw, poor Dorothy," she said, as if not noticing that everyone had gasped and cooed at the cake.

"Hey, May," Mitzi called out. "How'd last night go with the pharmacist?"

"Pharmacy tech," May corrected. "And he's way young. I felt creepy. Like I was babysitting or something."

"Ooh, our little May is robbing the cradle," Loretta

called from the other room, and while the ladies chuckled, Jean tried to give May a consoling look. "So, did you de-flower the kid?"

"Loretta! No!" May cried.

"Uh-oh, somebody's been reading Flavian Munney books again," Mitzi cackled, and Jean was glad for it, be-cause May's blush had gotten so deep, she almost looked like Janet.

May uncovered her cake and Jean took a break from arranging empanadas to admire it. "Looks delicious," she said.

"Coconut rum with an almond Irish cream ganache," May said. She crinkled her nose. "My date was with a baking blog." She and Jean exchanged smiles. "I love bak-ing blogs. They don't snore or steal your CDs."

"Enough with the primping already," Mitzi called from the dining room. "I have got to talk about this book or I'm gonna explode."

May reached over and patted the back of Jean's shoul-der, then sauntered toward the dining room. "Make you mad too?" she asked. "I seriously wanted to throw the book against the wall."

"Probably it was your hysterical uterus making you want to do that. You are a woman, after all, and thus prone to bouts of emotion that will someday take down man-kind," Mitzi answered. "According to R. Sebastian Thack-eray the Turd. Oops, I mean the Third."

"Ah, but I'm not a mother, so I get a reprieve," May

said. "It's you baby-poppers that make the world a horrible place to live. You'll probably mess up heaven too, if I recall correctly."

"Save it for the meeting," Loretta said again, then called, "Jeanie, are you coming out anytime soon? I can't hold these animals off much longer. They want blood."

"Be right there," Jean called. "Just as soon as I've got all the silverware out." The truth was she already had everything out. But she'd heard the floorboards squeaking above her head and knew that Bailey was roaming around upstairs. She hadn't seen the girl since last night, when Bailey graced Jean with her presence only long enough to snag a box of Pop-Tarts and take it upstairs, as usual. When Jean had tried to call her down for dinner, there'd been no response, and other than the toilet in Bailey's room flushing a few times during the night, it was almost like having nobody here at all. The girl hadn't come down for breakfast, and Jean worried that this meant she'd be getting hungry soon. The smell of food might bring her downstairs. And then what would she do? Jean hated that she didn't know. She couldn't predict, and Curt's predictions had been dire.

She tried to linger as long as she could, but soon she could hear the ladies' chairs scraping against the wood floor as they convened over the buffet, filling their plates and cooing over May's beautiful cake.

"I even brought dessert wine to go with it," she said,

pointing to the box she'd set on the floor next to the counter.

"Good thing I live close enough to walk home," Loretta joked.

"You mean stumble," Mitzi corrected, and Jean tried not to think about her daughter, with a broken wrist and no idea how it got that way.

"Har-har," Loretta responded, and they all carried their plates back to the table where they could get down to the business of letting recipes derail their book discussion.

They had just sat down when Janet arrived, glancing particularly sheepishly at Jean, who wasn't sure whether she was supposed to acknowledge that they'd seen each other at the supermarket or not. And especially not sure whether she should mention the behavior of Janet's manager.

Fortunately, Janet came in quietly and sat, her head bent over her plate. She never even added an uh-huh to the discussion about the book that she'd been so eager to discuss at the market.

"So clearly Thackeray is a misogynist," Mitzi said.

"He's definitely got mommy issues, at the very least," May agreed, around a bite of empanada. "Do you think he was abused? I think maybe he was abused. He's got a lot of anger."

"I can't even get into what I thought of the plot," Mitzi continued, "because I was so angry at the . . . the attitude."

"Did anybody else see him on *Sixty Minutes* the other night?" Loretta asked.

May pointed with her fork. "Yeah. He seemed so arrogant. And the thing is, he's kind of short and fat."

"Short-man syndrome," Mitzi singsonged. Mitzi had gone on more than once about short men, and all the women rolled their eyes and groaned when she said it. "What? It's a documented fact!" she argued, but heads had begun to turn toward the doorway to the kitchen.

"And to think you thought he was sexy, Loretta," May said.

Loretta shrugged. "They can't all be Flavian."

Jean turned just in time to see Bailey standing in the doorway, wearing nothing but a long T-shirt and underwear, her makeup smudged across her face. Her stomach dropped. *Not now. Please, not now.*

"Hi," May said brightly, and Bailey turned to her, but didn't reply.

"This is Bailey," Jean announced, noticing that her voice had a little quake in it. "She's Laura's daughter. My only granddaughter." She thought that continuing to talk might make her voice sound more commanding, but it only grew weaker.

"Yes, yes, hello," Loretta said, putting down her fork and wiping her mouth with a napkin. "Are you hungry? We've got Mexican."

"I am hungry, actually," Bailey said, wiping sleep from

her eyes. "Nobody eats around here." She glared at Jean, who tried to keep her smile pasted but felt it wilting on the corners.

"I wasn't sure if you wanted me to wake you up this morning," Jean said, then turned back to the table. "We're still getting to know each other's schedules. But we'll eventually get there!" She recognized that this last bit came out too brightly.

Bailey's face transformed into a huge smile, which she made even worse by twisting one index finger in a dimple. "Sure will, Grand-ma-ma," she said in a British accent, lacing the words with such sarcasm, the room went absolutely silent. "We shall sing show tunes in the parlor this evening. I hope you all can make it. Didn't anyone ever tell any of you that staring is rude?"

She turned and disappeared back into the kitchen. Jean couldn't bring herself to look up from her plate. She sat there, fork in hand and lips pressed in on themselves as humiliation ate through her insides. She waited for Mitzi to say something, bracing herself for it.

But after a moment of uncomfortable silence, when Mitzi finally spoke up, it was only to say, "And the way he ended this piece of trash. Instead of dying, they all lived, because death would be too kind for such lowly women? What a trite bunch of bunk. How could anyone glean anything positive from it? I'm positive I'd like to use the last thirty pages to line the litter box. How can this man's mother not be absolutely shrinking with shame right now? I wouldn't leave my house ever again. I would completely deny having given birth to that . . ."

She stopped in midsentence as Bailey reappeared. Jean turned and gasped. The girl stood in the doorway, one hand on a hip, the other clutching a hunk of May's cake. She had icing on her cheeks and nose and was chewing with her mouth open. Jean could see the cake on the counter behind her, a huge hole in one side, where Bailey had snatched her piece right out of it with her hand.

"This is pretty good, I guess," she said. Then she pointedly glared at Jean. "But it's probably not the healthiest breakfast in the world." She shoved another huge bite in her mouth, squishing cake up onto her cheeks and into her nostrils and through her fingers. Big dollops of it fell to the floor, some landing on Bailey's bare toes, some landing on the dining room carpet. When she was done, she held up her hand and squeezed it into a fist, watching as what was left in her hand fell to the floor. "It's a little dry, actually," she said around her mouthful, and then strode out.

The dining room was bathed in absolute silence. Jean could hear Bailey's feet slap across the hardwood kitchen floor and up the stairs and then, after a bit, her bedroom door slam. She closed her eyes with relief. It had been worse than she'd imagined it would be—she thought the girl might roll her eyes or not speak or be surly, but she never thought she'd make such a scene in front of everyone—but at least she was done for now.

She didn't know what to do. Did she try to defend herself? To tell them that she'd tried to wake Bailey every day and had gotten nothing but yelled at for her efforts? To mention that she had plenty of healthy breakfast food, that she wasn't so clueless about raising a child as to not know what she should have for her meals, but just that Bailey wouldn't eat anything? Did she pretend nothing ever happened? Jump up and clean the cake off the floor? Throttle Loretta for making her have the club here—hadn't she known this would happen?

Loretta cleared her throat and continued eating. Mitzi took a sip of wine. Janet sat and licked her lips repeatedly, glancing worriedly from the doorway to Jean to May and back again. She looked ready to bolt any minute.

But May, God love her, simply dug back into her nachos and took up the conversation as if it had never been interrupted. "Did you read any of the reviews? There are, like, a thousand five-star reviews on it. People are calling it 'an insightful social commentary.'"

"All men, undoubtedly," Mitzi added.

"I didn't think it was all so bad," Loretta said. "I mean, if you look at it ironically, like maybe he wasn't really blaming everything on women and mothers, but was making a statement that that's what our society has come to. We all do seem to blame the parents when a kid does something wrong. And we shouldn't be." She only glanced at Jean when she said this, but Jean heard her loud and clear, and it was enough to shake away some of the embarrassment of what had just happened.

Jean waited until the next time Loretta caught her eye and mouthed, *Thank you.* Loretta nodded just slightly.

"That is so not how he meant it," Mitzi plowed on. "He's a horrible little troll, and I hope to God that no woman ever allows him to procreate."

"So tell us how you really feel," Jean joked, and somehow the tension started to drain away. Somehow, eventually, she was even able to forget the glops of cake that were on the floor, waiting for the ladies to leave so she could clean them up.

The only thing she wasn't able to forget was that Bailey had barely just arrived.

TEN

Dear Judy Blume:

I am writing to you about your book *Blubber*. I didn't think I was going to like it because the title is kind of ugly, but it is the best book I have read in a long time. And trust me, I read a *lot* of books! Sometimes my mom yells at me for reading books instead of doing things like the dishes and stuff.

I am kind of fat. Not really huge or anything, but sometimes the kids say things to me about how my stomach wobbles when I run and that I can't jump rope too many times. It is not as bad as what Jill and her friends did to Linda in your book, but sometimes it makes me feel bad when they say mean things. I think I am ugly. The boys think so too. I wish I was as pretty as my mom.

Last year I read *Tales of a Fourth Grade Nothing*

because sometimes I feel like a nothing. But that book was really funny instead. I still liked it, though.

I hope you keep writing.

Signed,
Bailey Butler
Age eleven

Bailey lay on her bed and licked the icing off every centimeter of her fingers, going over them two, three times. Her stomach was growling so hard, it felt like thunder inside her body, and that cake had really been delicious.

But—and she didn't know why, exactly—she couldn't let them know that. As far as her grandmother's friends were concerned, it was . . . meh. And her grandmother had failed. Bailey had no excuse for it. No explanation for why she needed to do things like obliterate that cake. To make someone else feel like crap about herself. To totally negate her worth. It was not like doing those things made her feel any better about herself. Not after the initial rush had passed, anyway. It never failed—she would do something shocking, and it would be followed by that amazing, alive sensation that was both giddy and dark. But within hours, or sometimes even just minutes, that giddiness fell heavy in her gut, leaving her with just the darkness. That rumbling might not have been hunger after all, but more of her gut growing unsettled. Maybe it was the feeling of guilt. Maybe it was the feeling of anger. Maybe she was ruining herself from the inside out. She didn't know. She only knew that was what it felt like to be Bailey Butler these days—in constant, fluctuating states of fear, anger, euphoria, pain, and dread.

What was worse, she knew in her heart that her grandmother had been really making an effort and trying harder than anyone else. She'd heard her grandmother's knock this morning, followed by a soft voice: *Bailey, do you want some breakfast?* But she didn't answer. Had she become so closed off that she couldn't reach back to the people who were reaching for her? Had she become unreachable altogether? The thought made her feel all the more desperate. She flexed her hand a few times, feeling for sticky spots that she could lick again, then got up and shuffled into the bathroom and washed it, considering herself in the mirror.

Not long ago, not long before her mom pulled her going-into-work-wasted stunt, Bailey had overheard her talking to her friend Becky, the one who'd taken her to the hospital on Laura Butler's Great Big Embarrassing Day. They were both on the downhill side of drunk, which was what they did best, and were standing in the driveway.

It was prom night, and Bailey was going to be sitting at home alone, as usual, because what boy had any interest in a chubby, pissed-off girl with a drunk for a mother and ghost for a father, who was too ashamed of her house to ever invite anyone over? Bailey felt like the only girl at Cleveland Heights High School to have no prom date, not even a friend date. She tried not to let it hurt, tried not to even notice, but she noticed. She noticed every freaking day.

Even Chloe Roland, the dippy nerdgirl down the street, had landed herself a date. Bailey had seen them standing out in front of the flower bed, Chloe's mom snapping photos like Chloe was a celebrity, her lavender and silver dress poofing out behind her with every breath of wind. Her date wore a matching lavender bow tie and a top hat with a silver band. Nerdboy. Nerdlove.

Bailey had stood next to her garage door, idly listening to the moms relive their glory prom days, watching Chloe, and imagining herself in that lavender dress. It all felt so very Cinderella, and for a moment Bailey allowed herself to feel really sorry for herself. If only fairy godmothers really existed. If only one would swoop in and snatch her away and take her, not to prom, but to a different life where she had a mom who could stay sober long enough to take prom photos of her. A mom who could wave good-bye to the limousine without stumbling into the rhododendrons.

A mom who wouldn't, as the night fell and the rum kicked in, giving her a false sense of privacy, whisper loudly to her friends that if only Bailey would do some leg lifts or if only Bailey would put some makeup on or if only Bailey would smile every now and then, maybe she would have a prom date. Oh, how it broke Laura Butler's heart to not take her one and only daughter prom-dress shopping. Oh, how it embarrassed her, made her feel like a failure, to not be heading up the after-prom committee, because her own daughter couldn't even get the desperate boys to ask her out. *You know, even desperate boys have standards,* her mom whispered over the blazing fire pit, too sloshed to realize that Bailey was sunk into the shadows on the front porch, watching, listening like always, and also too sloshed to realize that whisper and Drunk Whisper were hardly the same thing. *Even those boys don't like a girl with heavy thighs and a constant scowl. Even those boys appreciate a girl who makes a little effort.*

How many of these very conversations had Bailey listened to? Conversations where her mother lamented how Bailey wasn't smart enough, or how she wasn't talented enough, or how she was too ugly for this or that. Once, her mother even said, *I don't know where she gets those genes! I swear to God I have more than once wondered if they switched her at birth!* Bailey was used to these overheard insults, and the laughs that followed, but that one stung. After that one, she'd gone into her mother's bedroom and had dipped each and every one of Laura's lipsticks into the toilet and then put them back in her makeup bag. And if she could have done it to the lipsticks of every chuckling, nodding, mmming mom out there, she would have.

So the prom conversation hadn't really been that big a deal, and in the end, Bailey was glad she didn't have a date, because being too ugly and too fat and too unmotivated to even turn the eye of the loserest loser in her high school was the best way to get back at her mom. Did the woman really not think she knew those things about herself? Did she really think that Bailey didn't notice she had no prom date, no friends outside of books? Did she really think for a second that Bailey wouldn't have traded places with one of the girls at the dance in a heartbeat?

The thing was, she knew her mother didn't remember saying these things. She definitely didn't know they'd been overheard. Her mother remembered them just as little as she remembered the times she threw her arms around Bailey's shoulders and leaned into her, breathing whiskey into her face and sobbing that she was the best daughter anyone could ever ask for. Thanking her. Calling her beautiful and kind and smart. Wishing aloud she could be a better mother for her. Patting her on the head like she was some stray dog. That was worse than her mother not remembering the mean things she'd said. She never remembered how awesome Bailey had been and how much she supposedly loved her, and that hurt most of all.

But at moments like this, when Bailey was hurting and scared and maybe even a little ashamed of her own behavior, she would look in the mirror and she would see it. She would see the things her mom talked about. She would see her pugged-up nose and her freckled forehead and the dullness in her eyes that practically screamed "loser." And in those moments, she wanted to scrub her face until it shone and draw highlights in her hair and be someone else. She wanted to take hot, steamy showers and wash off the hate, wash off the pain so that she was looking out at the world through fresh, pink skin. She wanted to run marathons and eat nothing but fruit and lose fifty pounds and wear sexy clothes that clung in all the right places while not looking slutty, and . . . she knew in the back of her mind that the person those things described was . . . her mom.

But more than anything in this world, she did not want to be Laura Butler.

She just wanted Laura Butler to notice her, and to remember having done so in the morning.

Back in the bedroom, she rummaged through the side pocket of her backpack—which was filled with mostly useless school assignments that she never bothered to complete—and pulled out a wadded-up piece of notebook paper. She flopped onto the bed on her stomach and smoothed it out, looking at the phone number in her dad's handwriting.

She'd dug it out of the trash back at home after her dad had plugged the number into his phone and thrown it away. It was the guest line at the rehab.

She pulled out her phone and dialed the number. It rang five times before someone picked up.

"Yuh?"

"Um . . . Laura Butler?" Bailey said into the phone, her heart pumping, creating lightning in her peripheral vision.

"What about her?"

"Can I talk to her? Um, please?"

There was a thumping, thudding sound, as if the phone had been dropped, and Bailey could hear someone shout, "Anybody know who Laura Buckner is?"

"Who?"

"Laura Buckner!"

Butler, you idiot. I didn't stutter, Bailey wanted to shout, but it would do no good. He was nowhere near the phone anymore as far as she could tell.

There was nothing for so long, Bailey was certain she'd been forgotten, but just as she was about the hang up, there was fumbling, and then a familiar voice.

"Hello?"

"Mom?"

"Bailey?"

Bailey smiled, despite herself. "Yeah."

"What's wrong? Why are you calling?"

"I just . . . I missed you."

"Oh. I miss you too, but . . . I really don't have time to talk right now. Group is in ten minutes, and I haven't journaled."

"Wait. Mom, Dad sent me to Kansas City."

"I know. I told him to."

Bailey paused, clenching and unclenching her hand, and it fell to the side, landing with a thump against something hard. Distracted, Bailey looked over. It was the Little Golden Book that she'd been sleeping with. "Why?" She picked up the book and propped it on her lap, her finger absently rubbing the illustration of the bunny. She'd rubbed that spot so many times over the years, she'd worn a white path over the ink. Touching the book and hearing her mother's voice at the same time were nearly too much. She almost thought she could smell her mother's perfume through the phone.

Her mother sighed. "He wasn't handling things well, and I thought you could use a little change of scenery and . . . Bailey, I really don't have time for this. We can sort it all out later."

"Well, you were wrong. I didn't need a change of scenery, and I want to go home. I don't want to sort it out later. I want to come home now. *Home*, home. Not Dad's apartment and not here."

"Well, you can't always get what you want, Bailey."

"When, then?!" Bailey shrieked into the phone. She found herself up on her knees in the middle of the bed, shaking, tears streaking down her face. The book landed facedown on the comforter next to her.

"You need to stop shouting, and—"

Bailey plowed over her mother. "Because I can't remember a time when I *ever* got what I wanted. Not once! It was all about you, you, you! Everything is always about Laura Butler the Great and what she wants."

"Okay, well, I can't talk to you when you're like this."

"Maybe you should go crack open a few beers, then. Can't shut you up when you've had a few of those. It's amazing, Mom, how ugly and disappointing I get when you've had a few of those."

"Bailey, now, that's not fair."

Bailey sat back onto her heels, her chest hitching. She felt sweat trickle down her lower back, and the cake that she'd eaten sat disagreeably and huge in her stomach. "No, I'll tell you what's not fair. Growing up being the mom because my mom is too drunk to be one," she said.

She pressed END CALL on her phone before Laura could even respond, then stared at the blank phone screen, watching her tears splat and spread across it, willing it to light up, willing her mother to call back so she could reject the call. So she could "not have time" to talk to her right now.

But the screen never lit up, and in a rage she picked up the book and heaved it toward the far wall. It landed with a clatter on the floor, and she blinked at the illustration that was showing—the bunny snuggling close to his new snowy white bunny friend, perfectly content. She stared, breathing heavy, for a few moments, then eventually sprawled out face-first on the comforter and cried it out.

ELEVEN

Laura arrived in the middle of the night. She pounded on Jean's door as if the place were on fire, scaring Jean, who raced to open the door, clutching her robe closed at the throat with one hand and a baseball bat with the other.

Bailey peeked out an open crack of her bedroom door as Jean dashed by. She wandered out, but only to the top of the stairs, where she stood, rubbing her eyes with the heel of one hand like a child, wearing the same rumpled clothes she'd had on for days. Jean only glanced back at her before opening the door.

"Oh, my . . . ," Jean said, stepping aside and throwing the door wide-open. "I had no idea you were coming. We were asleep."

Laura, carrying a beat-up trash bag, stepped in through the open door, her eyes bloodshot, her hair disheveled, looking the rattiest Jean had ever seen her daughter look.

In the driveway, a black Cadillac ticked and tinged as its engine cooled off.

"I couldn't stay there," Laura said, dropping her trash bag on the floor. "The house. It's so dark and empty. I was going to wait till morning to come out, but I just . . . He's doing something to it. He's knocked out all the spindles on the stairs. And just left them on the floor. He's thrown away all my dishes. He's ransacked my clothes, Bailey's. He's totally dismantling my life."

"I didn't know you were out of rehab," Jean said. "Curt never called."

"He doesn't know. I've been out for a few days, but after seeing what he did to my house, I just . . . I can't even think about him right now. It's all too depressing."

At that point, Laura's eyes tipped upward to the top of the stairs, and a look that Jean couldn't quite pinpoint— fear? Regret? Relief?—crossed her face.

"I'm sorry I woke you," Laura said. Bailey didn't respond, just dipped back into the shadowy hallway, moving backward until the sound of her bedroom door firmly shutting echoed downstairs.

Laura made a slurry shushing sound with her mouth and shook her head. "He's got her brainwashed against me, you know."

"She's having a hard time," Jean said, and then, sure she smelled something acidic on her daughter, asked, "Are you sober?"

Laura rolled her eyes. "Jesus, Mom, I didn't come here

for a lecture. If I'd wanted that, I'd have stayed in that ridiculous clinic."

"I'm sorry," Jean said. "Of course you're not here for that. I was just wondering if the rehab was a good move for you."

"It got everyone off my back. Isn't that what it was supposed to be about? But it destroyed me instead. Are you all happy now? Look at me." Laura leaned over and picked up the trash bag again. "Is my bedroom still a bedroom?"

"Of course it is," Jean said. "They both are. Kenny's room is where Bailey's staying."

"Good move. Mr. I Shit Rainbows and Unicorns won't likely be showing up in the middle of the night with gin on his breath, will he?" She trudged up the stairs, just as she'd done a million times before, and Jean watched with her mouth open, standing in the night-lit entryway, the front door wide-open and cool night air seeping in. It wasn't until she heard Laura's door shut that she finally closed the door and carried Kenny's old baseball bat back up to her bedroom, where she couldn't sleep anyway.

Neither Laura nor Bailey came down for breakfast, though Jean could hear movement and, once, a sneeze, upstairs. Jean tried not to think about what Laura's presence in the house would mean. Would things make a drastic turn for the better? Would Laura get herself together and help Bailey? Would they fix each other and go back to St. Louis, and, if so, where would that leave Jean? Back in her quiet house, with her book club?

Or would Laura's presence more likely mean outbursts? Would Jean be craving the quiet house and the book club in short order?

She poached herself an egg and ate it on toast as if it were any other morning. She went outside and watered her flowers just like always. She picked up the newspaper from the driveway and brought it in and read it.

She sank into the couch and leafed through the club's next book choice, which Loretta had insisted be the Flavian Munney book she'd just finished. *To soothe us after this Thackeray book,* she'd said. *Nothing makes you feel better than being bound and gagged by a hot millionaire genius.*

Speak for yourself, May had countered, but she'd giggled and added, *I prefer dog collars, anyway.*

I'd like to put a dog collar on Thackeray, Mitzi had muttered. *A shock collar.*

Oh, honey, Flavian's got those too, Loretta had stage-whispered, and they'd all laughed and agreed that a Flavian Munney book would be the best balm to soothe their aching egos after what they'd just gone through.

These weren't Jean's favorite kind of books, and she sometimes shrank at the thought of reading one aloud with Wayne. He and Chuck had teased Loretta mercilessly about them. Jean could hear him now: *Honestly, Jeanie? I thought you preferred a thinking man.* But she'd needed the escape badly, and she'd gotten so absorbed in it that she didn't notice Bailey roaming around in the kitchen upstairs until she heard the sound of luggage hitting the floor. She closed the book and laid it down, then went up the stairs tentatively.

Other than necessities ("My bathroom's out of soap") and some unpleasant encounters ("Did I tell you to change my bedsheets?"), Jean had still never gotten Bailey to open up to her. She'd tried. She'd made cookies, more than once. She'd gotten a movie—a teen drama that she had zero interest in, but hoped would be the icebreaker she and her granddaughter needed—and popped popcorn, only to have Bailey snatch both out of her hands and disappear into her bedroom with them. She'd invited Bailey every time she left the house. And nothing. Her granddaughter seemed to hate her just for existing.

But as she always did, she pasted on a timid smile as she came into the kitchen, hoping against all hope that the smile would disarm Bailey's foul moods and even fouler mouth. Bailey was leaning against the stove and eating a Pop-Tart. Jean glanced at the luggage that Bailey had parked in the entryway by the front door. Everything she'd come with, even the pillow and blanket she'd been holding when she arrived, was threaded through the handle of one suitcase. Jean felt a pang of something she couldn't quite pinpoint. Relief that she'd once again have her house to herself, lonely and quiet as it might be, and sadness that her granddaughter was leaving before they ever got a chance to connect, mixed together. Was there an emotion for that?

"You can take those with you," Jean said, motioning toward the Pop-Tart in Bailey's hand. "For the trip."

"Already done," Bailey said around a mouthful of Pop-Tart. "I also took the lotion in that bathroom because I like the way it smells. It's not too widowy."

From the beginning, the word *widow* always stung, and Jean hated hearing it. It made her feel old and gnarled and terribly alone. She hated the sympathetic and uncomfortable way people looked at her when they found out she was a widow. It always seemed to Jean that there was less finality to phrases like *passed away* or *moved on* or is *up in heaven*, because those phrases connoted movement, and thus existence. Words like *dead* and *died* and *widow* all seemed so dark and final. He was deader to her somehow when she thought of herself as a widow.

"That's fine. I'll buy a new lotion. You can take the perfume up there too. I think some of it was your mom's."

"It's skunky."

Jean moved to clean up some of the crumbs that Bailey had left on the counter, which, thankfully, forced her to turn her back to the girl, where she could hide everything she was thinking, everything she was feeling. There were so many things she wanted to say to Bailey—how she understood and felt her pain, how she wished she would let other people in and stop with this tough act, how she missed her and hoped that she would come back and that maybe someday they could have a real relationship, how she regretted the way she'd raised Laura if that had anything to do with why Laura drank herself, and her life, into oblivion. But none of those things felt safe to Jean. They all seemed attached to feelings rooted so deeply inside of her, she feared that if she said them, she might eviscerate herself right there on the kitchen floor.

Soon there was the sound of footsteps coming down the stairs, and Laura plodded in, wearing a torn and filthy old sleep shirt and looking like hell.

"Coffee?" she croaked, turning in circles, searching for a coffeemaker.

"I've already tossed the pot. It was cold. I'll make another," Jean said, reaching for the carafe.

"Don't bother," Laura said. "I'll just go back to bed. My head is killing me."

"When are we leaving, then?" Bailey asked, swallowing the last of her Pop-Tart and sipping a glass of milk.

"For what?" Laura peered up at her daughter—who was taller than she was, Jean just noticed—out of one squinted eye.

Bailey let her shoulders drop downward impatiently. "Home. Duh."

Laura shook her head, scratched her neck. "We're not going home. Not right now. We're staying here until I can get back on my feet." She turned to Jean. "I assume that's okay?"

Flustered, Jean didn't even have time to think before she found herself nodding yes and saying, "As long as you need."

"No, it's not okay," Bailey countered. "I want to go home. This place is lame. What did you come here for if it wasn't to get me?"

"To get control," Laura said, sounding frustrated and weary, then rubbed her hand over her forehead. "I don't know. To get away. To get . . . better, I guess."

"I thought that's what rehab was for," Bailey said. "I thought you were all 'cured' or whatever." She made quote marks with her fingers when she said "cured," and Jean half expected the milk glass to slip out of her hand and shatter on the floor.

"I did. I am."

"Then why can't you 'get better' "—again with the air quotes—"at home?"

"Bailey, you don't understand. Your dad left me with a lot of things to handle, and I just don't think I can do it right now. I want to get some rest before I go back." Laura pulled her hand away from her face. She seemed to sink down into herself, getting smaller and smaller before Jean's very eyes. She'd never seen her daughter look lost and helpless before—not even when she was little. She was an angry infant, a bold toddler, a precocious little girl, but never once had she ever been helpless.

"But I mean, why can't it ever be about what I want?" Bailey countered. "Why can't I ever have any sort of say in my own life? I'm not the one who got all hooked on booze, so why am I the one who's always suffering? It's not fair. I don't see why—"

"Because I can't do it, okay?" Laura had gone taut like a fire hose, her voice, loud and sharp, bouncing off the kitchen cabinets. "I can't do it all alone, Bailey. You know what it was like over there. Trash and dishes and the bill collectors and the water turned off. The house is broken and I feel broken, and now I'm afraid every time I drink, everyone will be eyeing me, judging me, saying I need to go back to rehab. Especially your dad. I can't do that anymore."

"But you're sober now. You'll do better," Bailey said.

"I was not falling apart because I was drinking too much!" Laura shrieked, her hands balled up in fists at her sides. "I was falling apart because I was alone to do it all. I was falling apart because everyone expects me to just be able to handle everything with no help."

Jean could see Bailey's chin quiver. "Lies," she finally said in a very quiet voice.

Laura closed her eyes and steadied her voice. "I just didn't get much sleep there and need some time to get back on my feet. To work up a plan. We'll go back when I get caught up on sleep. Everything will be better then." Laura turned and rummaged through the pantry, then came out with a sleeve of saltines. "I'll make some coffee later," she said, and then trudged back upstairs.

After she'd gone, Jean felt more in the way than ever. She wasn't sure what to make of Laura's denial. Maybe Curt was making things sound worse than they were. Maybe Laura was simply heartbroken and overwhelmed, and couldn't Jean, more than anyone, understand how that felt? But yet . . . Bailey was so very angry. Clearly there was more to it than maybe even Laura understood. Maybe it was possible that Laura truly didn't realize she had fallen so far down into the hole she was in. Meanwhile, Bailey's anger came off her in sheets and oozed out beneath their feet. Jean almost felt light-headed from it.

"Would you like to go to the pool today?" Jean asked quietly, knowing this question would do nothing but anger Bailey, but unsure what she could say that wouldn't, and also unsure what silence would do.

Bailey gazed at her, teeth gritted, as if she'd never seen the woman before, and then lifted her milk glass and chugged what was left. When she finished, she slammed the glass in the sink so hard Jean winced and braced herself for flying broken shards of glass, which never came. "Bullshit," Bailey mumbled, then spun on her heel and went the way her mother had just gone. "This is not fair!" she cried, much louder, when she reached the top of the stairs. The outburst was followed by yet another slammed door. If this kept up, Jean would have a splintered door on her hands.

But that would be the least of her worries.

TWELVE

Jean had just finished cleaning up the dishes from her egg salad sandwich, to which she'd added capers as a trial run for a possible future club dish, when Bailey came into the kitchen. Jean didn't acknowledge her. She'd learned her lesson one too many times now. Engaging with Bailey meant opening oneself up to all manner of abuse, and after the shrieking match between Laura and Bailey in the kitchen that morning, Jean just didn't think she had it in her.

She knew she couldn't ignore the situation forever. At some point she would need to talk to Laura, find out how long she planned to stay, find out what exactly the plan was and how she could help. But today was not that day. Laura was hungover and pissed off and, short of calling Curt, who was unlikely to do anything, Jean was at a loss how to deal with any of that.

Wayne would have known. Wayne seemed to always know. And he had a way of getting Laura to listen to him. If only she could get Kenneth to come home while Laura was here. Maybe he would be able to get Laura to listen to him too.

"So when are we leaving?" Bailey asked.

Jean turned, still holding the dishrag in her hand, and tried to paste on a smile, though that was getting harder and harder with Bailey. "What?"

Bailey grunted and shook her head as if Jean were possibly the dumbest person who ever walked the face of the earth. "Swimming?" She mimed doing a breaststroke. "You said we were going swimming?"

"Oh. I didn't think you'd want to go."

"I don't. But it's better than sitting around here all day. With her." Bailey gave a quick glance over her shoulder at the stairs.

"Okay," Jean said, wringing out the dishrag and draping it over the faucet. "We'll go. Just let me . . ." She found herself strangely rattled by this sudden request for together time, still wanting to do things right. Still hoping that doing things right was a possibility. She tried to move five directions at once, bobbing and weaving this way and that. She patted the sides of her hair and felt her shorts pockets—for no particular reason other than she didn't know what else to do—until her brain kicked in. "Let me get ready," she finally said, and that seemed to be what it took to get her moving. She picked up her book and put it down again. "Do you need something to eat?"

"I ate a Pop-Tart. Remember?"

"That was hours ago."

Bailey rolled her eyes and sighed with annoyance. "I ate four of them, okay? Are we gonna go, or are we gonna talk about the History of Bailey's Stomach Contents?"

Jean nodded, started to move past her granddaughter. "Do you swim?" she asked as she passed.

"No, I'm planning to drown myself in your neighborhood pool," Bailey said.

Jean tried not to smile. She knew Bailey was trying to be tough, to be abrasive. But something about the way she'd said it led Jean to believe that just maybe she might be breaking through that angry exterior after all.

Jean rushed upstairs to her bedroom, pausing only briefly to listen at Laura's door. Hearing nothing but silence, she moved on. She would leave Laura a note, invite her to join them, even though she knew Laura wouldn't.

Jean pawed through her dresser drawer, rifling past clothing items she hadn't worn in years—a clutch of slips that her mother had insisted she buy when she first got married, though she never wore dresses, a knotted pair of panty hose, a lacy negligee that Wayne had loved (she'd last worn it for him the week after he was diagnosed, for what Jean would always think of as their farewell love-making session, even though they'd made clunky, clumsy, half-sick love several times after that). Scrunched in the very back, half-stuck behind the drawer, was her old swimsuit, a black and gold skirted thing that practically screamed *old lady*. She held it up over her torso and studied herself in the mirror, shuddering at the very idea of squeezing into it. She hadn't swum in years—maybe not in a decade. And she certainly didn't plan to start today.

But if Bailey wanted to go down to the pool, she would go. She would wear the suit and she would sit in a lawn chair and she would be thrilled to do it, if it meant a few minutes of happiness for her granddaughter—and peace and control for her.

When she finally sucked up enough courage to face the world in her swimsuit and found her floppy sun hat, Jean headed back downstairs, where she found Bailey leaning over the bar, eating pickle chips out of a jar and thumbing through the Flavian Munney book.

"You ready to go?"

"This is stupid. You actually read this?"

Jean felt her face flush. "You mind if I call my friend Loretta to go with us?" she asked, reaching for the phone.

Bailey picked up the book and turned so that she was resting backward against the counter. She held it up in front of her face. *"Flavian's chest heaved under Roberta's shaky touch. She let her fingers dip into the playground of a divot at the top of his six-pack, and she shuddered, moaning aloud and swirling her finger in the pool of sweat that had gathered there,"* she read aloud. "Gross! Who wants to play with sweaty man nipples?"

"I'm going to call," Jean said, dialing Loretta's phone number.

Bailey continued to read, her voice going low and sultry. *"Roberta let her hand trail down his stomach, over the muscles that rose and lowered with his every breath, toward the erection that was unrolling to meet her just above his belly button."* She laughed out loud. "Unrolling? Makes it sound like one of those party favor things you blow into."

"I don't read them normally," Jean explained, her face burning. "The club voted . . ."

But Loretta picked up the other end of the line, rescuing Jean from having to explain further, and fortunately by the time she was off the phone, Bailey had finished her pickle chip and had laid the book down while she rooted around in the pickle jar for another one. Jean grabbed the book and stuffed it into her purse, as if she were dying to read it at the pool, but knowing she was simply hiding it from further humiliating read-alouds.

"Loretta will meet us down there," she said. "Do you have your swimsuit on?"

"Duh," Bailey answered, finally fishing out a pickle and devouring it in one bite.

Maybe because it was still early in the day, or maybe because the neighborhood had all grown up and moved out, or maybe because it wasn't all that hot that day, the pool was nearly deserted when Jean and Bailey arrived. A lone lifeguard sat at a round patio table, listening to music and chewing on a thumbnail so intently, Jean wondered how it wasn't hurting him.

He pulled the earbuds out of his ears when they opened the gate.

"Hey," he said as Jean signed them in. "Nice day, huh?"

"Very," Jean said, and it was true. The sky was brilliant blue, with just enough clouds to make it look interesting. The sun washed over the pool deck, giving it a bathed, glittery look that suggested excitement ahead. That had once been Jean's favorite part about early summer—the promise that it held. But ever since Wayne died, she'd had so little to look forward to. What promises mattered when that one—the one that they'd be together until they were old and dotty—had been broken? She would be old and dotty alone. "Where is everyone?" she asked.

The guard shrugged his tanned shoulders and popped a handful of sunflower seeds, which he'd seemed to produce out of nowhere, into his mouth. "Been dead all week. Got the pool to yourself."

"Awesome, dude," Bailey snarked.

Jean offered him an apologetic smile and took her things to a deck chair. Suddenly she didn't know why she hadn't been to the pool in so long. Sitting in the sun for an hour or two would feel good. Had she gotten any sun on her face since Wayne died? She couldn't remember. In some ways, it was as if the sun had died right along with him.

Loretta barreled through the gate just as Jean was getting settled, a giant bag dangling from her arm and an even bigger pair of sunglasses dwarfing the top half of her face. She signed in and made her way to Jean and Bailey, waving the whole way.

"How do you like our private pool?" Jean called.

"If I'd known, I'd have worn my bikini," Loretta answered, and out of the corner of her eye, Jean could see Bailey make a gagging gesture with her finger. Loretta must have seen it too, because she leaned toward Bailey and said, "The thong one." Jean tried hard not to giggle as Bailey shot daggers into Loretta with her eyes.

"I brought Flavian with me," Jean said.

"Flavian in a Speedo—now, that's my kind of after-lunch aperitif," Loretta answered, pulling an oversized towel out of her bag and spreading it over the chair before settling into it. "What do you think of it so far?"

"You know the rules. No talking about a book before the club meets."

Loretta pulled a sweating plastic cup out of her bag and took a healthy sip through the straw. "My rule. I can break it."

"Nope. You have to wait, just like everyone else, if you want to hear my deep thoughts about Flavian Munney."

"Don't say *deep* and *Flavian Munney* in the same sentence. You'll give me a hot flash." Loretta took another sip as Bailey, making retching noises, got up from the deck chair and sat on the edge of the pool, down by the diving board, out of their earshot.

"So I see she's warming up nicely," Loretta said, gesturing to Bailey with her cup.

Jean leaned her head back against the vinyl strap of the chair. "I've given up. She's sour and mad all the time, and her eating habits are atrocious. And she does the strangest things. Things you and I would never think of doing. Like the cake thing. That was just bizarre, wasn't it?"

Loretta shrugged. "She's trying to shock everyone because when she does, she gets attention."

"Well, she's losing mine. I just don't have the energy for it. And to make it worse, now Laura has shown up. Drunk, of course, and having driven herself all the way across the state like that."

"Oh, my, the prodigal daughter returns."

"Yes, so what did they have first thing this morning? A screaming match in my kitchen. Wayne is probably rolling over in his grave just listening to it. He would have known how to handle all of this, and obviously I'm not doing a very good job of it. It's hard to handle someone you barely know."

"Don't bring Wayne into it. You'll just make yourself miserable. You're doing just fine. Remember? You were two halves of the same whole, so anything he could have and would have done, you can do just as well. We've discussed this so many times."

"I know, I know," Jean said. "And I'm doing it. I just hate doing it alone."

Loretta leaned over and set her drink on the ground next to her chair, then reached over and patted Jean's arm. "That will never go away," she said. "And you wouldn't want it to."

"Thank you, Dr. Optimist. Am I going to die a lonely and crazy old cat lady with no teeth too?"

"No, of course not," Loretta said. "You'll have a few teeth." She reached into her bag and produced another Flavian Munney novel, which she dropped into Jean's lap. "Take two of these and call me in the morning and you'll be just fine."

Jean ran her fingers over the book cover. "Dear God, is he wearing chaps?"

Loretta grinned wickedly. "Rodeo-Lovin' Flavian. Rope me up, cowboy! Yeeeehaw!" This last she yelled while waving her arm over her head as if swinging a lasso. Her voice echoed off the walls, and even the lifeguard looked up. Bailey made a disgusted noise and slid into the deep end, the water rippling up over her head.

Jean laughed, despite herself. "How many of these things are there?"

Loretta took the book and rubbed the cover as if she were buffing off Jean's fingerprints. "Not enough. Never enough."

"You must have hundreds."

"At least one for every month of next year's club reading pleasure."

"I think Mitzi would kill you."

"Probably," Loretta said. "But she'd kill me with a satisfied smile on her face."

Jean burst out laughing. She loved how Loretta could take even the most stressful day and turn it into something fun.

"Besides, these are so much more fun than that tired Thackeray crap."

"Oh," Jean said. "Did I tell you about my run-in with Janet? She seemed to have a similar opinion of the Thackeray novel."

"Not surprising. It really was terrible. What did she say about it? She didn't make a peep about it at the meeting."

"That was the thing. She didn't get to say anything. The minute she started to talk to me, her horrible boss appeared out of nowhere and just lit into her."

"Lit into her? About what?"

"About everything. It was really just so awkward. Almost inappropriate."

"Oh, wait, was he the bald one? I've seen him before. Walks like he's got a nine-foot pole crammed up his nethers."

Jean nodded. "That's him. I probably should have said something. Poor thing was so embarrassed."

"To hell with turning him in. We should get him back. One time my friends Dolly, Jane, and Lily and I got fed up with our boss, so we kidnapped him and tied him up in a bedroom so we could run the company without him. True story." She took a sip of her drink.

Jean studied her friend for a beat. "You did not. That's the movie *Nine to Five*," she said. "You never had a boss."

"Not true. Before I married Chuck, I had bosses," Loretta countered.

"I stand corrected."

"I just never had a boss I didn't sleep with."

And that had turned into a true story about a gay boss that Loretta had once tried to sex straight, and how it almost worked, except he never could figure out how to undo women's clothes, and they were so wrapped up in their conversation, they never saw the lifeguard get up and walk over to the deep end, where he crouched down and said, "Hey, you're not allowed to wear street clothes in the pool." And they didn't see Bailey give him the double bird and do a lazy backflip, her cutoff jean shorts and tank top sticking to her body.

They chatted and had a good time, and Jean had just been thinking that maybe they could make this a regular thing, that maybe this was what would bring her back to the world of the living, back into the sun, when they heard a "Hey!"

They both turned just in time to see something fly from the deep end right onto the lifeguard's table with a splash.

"Hey!" he yelled again, his shoulders hunched up and

his hands held out defensively. "Whoa! You can't . . ." Something else flew at him, and then another thing and another, all landing with splashes on the table, on the deck next to the table, and on the lifeguard himself.

"What the . . . ?" Loretta said in a low voice. "Is that . . . ?"

But Jean could see what it was clearly, and her mouth went dry, the laughter evaporating from it instantly. "Bailey's shorts," she said.

The lifeguard jumped up, but didn't seem to know what to do. He peeled a pair of underwear off his chest and dropped them to the ground. He looked up at Jean and Loretta, but Jean was too afraid to even look in the pool to see what she knew she'd see there.

Finally the lifeguard seemed to find his voice. "Dude, you have to have a swimsuit on . . . This is a family pool," he said to Bailey. "She can't do that here!" he yelled across to Jean.

"Oh, dear Lord, that child is naked as the day she was born," Loretta said.

Finally Jean forced herself to look into the pool, and there was Bailey, swimming defiantly to the pool wall. She crossed her elbows on the pool deck and rested her chin on her arms. "You said I couldn't swim in my clothes," she said.

"That's not what I meant. You have to wear *some* clothes," the lifeguard responded. He directed his next words to Jean: "I'm gonna have to ask you to leave," he said. "Sorry, but swimsuits are policy."

Loretta burst out laughing, as if *Sorry, swimsuits are policy* was the funniest thing she'd heard all day.

So much for a regular thing, Jean thought, and with a sigh got up and carried a towel over to the side of the pool where Bailey was treading water. Jean wordlessly bent by the ladder and opened the towel for Bailey to cover with on the way out.

But the girl paid no attention to her grandmother. She swam to the shallow end of the pool and took the steps, very deliberately, and, to Jean's eyes, very slowly. She sauntered over to the lifeguard and picked up her clothes.

"Sorry. I guess I misunderstood," she said, then yelled over her shoulder, "I'll wait in the car!"

Jean stood by the pool, towel still outstretched, and watched as her granddaughter strode across the parking lot, covering herself with wads of sopping clothes, and got into Jean's car. Jean and Loretta exchanged a look across the deck.

Loretta pointed at the car. "Wayne would not have known what to do about that!" she said.

Jean couldn't argue. She could only fold the towel and, not daring to so much as look up, slink past the lifeguard to the car.

THIRTEEN

Dear J. K. Rowling:

I suppose you get fan e-mails all the time. You probably get so many of them, there is no possible way you can even look at them all. I know there is pretty much no chance you'll see this, but I'm going to write it anyway.

I love your books. And, no, I don't mean that I love the movies of your books like all the other kids. I mean I love your books. I've been reading them pretty much my whole life. Okay, maybe not my *whole* whole life, but since I was pretty little.

My mom and I read *Harry Potter and the Sorcerer's Stone* out loud together. Every night she would sit on the edge of my bed, just like I was still a little kid, and she would read a chapter. And then I would beg her to read another chapter when she was done. And another when she finished that one too. And soon it was way past my bedtime, but we didn't care because the book was so good.

That was the last book my mom and I ever read together—can you believe it? I guess things happened. Also, turning fifteen happened. It's probably a little immature to have your mom read stories to you out loud at bedtime when you're fifteen. Not that I would care, but maybe she did. I don't know. Probably not.

I know Harry was the hero of your books, but honestly my hero was always Hermione. She was smart and brave and loyal. But she was also kind of serious too. I'm like that. Serious. I don't know about the other stuff. I like to believe I'm smart and brave and loyal, but it's been so long since I've just been allowed to be me, it's hard to tell. But it was good to see a girl that could be those things without being all giggly and ditzy too.

I think it would be cool to just be able to make things happen with a flick of my wrist. It would be really cool to have a time-turner too.

So if you're reading this, you don't need to answer me or anything. I just wanted to tell you thank you. Keep writing!

Sincerely,
Bailey Butler

The lifeguard had a name. Noah. Ironic, Bailey thought. Like the guy in the Bible, rescuing the animals from the flood waters. Only this Noah had rescued her from the boredom of having to live in this place.

Not that her grandmother was all bad. She was old. She was boring. She was constantly trying to cram food down Bailey's throat. But at least she knew Bailey was there. She was . . . predictable. Predictable could be good. She had forgotten what predictable felt like.

Bailey had even been considering giving the poor woman a break had her mom not shown up. Not that Bailey would've wanted to be there without her mom, but just that with her mom there and still not paying any attention to anyone but herself, it was kind of a slap in the face.

This was what her mom did all day every day:

1. Sleep.

2. Walk around looking like a zombie, which was scary as hell. If Bailey had told anyone who knew Laura Butler that the woman hadn't showered in, like, two weeks, they probably would have joined a church right away and waited for the Apocalypse to get here. And, not for nothing, but the perfect-skinned, perfect-smiled, perfectly perfect Laura Butler looked pretty not perfect at the moment. She might have even made Bailey look good, and Bailey had to force herself to keep from sniping, *I don't*

*know where I got these genes! I swear to God I have
more than once wondered if they switched me with
some other baby!* But she'd have to be speaking
with her mom to say that.

3. Yell at people.

Bill collectors: "I don't care what your policy is! Where's
the heart? Where's the caring for a sick single mother, huh?
I've been in the hospital for a month, and you're talking to me
about your goddamn policy? How do you sleep at night? I
know it's not your personal policy, but I would never be able
to work for a company that treated people the way your company treats people, and you know why? I have a conscience!"

Various managers and employees at Bradley Electronics:
"I'm on a leave of absence, Syl; I'm not dead. I know you
have to take care of things while I'm away, but don't treat me
like a corpse. Well, Henry can get another job if he doesn't
like it. I wonder how Carolyn and the kids will like it when
they find out he pissed away his career because he was too
impatient to wait for his boss to come back. How about you
bring that up as new business at the next board meeting, Syl,
and see how it goes? Well, then stop treating me like I'm
some sort of plague on the company and start giving me the
respect I've earned. I don't care what I did a month ago—it's
not about what I did in one day, but what I've done over the
course of sixteen years!"

And, especially, her soon-to-be-ex-husband, the Ghost

Dad: "No, I will not calm down! I don't have to calm down! You lost the right to tell me to calm down the minute you walked out of that house. No, I won't lower my voice. I don't care if someone else hears me. What do I have to be ashamed of, Curt? Not nearly as much as you do!"

And then repeat it all on a loop. Back to the bill collectors, back to the office, back to Ghost Dad. Over and over and over again until Bailey got tired of eavesdropping, until her brain hurt trying to keep up with the long list of People Who've Wronged Laura Butler. God, the woman was even perfect at being a victim. It was sickening.

And you know who she wasn't yelling at?

Bailey. Of course. Because she'd have to actually know Bailey existed to yell at her. That would be way too much trouble.

But Noah the lifeguard noticed her. If she'd only known that standing naked in front of a guy would make him notice her, she might have done it years ago.

She still couldn't believe she'd done it. It was one thing to drop a glass jar on a hospital floor; it was another to get naked in front of the whole world in the middle of a Wednesday afternoon, and she was beginning to wonder if she really was just flat-out losing it. One minute she'd been paddling around and thinking about mermaids— mermaids! Like a little kid would do!—and the next she was throwing her clothes at a guy she'd never seen before in her life.

And walking toward the lifeguard, not even worrying

whether she looked fat or frumpy or whether he could see the freckles on her thighs or whether he was grossed out by the pudge on her lower belly.

She'd sat in the car and laughed one of those laughs that was a half cry, because she'd realized at that moment that she'd somehow gone from pretending she didn't care to actually not caring. And somehow that seemed scary and really hopeless to her.

She'd left her bra down there. She hadn't meant to, but when she went back the next day to retrieve it, she found out that she had some things in common with Noah. For example, he didn't like to think about heavy things, and she was trying to escape them. He liked to listen to stoner music around the pool, and she liked to read to a brainless beat. He liked to smoke a lot of dope, and she liked to pretend she did.

She started hanging out with him every day. He'd light up a joint, and she'd complain that she could only smoke it at night because it made her want to sleep. Then he'd give her a baggie for later, because he was generous that way, and she'd stuff it in her pocket. The dope would kick in and he'd start talking all this philosophical crap; she'd act like she cared, and then he'd turn on some music and she'd pull a paperback out of her backpack and prop it on her knees and get lost in a story the way she'd always done. Sometimes he would get the stoned giggles and they would laugh over the dumbest things. It felt good to laugh with someone, someone who didn't have a clue what her life was really like.

And she would come home, sun-drenched and chlorine-soaked, and her grandmother would practically fall all over herself with happiness that Bailey was "getting out and making friends." Bailey wasn't sure if Noah really fell into the category of "friend," mostly because it had been so long since she'd had a real one of those. Could someone who didn't know you at all be your friend? Could someone who was stoned one hundred percent of the time you hung out together really offer any friendship potential? She didn't know, but he didn't judge her and she didn't question him; as far as she could see, these days that was close enough to friendship.

And sometimes she would lie back on the chaise lounge and close her eyes against the sun, old Led Zepplin songs pulsing over the overhead pool speakers. She would imagine herself in a lavender and silver prom gown, a stoned Noah standing next to her in a tux, awkwardly clutching a wrist corsage in a plastic box, and the image seemed okay, like it could even possibly have happened in an alternate life.

And after his shift, he would invite her to get pizza or go hang at his house, but she'd beg off—scared to be alone and away from her grandmother, even if she didn't quite understand why—and make him drop her off at home, where she'd dump the pot he'd given her in an ugly ceramic vase that sat on a shelf above the coatrack in the kitchen.

"What's that?" Noah asked one day. She was tucked into a deck chair, a book propped up on her knees as usual.

"Huh?" She didn't look up.

"What's that?" he repeated, smacking the book with the back of his hand. It wobbled.

"Stop—it's a book, dumbass. This is your brain on drugs." She gestured to his head but still didn't look up.

He was silent for a moment, bending and flexing his knees restlessly. It was overcast, and the one person who'd come to the pool had packed up and left an hour ago.

"Let's smoke some," Noah said.

Bailey didn't answer, just turned the page.

He smacked the book cover with the back of his hand again. "Come on, you never join me. I'm tired of getting high alone."

"Stop. In a minute," she mumbled.

He was silent for another minute, then, with surprising quickness and agility, reached over and snatched the book out of Bailey's hand. "I think you're afraid," he teased.

"Stop it!" she cried, smacking at him, at first playfully, but when he didn't give the book back, she started to get angry. "Give me the book. I'm serious."

He grinned. "I love it when you get mad. It's cute." He stood up and held the book high, out of Bailey's reach.

She jumped off the lounge, her teeth bared, and slapped at his arms, his stomach, his hands. "I'm not kidding. That's not even my book. I borrowed it from my grandmother. Give it back."

But he held it even higher and started across the deck with it. And she could feel it coming, rolling in on her like a wave—the anger, the ridiculous, blinding ugliness that seemed to push itself in on her so often these days. It was the same rage that made her smash her mother's TV screen in or bust the slats in the backyard fence or tamp out a cigarette on her father's pillow. She couldn't stop it, even though she wanted to, even though she knew that it never turned out well for her. She was powerless against it.

In one motion, she grabbed Noah's cell phone off the patio table and chucked it into the deep end. It went under with a *ploomp*.

Noah's eyes went huge, the book going slack at his side. "What the fuck? Are you kidding me?"

"I told you to give it back," Bailey said, marching over and pulling the book out of his hand.

She walked home, her nose buried in the book the whole way. But she wasn't reading the words. She couldn't through the remorseful tears that streamed down her face. So much for friendship. So much for lavender gowns.

The real kicker was that she hated the stupid book. It was called *Blame*, and it was written by some nitwit with about ten names. She'd found it on the end table in the living room and had picked it up out of curiosity. She knew it was the book her grandmother's book club had been talking about at the last meeting.

About three paragraphs in, she was already pissed. *Blanche sat on the toilet, smoking a cigarette, gazing through the doorway at the doughy arm of her last trick, which had slipped through the sheets and pointed toward the overturned gin bottle on the floor. When she was done with her cigarette, she knew she'd crawl to that bottle and drink the dregs, no matter that her most recent "partner" made her stomach churn with revulsion, no matter that his lips had last suckled it. She knew she would do it, and as pathetically as her mother had done. She knew this precisely because it was what her mother had done. She would be powerless to do anything else.*

This Thackeray idiot had no idea what he was even talking about.

Yet she couldn't stop reading.

She came home, stripped out of her clothes, put on her pajamas, and propped her back against two pillows and read.

By night's end, she'd finished the book.

And had begun to formulate a plan.

FOURTEEN

Jean stood outside the shed, trying to work up the courage to go inside. Summer had elbowed spring out of the way over the course of just days, and had pushed its way in fully, the sun strong, making everything look bleached and suffering, and she felt sweat rolling down the small of her back, beneath the flannel shirt she'd always worn to do yard work.

It was something they'd done together, yard work. Wayne would fire up the riding mower and swoop circles around the property while she dug holes along the sides of the house and patted plants and seeds and roots and bulbs in little puddle-shaped gardens. They would water together, spread mulch together, and stand back with their hands on their hips to admire their work together.

At the end of the day, it had almost felt as intimate to Jean as making love. Everything about them matched.

Their muscles ached the same; their eyes and cheekbones and noses wore matching shades of sunburn. Even the grime under their fingernails, up their forearms, and caked with sweat in the creases of their wrists and necks and elbows looked like twin sets. They panted and perspired and stood over the sink and gulped water together. And afterward, they felt good together.

They would shower together, wrap themselves in robes. Jean would make them a light dinner, then fix them both tea, and they would recline in the living room, watching a baseball game or reading, or, when the kids still lived at home, playing a game of Monopoly, their hands brushing against each other, both of them feeling so comfortable, feeling ownership of their home, their lives, more than ever.

Feeling like this, this was the place where they belonged.

Jean hadn't done yard work since the diagnosis.

At first she'd told herself that it was because she was too busy, running Wayne to doctor appointments and chemo treatments, buying his meds, keeping up with his needs. And then after the appointments stopped and the running out to do anything stopped and Wayne's whole existence resided in the bed in the dining room where Jean and the home nurse could keep track of him, she told herself she didn't have time because caring for him was too cumbersome. And then in those final weeks, those final morphine-haze days, she told herself that she couldn't possibly go anywhere, because the moments when Wayne was lucid and recognized her were far too precious to miss.

And then there had been the funeral, the people, Kenneth staying on. She was too busy again. And then too horrified by the depth and scope of her loneliness to even think about digging in the dirt.

She hired a kid down the street to mow the lawn. She let the annuals die and the perennials become strangled by weeds. She told the kid to mow over the puddle-shaped flower beds. She let it all go.

But those Knock Out roses. Wayne's Knock Outs. They still lived on. They flourished! They didn't mind the weeds; they didn't suffocate; they didn't shrivel with thirst. They grew. And when Jean had noticed them the other day, when she'd picked a rose and sniffed it, she'd felt guilty.

Wayne loved those roses. Maybe he was sending her a message with them.

A bird squalled at her repeatedly from a branch hanging over the shed. She looked up, tried to find it, tried to spot the nest it was protecting, but she couldn't. She went back to staring at the shed door. Wayne's shed. It hadn't been open since he last opened it. It would smell like those intimate gardening days. It would remind her of him, and the very thought nearly made her nauseated with dread, but she knew she had to go in there.

It wasn't just the roses. It was Bailey too. And Laura. Neither of their situations seemed to be improving at all. Laura still stayed locked in her bedroom most of the day, screaming into the phone, watching daytime talk shows at earsplitting volume, and barely eating. She would creep downstairs in the evening, looking pale and sickly and so thin, her joints stuck out. She wasn't showering. She wasn't moving forward. She wasn't speaking to Jean. And other than to scream, she wasn't speaking to Bailey.

But in the evenings she would leave, wrapped up in too-big button-downs and paint-stained sweatpants, only to come home half an hour later, saying nothing about where she'd been and sinking right back into the darkened TV-saturated bedroom for the rest of the night. Sometimes Jean could hear her laugh at the TV late into the night. She suspected that Laura's nightly treks had been to buy alcohol, but she was too afraid to say anything. Laura had been so volatile. Not to mention, when did you stop stepping into your kids' lives?

And then there was Bailey, who did way too much speaking, only not to Jean specifically, and never with anything pleasant or positive. She'd been spending a lot of time down at the swimming pool, and though Jean acted as if she were excited that Bailey had found a friend, she had begun to suspect that Bailey might be doing things that could get her into trouble. Or, even more likely, things to get the poor lifeguard in trouble.

She worried about what having Bailey's mother in the house might do to the child. She had already been so angry; Laura's presence only seemed to make it worse. Once, Jean had even walked past Bailey's not-quite-closed bedroom door and seen Bailey sitting on her bed, her knees pulled up, her arms wrapped around them tightly, biting herself repeatedly on the wrists, on the legs, leaving welts, inspecting them, and biting herself again. Jean had also noticed that same children's book open on the bed next to her. Was it healthy for a girl Bailey's age to be so attached to a book intended for a toddler? Jean didn't know.

Both of them were in such pain, and Jean could do nothing about it. And she couldn't help but think that Wayne would be expecting her to do something. But what? What would he expect her to do?

The feeling was so hopeless, as if she suddenly couldn't feel him anymore. As if he were further away from her than ever before. What did it mean when you suddenly lost a presence that may have been there only in your imagination anyway? Had she been closer to him, had she been a better wife, maybe she would still be able to feel his presence; maybe she would know what he would do. Maybe he would tell her.

The very thought made her feel so frantic, all she could think about were the rosebushes and the yard that desperately needed gardening.

But standing in front of the closed shed doors, she didn't know how she would ever reach out and pull them open. The effort seemed so massive, so impossible.

Slowly, she extended her hand and touched the padlock, her fingers initially jumping back involuntarily, as if she'd received an electric shock. But she knew that was all in her mind and she forced them to curl around the lock, then took a deep breath and stabbed the key into it before she could talk herself out of it. *You're being silly, Jean,* she told herself.

The lock opened easily, as if it had been only a weekend since it had last been opened, rather than years, and she tugged it off the door handle, the reverberations of the movement all up and down the metal door a familiar music. She let out a breath—not realizing that she'd been holding it until she started to feel dizzy—and twisted the door handle, then pulled the door open with a squeak.

"Oh, God. Wayne," she said when the smell of the shed greeted her. It was amazing what parts of the brain could be awakened by scent alone. She'd first experienced this when she'd found an old shaving cream can in the bathroom cabinet two months after he'd died. She'd pulled off the lid, buckled to the floor, and cried, lifting the can to her nose over and over again, imagining the rough red spots on Wayne's neck, just above his collar, when they'd go out somewhere special. Imagining him humming along to the radio while he shaved.

She felt like falling to the floor now. The grass clippings, the lawn mower, the oil, the gasoline. Those were the aroma of their daily life together. Those were the smell of happy weekends, of the future, of hopes and of making their two lives a life together—one weekend, one chore, one flower at a time.

Somehow she managed to move her legs forward, sucking in a breath and trying to shake the grief from her brain. *You can miss him forever,* her therapist had told her, back in those early days after his death. *But you can't mourn him forever.* But sometimes it felt as if she would.

She stepped forward, one step, two, running her fingers along the fender of Wayne's riding mower. She should have sold it by now—the kid who mowed her lawn used his own mower—but she could never bring herself to it. Wayne had loved that thing.

Her hands tried to trick her into believing that it still felt warm under her fingers, as if he'd just finished using it, but she knew better. Besides, she wasn't in the shed for the old mower anyway. She moved beyond the mower to the shelves along the far wall, the ones that held watering cans and terra-cotta pots and hardened bags of dirt and fertilizer and plant food and . . .

There they were. Her gardening gloves, the ends of their fingers stained deep brown. They were lying right in the palms of Wayne's gardening gloves, the fingers of each looking almost intertwined as if he were holding her hands in his.

Jean let out a croak and reached for them, the tips of her fingers barely brushing against the fabric of the gloves, barely whisking past his. To touch those gloves would feel too much like touching his hand again. She would be crushed under the weight of memory.

Instead, she backed out of the shed, leaving the gloves,

and the mower, right where they were. She stumbled over the lip of the doorway and fell backward onto her hands and butt, the jolt of pain in her wrist breaking the spell, at least enough for her to glance around, to see if anyone had witnessed her fall.

But nobody was around. Just the damn bird, which continued to shriek above her.

"Oh, shut up, you," she said, trying again (and failing again) to spot the bird in the tree. "Haven't you ever seen someone do yard work before?"

But as she pulled herself up to standing and brushed off the back of her jeans, Jean knew that she would be doing no yard work. Not today, maybe not ever again. She couldn't separate those gloves. And she couldn't buy new ones, either. This was what her life had been reduced to—everything so rooted in meaning and memory, she was unable to complete even the smallest task. If she was being honest with herself, she would admit that she didn't even care for capers or macaroni and cheese with feta and roasted red peppers—she liked them just because they were one of the few things in this world that represented absolutely nothing to her.

She closed the shed door and locked it, feeling emptied. Feeling as if all the work she'd done had been reversed.

She headed back to the house, sweat beading on her forehead and upper lip now. She needed a cold drink. And then maybe she'd lie down. But as she crossed the yard, she saw light glint off the windshield of a familiar car turning slowly into her driveway. She changed course and went around the house to the front, just as the car rolled to a stop.

"Hello!" Mitzi called through the driver's side window as she geared the car into park.

"Hi there," Jean said. "I wasn't expecting you."

"Lunch break." Mitzi got out of her car, the door opening with a creak. Her skirt stuck to the sweat on her legs, and she brushed at it impatiently. "So hot. Thought I'd drop by for a quick visit." She glanced at her watch as she said this. "My usual lunch date is otherwise occupied."

"Court?" Jean asked.

"Meeting with a principal," Mitzi said. "Apparently Russell has been engaging in some less-than-savory activities in the school parking lot during lunch shift. Always something."

"Poor Dorothy," Jean said. "It really is, isn't it?" *For all of us,* she wanted to finish. *Whether we like it or not. Whether we can even handle it or not.*

Mitzi ducked her head to look into Jean's eyes. "You okay? You seem a little off."

Jean tried on a wobbly smile. She could hear the bird, still shrieking in the backyard. "It's just the heat," she said. "I've been . . . doing yard work."

But Mitzi shook her head. "Nice try, but I'm not buying it. I know you. There's something more. Spill. Is it Bailey?"

Jean sagged back against Mitzi's car. The heat beat

down on the metal, and she could feel it sear through her clothes, but she didn't make a move to pull away. "It's Bailey, it's Laura, it's Wayne, it's everything," she said. "Been a rough few weeks, I suppose."

Mitzi leaned back next to Jean. "Wayne? What about him?"

Jean hesitated, still unsure about how much to let Mitzi in. She sighed. "It's so silly, after all this time, isn't it? I should be used to it. I should be able to touch the damn gloves."

Mitzi shook her head again, confused. "Gloves? I'm not following."

Jean offered Mitzi another smile. "I'm sorry," she said. "I suppose I'm just a little bit down right now with all that's going on with Laura and Bailey. I just wish Wayne was here to help me out. I miss him. I don't think I'll ever stop missing him."

"Ah," Mitzi said. She checked her watch again. "I get that. I would be lost without Frank. And, of course, without a little help from my local pharmaceutical friends." Jean gave her a quizzical look, and Mitzi laughed. "I don't mean *drugs*. I mean . . . drugs. Antidepressants. Might help you too."

Jean knew it was rude to act so shocked, but she truly was. This was Mitzi—the one they were all afraid would judge them. She had to remind herself to close her mouth.

"Well, it's not that big of a deal," Mitzi said.

"No, no, of course it isn't," Jean said. "It's just that I had no idea. You seem so happy and put together."

"I am happy," Mitzi said. "I'm very happy. But nobody is put together. We're sure all expected to act like it, though, aren't we? It's kind of ridiculous if you think about it. Nobody admitting their weaknesses, everybody taking so much responsibility for everything. Life is stressful. It's terrible the way we boil everything down to *should* and *shouldn't*. I do it more than most. You should vote for this person or that person. You should make your decisions based on this moral code or that one. You should be just like me. When I say it out loud like that, it's all so obnoxious."

"It's not obnoxious," Jean said, and then she and Mitzi locked eyes, and both of them let out breathy laughs. "Okay, it can occasionally be a little obnoxious."

"I'm a jerk, I know. But I don't mean to be. It's sort of like that Thackeray book. The whole book was about being trapped by your mistakes and blah blah blah. But you know what he got wrong?"

Jean rolled her eyes. "So many things."

"Dorothy couldn't think more polar opposite of the way I think if she tried, but she's still my best friend and I love her and none of that other stuff matters. She accepts that I'm a jerk, and I accept that she does everything exactly how I wouldn't. That's what he got wrong. Human connection. But tell that to my gut when I'm lying awake at night, stressing about whether I've done the right things in my life."

"Me and you both," Jean said. She wiped the sweat that was rolling down her temples. "Would you like to come inside? Much cooler in there. I'll get you something cold to drink."

Mitzi looked at her watch again and grimaced. "Nope. I've got to get back to the salt mines." She stood up straight and patted her backside. "Besides, my buns are about half-baked by now anyway. You sure you're gonna be okay? I can call in sick. Say I got a bad chicken sandwich under-cooked by a bleeding heart free-range freak." She grinned and winked.

"Actually," Jean said, "I'm feeling a little better." And she was. Certainly not great, but a little better. She could still feel a little twist in her heart with the memory of Wayne's gardening gloves. She could still feel the anxiety over what would happen with Laura and Bailey. But in a way she felt lighter too. Not because Mitzi, the most put-together woman in the group, had a weakness. But because Mitzi, the most put-together woman in the group, had a weakness and had shared it with her.

She stood in the driveway and waved good-bye as Mitzi pulled down the street. The sun pounded into the top of her head, and she could feel sweat bead on her lower back and slide down into her waistband. She really could think of doing not much else besides grabbing a cold glass of water and lying down for a few minutes to shake this terrible afternoon.

She went around the house and through the back door, the one right off the living room, and was immediately struck by how much cooler the house felt compared to the outside. But her relief was short-lived, when she was struck with something else.

At first it didn't make sense what she was seeing. At first the best her brain could do was articulate the words, *That shouldn't be happening!* but it took a few seconds for the rest of her to catch up on what was going on.

Bailey was lounging across the couch on her back, one leg dangling toward the floor, her right hand holding a book above her head. In her left hand, she absentmindedly swung something around and around in lazy circles.

Jean's eyes darted to the end table.

The glasses. They were gone.

Bailey was swinging Wayne's glasses around in circles.

"What are you doing?" Jean barked, aware of how she sounded, but unable to control herself. The scent of the mower still lingered in her nose. The vision of his gloved hands holding hers still rolled around in her gut. And now this insolent granddaughter of theirs had moved his glasses from where they'd sat for more than two years undisturbed, and was waving them around as idly as if they were a toy.

Bailey turned her head, a curious expression on her

face. She stopped swinging the glasses, which hung loosely from her fingers now. "What? I'm reading. And I gotta tell you, this stuff is—"

Jean pointed. "Those," she said. "They're not for playing."

Bailey looked curiously at the glasses. "I wasn't playing with them. I had them on because I was getting a headache and Father of the Year forgot to pack mine, but old Gramps was even blinder than I am."

"Put them down," Jean said, her voice gruff, and louder than she wanted it to be. "They aren't supposed to be moved. Put them back."

Bailey's eyes went wide and then narrowed into little slits, the look Jean knew best on her granddaughter. "Okay. Whatever. What's your problem? It's not like he's going to need them or anything."

Jean's hands clenched into fists. Sweat rolled down over one eyelid. "And stop doing that. Stop saying things like that." She stormed over to where Bailey was lying down and snatched the glasses out of her hand. "He was a wonderful man, and you may not disrespect him in this house."

Bailey sat up, the book closing in her lap. "Whoa. How did I disrespect a dead dude?"

"By doing that," Jean said, pointing, as if tracking the words in the air. "By calling him the dead dude and Zombie Grandpa and saying that he kicked the bucket and took a dirt nap and all the other things you say and do to impress yourself. It's not impressive. It's disrespectful. And it . . ." She stopped, pressed her lips together. *Hurts,* she was about to finish. *And it hurts.* But a lump had suddenly appeared in her throat, and she could feel the metal of his frames burning into her hand, could feel the sweat from her palms making them slick.

She couldn't put them back on the end table. Not now. They'd been moved. They'd been moved, and he hadn't come in asking where they were. He hadn't needed to put them on to read a scene out of his favorite Preston and Child book. Bailey had been playing with his glasses, and nobody had noticed because he wasn't around to care.

In the meantime, Bailey had pulled herself to standing. "This place sucks," she said. "I can't wait to leave."

Jean said nothing, the fight drained out of her, as Bailey walked around the couch and sped past her, up to the kitchen, the book she'd been reading tucked into the crook of her arm.

"Oh, good, you're up. This is gonna be a real treat," Jean heard Bailey say when she got to the kitchen. Jean shuffled a few steps to the side and peered up the stairs, where she saw Laura, a glass of water sweating in her hand, her back to Jean.

"Good morning to you too, sunshine," Laura responded in her usual flat voice.

"Morning? It's, like, one. When are we going home? I want to go home. You have to take me home," Bailey said, her voice ratcheting up with every word. Jean recognized the same hysteria coming on that seemed to happen between Laura and Bailey every day at about this time. She didn't want it. She wanted to put her hands over her ears and tune it out.

"Bailey, I've told you. We'll go home soon, okay? Can I not be sick for a while?"

"But you're not sick! You embarrassed yourself in front of everyone, and now you're acting like it's all some big terminal illness that made you do it, but it's not. You're hungover. Tonight you'll feel great, just in time to drink again. Don't think everyone in this house doesn't know it."

Jean blinked, hearing Bailey voice her own thoughts, her own worries.

"Don't talk to me that way," Laura warned. "I'm not your grandmother. You won't get away with it."

"Oh! And speaking of. She's nuts. Just went ballistic on me over a pair of stupid glasses. This place is so messed up! This is abuse. It's got to be abuse to keep me here."

"Nobody's abusing you." Now Laura's voice was edging upward, and Jean's head started to pound with every syllable. "You're so spoiled."

"Oh, really, Mom? Spoiled like a CEO's daughter, or spoiled like someone else's baby? Because you know I was switched at birth!"

"What are you talking about?"

"You know! You know what I'm talking about!"

Jean started up the stairs, but by the time she got to the top, Bailey was already storming out of the room and to her bedroom. Jean heard a few steps and then a slam, a sound she had gotten used to.

Laura shook her head, rubbing her temples with a thumb and forefinger. "What did you do?" she asked Jean when she finally looked up again.

"I told her to put down your father's glasses," Jean said defiantly, her hand still shaking around the glasses. How would she bear to look at that table ever again without them there?

Laura rolled her eyes. "Really? All this over Dad's glasses? It's so morbid, you know, the way you hang on to his stuff like he's coming back."

"Yes, you've told me."

"Can't you just leave well enough alone with her? Can't you just . . . focus on the living people in this house, Mom? It's like you're living with a ghost, and he's your only friend in the world."

Jean opened her mouth to protest, but then snapped it shut again when she realized the only thing that might have come out of it were the words, *You have no idea how right you are.* "It's my house," she finally said.

"Oh, okay, so now I get it. We've worn out our welcome. You want us gone. Very nice. Glad to know I have someplace to come home to when I'm sick."

"That's not what I meant at all. You know that. You can always come here, sick or not."

Laura nodded, unconvinced. "No. Kenny is always

welcome here. But Laura. Oh, well, we don't have to worry about her, because she's got it all together, man. She can handle whatever is thrown her way."

"I never said that."

"You didn't have to. Every move you made, my whole life, has said it for you. Why do you think I drink, Mom? Because it's the only time I get to just be Laura, not Laura the Perfect."

"We never expected you to be perfect."

"There is no more we! You need to come to grips with that, Mom! He's gone, and my daughter is upstairs, angry because his glasses were more important to you than she is."

For a moment, Jean simply gawked at her daughter, almost unable to believe what had just come out of the woman's mouth. *What about you?* Jean wanted to ask. *What part of this is your fault? I wasn't the one drinking. I wasn't the one who got her so angry in the first place!*

But what came out of her mouth might have been even more surprising. "What is your plan?"

"What?"

Jean curled her fingers tighter around the glasses. "What is your plan? When do you go back to work? When do you get . . . better?"

Laura blinked a few times, her mouth hanging wide-open. "You want me out," she said. "Very nice. I guess I know how you feel now. Okay. Okay. You want to creep around here in your little shrine to the Great Wayne God, then fine."

"No, of course not," Jean said. "I want you to get back to your life." But it was useless. Talking to Laura had become useless. Talking to Bailey had become useless. Every bit of the situation seemed useless. Plus, she wasn't sure if maybe Laura was right. Maybe she had made this a shrine to Wayne, without even thinking about it. Maybe as he faded away from her, she only tried to hang on to him tighter—so tightly it was all anyone else could see.

Laura refilled her glass under the faucet and stomped up the stairs—just as Bailey had done a few minutes before—and Jean was alone.

At first she stood in the silent kitchen, listening to ice crash into place in the freezer and the mumbling of TV voices upstairs. But after a while she too trudged up the stairs and shut her bedroom door.

Her legs felt so heavy. Her eyes felt heavy. Her stomach, her breasts, everything felt as if it were being pulled to the ground. She hadn't felt this way since right after Wayne died.

Jean walked to his dresser, which she'd emptied of his T-shirts and boxer shorts and socks long ago. She'd stored her sweaters there, but then had spent last winter chronically cold because she couldn't find the strength to open his dresser and take a sweater out.

But the top drawer she'd opened many times. Three times a day for the first month, twice a day for the second month, once a day for the third and fourth months. Once a week for the fifth. And then she'd . . . stopped.

She opened it now and peered down at the contents inside. Wayne's wallet, including snapshots of both kids, of Bailey at age seven, of Wayne and Jean at a flower show, a snapshot of Jean holding a diapered chimp. She'd had that one taken at a festival down on the riverfront; Wayne had loved it, had always joked that it was a photo of the two of them together. She opened the wallet, lifted it to her nose and closed her eyes, smelled the leather. She rifled past his driver's license and his credit cards (all canceled now, of course), his voter registration card. She pulled out the yellowed newspaper clipping he'd kept in there—his mother's obituary—then refolded it and put it back.

She touched his wedding ring, the pinkie ring she'd given him for their first Christmas and he'd never worn, the rosary with the wooden beads his grandmother had given him as an infant. She picked up his autographed DiMaggio baseball, the one he was so proud of, and turned it around in her hand, inspecting the signature. She remembered when her father had suggested that the signature was a fake how angry Wayne had gotten, how they had almost come to blows. She laid the ball back in the drawer and picked up his bartending book that she'd kept because he'd sketched so many notes in it and she didn't want to forget his handwriting. She flipped through the pages, looking at nothing, but seeing it all—*oranges, triple sec, great Christmas cocktail, try this at Jean's birthday party, no to the vodka, too sweet.*

Handkerchiefs, watches, coins, his handwritten wedding vows, the wristband he'd worn at the hospital when Laura was born, a lifetime of memories and treasures, a person's life boiled down to just enough to fit in a top dresser drawer.

Jean's Crying Time drawer.

In the beginning when she felt like she was drowning in grief, her therapist gave her permission to cry, but only during specific times.

It's healthy to grieve, he'd said, *but it's unhealthy to grieve too much. Schedule crying times, say, noon to one, every day, you will think about him and cry your eyes out. But by one-oh-one, your eyes have to be dry and you have to be moving on. Understand? Give yourself a few times a day these first few weeks, and we'll pare it back later.*

And so she did. During the days, she gathered up Wayne's everyday things and took them to Goodwill. She packed his clothes in boxes and stuffed his shoes in garbage bags and gave away his CDs to friends and donated his coats to charity. She erased him from the house, dry-eyed all the while. And then she put the small treasures—the things she wanted to keep, that she thought he would want her to keep—into his top dresser drawer, and she would touch them and smell them and curl up with them and cry with all she had.

Three times a day for the first month.

Two times a day, which didn't seem like nearly enough, for the second month.

One time a day for the third month.

And so on, until one day she realized she'd forgotten to have a Crying Time for several weeks. And the realization felt like betrayal so fierce, she raced upstairs and tried to force one out. And then got to laughing when she thought of what Wayne would have thought, seeing her writhing around on their bed, clutching his old DiMaggio baseball and making gaggy whining noises meant to instigate tears.

And that had been the end of Jean's Crying Time.

Until today.

FIFTEEN

Jean felt like it was cheating to use packaged tikka masala sauce. She waved her spatula over the bubbling
pan and sniffed. It smelled just like what they used to get
at the Indian restaurant down the street. She would choose
the vegetable korma, and Wayne would pick something
called chili chicken, and they would stuff themselves with
garlic onion naan. But all of that had been handmade—
you could see the chefs in the back, working cooktops
directly behind the buffet table. No packaged tikka masala
there.

Using prepackaged food really went against Jean's desire to be "chefy," as Loretta liked to put it. But she couldn't
help it. She didn't know the first thing about Indian cooking, and it was impossible to try to learn new things in the
house as it was now.

Fortunately, Laura hadn't left the house, hadn't had a

drink in five days. She had showered and was coming out of her room more. Unfortunately, her mood hadn't improved any, and it seemed to Jean that Laura and Bailey couldn't be in the same room together for five minutes without one or both of them blowing up. And both of them ignoring her, except to sneer at her or roll their eyes at something she'd said or huff angrily over something she'd done.

"Why do you let them treat you like that? Tell them to get out," Kenneth had said on the phone last night.

"They don't have anywhere to go. Laura says she can't keep up with the house without Curt."

"She's forty, Mom. That's her problem. You have your own house to deal with. Tell her not to let the door hit her on the way out."

"You know I can't do that."

He'd sighed. "I know. You're too kind for your own good. Dad always said it, and he was right."

She'd forgotten about that, about how Wayne had told her that strays and hard cases could sniff her out like a dog on a rotten sandwich. It had frustrated him, how Jean would be treated by someone she was helping, but at the same time, he'd said, it only made him love her more.

She'd felt tears prick the corners of her eyelids and had only barely held them off, promising herself that later she would remember those words during her Crying Time. And trying not to think about the fact that she was back to a twice-daily Crying Time.

"When are you getting out?" Kenneth had asked her next.

Jean had hesitated. "I'm kept pretty busy here. I have the book club."

"That's not getting out. You can't sit in that house babysitting those two and not ever have a life of your own, Mom. You have to be active."

"We've been meeting here. It's been enough."

"What about Loretta?"

"She's been around." Which was normally the truth, but even Loretta hadn't been over as much as usual. The tension in the air made it too unpleasant. She'd told Jean, *I feel like any minute a frying pan's gonna crash down on my head.* Not that Jean could blame her—she felt that very way herself more times than not, as if she were creeping around her own house surrounded by broken glass and hoping not to get cut. "I'm fine, Kenneth. I really am."

But as she put the lid back on the tikka masala, she wasn't so sure she was fine. She felt jumpy and anxious and like at any moment, everything could explode. And she wasn't sure she wouldn't be the one doing the exploding.

"Gross. What's that nas-assty smell?" Bailey asked, schlumping into the kitchen, still in her pajamas. Ever since she'd suddenly stopped spending her days at the pool, Bailey had barely had reason to wake up in the morning, it seemed, just like her mom.

"It's Indian food," Jean said, turning back the heat. "Have you ever had it?"

"Why would I eat something that smells like that?" She opened the pantry and pulled out a Pop-Tart, in which, it seemed to Jean, the girl ate her weight daily.

"You should try new things," Jean said. "You might be surprised what you like."

Bailey took a huge bite out of her Pop-Tart. "You should try minding our own business," she said around the food in her mouth. "That would be new."

Jean clamped her mouth shut, bracing herself against her granddaughter's hurtful words. She didn't understand what it was that made Bailey talk to her like that. She had never done anything to hurt her. Kenneth's words rang in her head—*You are too kind for your own good*—followed by Wayne's voice, urging her on: *Don't let her talk to you that way. Say something!*

"And you should try some manners," Jean said before she could stop herself. "That would be new too."

Bailey's eyes grew wide with surprise, but before she could react, there was a knock at the door, followed by the door opening.

"Knock, knock!" Loretta called, coming in. She rounded the corner, her brow creased. "Indian food? I thought we were all going Flavian Munney aphrodisiac themed." She held up a small silver bucket, one Jean recognized as Chuck's beer bucket that he would fill with ice and beer bottles while outside cleaning the fish he'd caught that morning. "Oysters!" Loretta proclaimed.

Bailey rolled her eyes. "Oh, God, is it another old-biddies-with-books meeting?"

Loretta set her bucket on the counter, snapped her fingers. "We should call ourselves that. OBWB. We could get T-shirts—what do you think, Jean? Has a nice ring to it."

"I'm not an old biddy," Jean responded, pulling plates out of the cabinet. What she really wanted to say was, *Don't encourage her, Loretta. She's like a rabid dog—don't make eye contact, and hope she just sniffs around you and goes away.*

"Well, if I'm one, you're one. That's all I know," Loretta said.

"Take it from me—you're all one," Bailey added. "And I looked at that book you guys read for this meeting. Nauseating. You must be a bunch of perverts if you like that."

"Perverts with aphrodisiacs," Loretta corrected. "Did you know that oysters are an aphrodisiac because they're reminiscent of a vagina?"

Bailey made a gagging noise. "Speak for yourself. I'm out."

She left, making dramatic retching noises all the way down the stairs to the living room, where she promptly turned on the TV.

"I know how to clear a room, huh?" Loretta said, smiling and sidling up to Jean.

"You did a nice job," Jean answered. "And I think Indian food is very sexy. It's spicy and saucy, just like Flavian Munney's boxers."

Loretta laughed, slapped her hand on the counter. "Oh! I almost forgot." She went over and picked up a tote bag she'd left by the door. She set the bag on the counter and proceeded to pull three bottles of wine out of it. "Chocolate wine."

Jean picked up one of the bottles. "Yum!"

"Did I hear someone say chocolate and wine in the same sentence?" a voice came from the entryway, and before Jean knew it, the whole club had arrived, each member carrying her own Flavian Munney book and a seductive dish. Chocolate soup, strawberries with whipped cream, silky cheeses with brioche and caviar. Jean's tikka masala was delicious, but it stayed on the stove, a wooden spoon propped against the side of the pan, barely touched. Jean tried not to tell herself that this was because the sauce was prepackaged.

"Should we talk about the literary merits of Flavian of the Month?" Jean said around a bite of May's oyster salad, which was sweet and briny and divine.

"It ended. That was the only merit I saw," Mitzi said.

"Don't let her fool you," Dorothy said, licking her fingers. "I caught her more than once reading it at her desk at lunchtime." She pointed to Mitzi. "You know you were."

"I was trying to get it over with," Mitzi responded, but a blush had crept high on her cheeks.

"Well, I for one thought it was a perfect read after that Thackeray crap," Dorothy said, and there were groans around the table.

"Let's not go there," Mitzi said. "I don't want to get my blood pressure up again. Talk about a book with no literary merit."

"But to listen to everyone speak, he's the only writer out there with any merit, literary or otherwise," Loretta said.

"I'm not kidding; don't get me started," Mitzi warned again. "Continue with Flavian, please."

"Oh, come on, I missed the discussion," Dorothy whined. "I had lots to say too. For instance, did anyone else think the way the knight-on-a-white-horse love interest was described sounded a lot like Thackeray himself?"

"Oh, my God, I didn't notice, but you're right. It totally did," May said, and doubled over, laughing. "Who does that?"

"Egomaniacs like Sebastian Thackeray, that's who," Mitzi said. "Nobody loves him as much as he loves him."

"You didn't miss anything, Dorothy," Jean said. "We hated it. That's about it."

"You didn't think it had some sort of bigger message that we probably all should hear?" Dorothy asked, then after a moment of more groans, said, "Yeah, I guess you're right. I'm probably just sensitive to the whole mommy thing. Been a rough few years at my house."

"But back to the Flavian novel," Jean said. "I thought this one was better than the last one because Flavian seemed a little more humble, and—"

"Yeah, there was a message, all right." The voice came up over the railing that separated the dining room from the living room down below. All the women stopped eating and glanced at the rail. Was that Bailey?

"What did she say?" May whispered.

Bailey came halfway up the stairs, just far enough so the ladies could see her top half. "The Thackeray book? It had a message. The message was, 'I'm a douche bag who deserves to have my ass kicked up between my pointy little elfin ears.'"

Loretta chuckled again, shaking her head and diving back into her chocolate soup.

"I'm sorry," Jean mumbled to the ladies. "Bailey, please," she hissed. "Not now."

"No, she's right, though," Mitzi said. "She's on the money."

"Of course I'm right," Bailey said from the stairs. "Don't sound so surprised." She adopted a high-pitched kindergarten teacher voice. "You know, sometimes we children types have a brain and think for ourselves. Despite what Dickface Thackeray seems to think."

"Language, Bailey," Jean said.

"What? Everything I'm saying is true. The guy should have his nuts—if he has any—kicked so hard, he burps pubic hair."

At this, Loretta burst out laughing and had to cover her mouth to hold in the giggles as Jean shot a look at her.

"Bailey! We're not talking about that book anymore," Jean said, trying to be as delicate as possible. She was over her granddaughter's insolent attitude. "And you're being rude."

"Right. I know. You're talking about the penis party favor book. So much more worth your time. Good call." She gave a double thumbs-up.

"Penis party favor?" May asked, but Jean shook her head curtly and May pressed her lips together.

"But hear me out. I've been thinking about this, and you know what I think you should do? I think you should get Mr. R. Sebastian Thackeray to come to your next meeting," Bailey said.

"Oooh, good idea," Mitzi said. "I wouldn't mind having a little one-on-one with that guy."

"I'd prefer my one-on-one to be with Flavian, personally," Loretta cracked.

"Go to the paint store," May said, and everyone except Jean laughed. But it was an uncomfortable laugh. Nobody, including Jean, seemed to really know how to handle Bailey's intrusion on the meeting.

"I'm serious. I've heard of authors visiting book clubs before. They're attention whores—they'll go anywhere if they think somebody's gonna stroke their egos a little."

"Bailey!" Jean said, feeling anger bubble up. "That's enough of this topic. You're rudely interrupting our meeting. I've had enough of your bad manners."

Bailey's fists were clenched and on her hips. "God, it was just an idea. You guys were all pissed off, and I thought it might be fun to get a chance to tell him that to his face. You can keep pretending this club is about books. But we all know what it's really about—stuffing your faces and getting tipsy on a Tuesday afternoon. How does that make you any different from that zombie upstairs, huh?"

"Okay," Jean said, moving toward her granddaughter.

"You're done now. You need to leave. Go . . . Go back up to your room until the meeting is over." Jean felt electricity run through her. It took restraint for her to hold her voice down, to keep it from breaking.

Bailey let out a husky laugh. "You're sending me to my room? Like you're my mom or something? I don't have a mom! I haven't had a mom pretty much my whole life! And you raised her, so what does that say about you?" Bailey was yelling now—her specialty. She pounded the rest of the way up the stairs, and turned just as she passed the dining table. "Oh, and also? Just so you know, you should never leave two unopened bottles of wine on the kitchen counter when you live in a house with an alcoholic. You'd know that if you grew up in my house."

Jean set down the book she was clutching to her chest. All heads turned toward the kitchen, where, sure enough, one of the wine bottles was missing.

Laura.

"You're so blind," Bailey whispered. She reached out with one arm and grasped the neck of the remaining bottle. Jean heard someone at the table gasp just seconds before Bailey raised the bottle over her head and slammed it to the floor. It landed with a great crash, wine splashing so hard and so far, it snaked up Jean's legs. Shards of glass slid to a stop under the dining room table. Dorothy jumped as a piece bounced against her shoulder. Bailey shook her head disgustedly, then stormed out, only this time instead of stomping up to her bedroom, she left through the front door, leaving the house so quiet, they could hear Laura's TV upstairs.

Nobody seemed to know what to say. Mitzi and Dorothy traded worried glances. Loretta let her fork clatter to her plate, and leaned back, wiping her mouth with her napkin. May cleared her throat twice. Janet stared intently into her plate. Jean stood with her back to the dining table, afraid to turn and face them.

Embarrassed. Angry. On the verge of tears.

So alone. So, so alone, even in the midst of all her friends.

Maybe Kenneth was right—maybe they weren't enough—because all she wanted was them to leave. All she wanted was to crawl upstairs and open the top drawer and cry. All she wanted was to shake her daughter, to slap her granddaughter, to knock some sense into both of them. To take back time, to try it all over again. If she started her life anew, would Wayne have still gotten sick, left her? Would she have known enough to warn him, to talk him into getting tested sooner, catching the cancer earlier?

She didn't know. She couldn't know, because she'd been dealt this life, and it was the only one she was going to get, whether it was fair or not.

"We should go," May finally said, and Jean tried, with great effort, to put on her best hostess smile, as if a puddle of dark wine weren't staining her hardwood at that very moment. Loretta tossed a handful of napkins on the mess and started to crouch down, but Jean told her to leave it.

"It's okay," Jean said. "I'll handle it."

She expected Loretta to say something witty, something about handling Flavian Munney or who knew what else, but instead, she just pressed her lips together and grabbed her oyster bucket, patting Jean's back twice on her way out. Jean knew it was bad when even Loretta Murphy didn't know what to say.

"We'll do an e-mail vote on the next book," Jean said, trying to keep some semblance of protocol as she followed the ladies toward the door. This was the second time in as many months that they'd been unable to choose a book because their meeting had been destroyed by Jean's family problems, and she hated it.

"Maybe we should skip a month, give you some time to get things . . . worked out," May said, and sweet May smiled at Jean in a way that made Jean feel pitied, which only deepened Jean's guilt and humiliation.

Everyone seemed to get out of the house in record time, and it wasn't until Jean shut the door and turned back to the kitchen and dining room that she could see that all the plates were still on the table. It seemed like they left quickly because they had.

She grabbed a black towel out of the guest bathroom, carried it over to the puddle, and threw it on top. She crouched next to it and watched as the towel sank into the liquid. It smelled terrible, so concentrated, so bitter.

She sank backward onto her bottom, her back leaning against the island, and closed her eyes. The ladies were probably gathering in Loretta's house right now, speculating, feeling sorry for her, talking about what she should do, talking about her family. She loved the ladies, but having them witness this dark moment of hers felt so personal, and she didn't like it.

She didn't like any of it, actually. Her carefully constructed life, the control that she'd taken after Wayne's death . . . It was all falling apart on her. She was crying every day again; she was yelling at her granddaughter in front of the book club. She felt on the verge of something, as if she never got it right and as if she never would.

She opened her eyes and reached forward to wipe up the rest of the wine with the now-soaked towel. The damage to the floor was worse than she thought it might be. The wine had left a light purple stain, gray against the brown floor, and in the middle of it was a deep chunk taken out of the wood, presumably where the bottle hit. Jean picked splinters out of the gouge, and it was then that the tears started.

She pulled herself up and got the dustpan and trash can from the mudroom, then brought them back to the damage, hiccupping and emitting loud, wet snorts the entire time. She picked up big hunks of glass and tossed them into the can, mumbling to herself, mostly angry, self-pitying words like *unfair* and *give up*.

And then she heard the front door open and close again softly. At first she thought it must be Loretta, back to check up on her, but she was crying too hard to call out.

But a pair of black flip-flops and blue, shimmery toe-nails, the polish chipped, came into view. Bailey. Without a word, Bailey crouched down next to Jean. She picked up a large chunk of glass and tossed it into the garbage pail, then picked up and threw away another and another.

She never spoke. She never apologized or cried or raged or did any of the things Jean would expect her to do. Slowly, Jean's tears stopped, and she went back to work picking up the glass, sweeping smaller pieces into the dust-pan with the edge of the towel, working side by side with her granddaughter.

At one point, she glanced up at Bailey, whose eyes flicked up and shone from behind her hair. But they only stared at each other for that one short beat, something passing between them, some unspoken sentence, some truth that neither of them could put into words but that both of them understood, and then they went back to their cleaning.

Once they had finished their work and the glass shards had been all thrown away, the towel had been wadded up and readied to toss in the wash, and all that remained was the gray stain and the hole in the floor, Bailey stood and walked steadily to her room.

She did not slam the door.

SIXTEEN

Dear Mr. Thackeray:

My name is Bailey Butler. I'm sixteen, and recently my grandma's book club read your book *Blame*. We had so many things to discuss about it, and we still ended up with lots of unanswered questions. We would like to speak with you about it, so you can help us understand the true meaning behind your work. I know you do the hermit thing, but would you please be willing to consider stopping by our book club sometime? We have great food.

Sincerely,
Bailey Butler

Dear Fan:

Thank you for reading my book. Due to time constraints, I am unable to answer reader correspondence individually. Please feel free to visit my publisher's Web site for more information about where to find my books.

Sincerely,
R. Sebastian Thackeray III, Author

Dear Mr. Thackeray:

I know you can't answer every single e-mail, but this one is different, I promise.

You see, my grandmother is dying, and you're her favorite author of all time. She has all your books, and she rereads them all, over and over again, during her dialysis treatments.

She wants the chance to tell you in person how much she admires your work before she goes. Think of this as one of those wish thingies they do for dying kids.

Sincerely,
Bailey A. Butler I

Dear Fan:

Thank you for reading my book. Due to time constraints, I am unable to answer reader correspondence individually. Please feel free to visit my publisher's Web site for more information about where to find my books.

Sincerely,
R. Sebastian Thackeray III, Author

Dear Mr. Thackeray:

I'm not giving up. My grandmother is now losing her eyesight. She may not be able to see very much longer and won't be able to read your books, so telling me where to find more of them is pointless.

Please come before it's too late. Do it for me, a mere child who's going to miss her grandmammy something fierce.

Sincerely,
Bailey Butler

Dear Fan:

Thank you for inquiring about my books. Please check my publisher's Web site for a listing of Braille versions of my work.

Sincerely,
R. Sebastian Thackeray III, Author

Dear Thack:

Is it okay if I call you Thack? I think we've e-mailed back and forth enough times now for me to call you Thack. Or to call you R. What does R stand for, anyway? Robert? Randolph? Rufus? You look like a Rufus.

So here's the deal. The doctors think she may only have a few months left. This is her last chance to meet her idol. I know you're a decent guy. And I know you say you don't do fan mail, but I think you actually do. I think you actually do because deep down inside you care. No, I don't think it. I know it. Because I can read it between the lines in your books.

Please let my grandmother tell you how much she loves you. Come to our meeting. You can meet my grandma's dog, Riptide (named, of course, after your 1994 Pulitzer Prize–winning novel).

Hey. Maybe that's what your R stands for?

Sincerely,
Bailey Butler

Dear Fan:

Thank you for reading *Riptide*. For more information on author appearances, please consult my publisher's Web site.

Sincerely,
R. Sebastian Thackeray III, Author

Howdy, Thack!

Boy, I do feel we're having a major connection right now, don't you? I mean, the way you keep pointing me to your publisher's web site? So intimate! I feel so very taken care of!

So here's the deal, Thack. I know you're seeing these e-mails. I also know you're pretending this is some random-e-mail-answering generator you've got set up here, but I'm not fooled.

I know you're reading them, and I know you're reading them specifically because you like hearing how awesome my grandma thinks you are.

And she does. The poor, old, coughing, choking, last-breath-shuddering lady really, really does.

You can find out in person when you show up at our book club.

It would probably give her a heart attack to see you and put her out of her pain and misery sooner.

Please say yes.

Sincerely,
Bailey

Dear Fan:

Thank you for reading my book. This is an automatic e-mail generator. Please do not respond. I've already told you where to look for further information.

Sincerely,
R. Sebastian Thackeray III, Author

Thack, Thack, Thack:

Did you actually read that last email before you hit send?

I know you're reading this. You know you want to

meet with us. You know you want to make my granny's dying wishes come true. The cancer is spreading. Think of poor little Riptide, man (photo attached)!

Think of me, your biggest fan.

Sincerely,
Bailey

Dear Fan:

Cut the crap. Your grandmother isn't dying. That dog was on *America's Funniest Home Videos* last night. You took a screen shot.

Sincerely,
MR. R. Sebastian Thackeray III, Author

Dear *MISTER* Thackeray:

Okay, you caught me. Nobody is dying. Except me. I'm dying to talk to you about your book. We all are. You'll like Kansas City in summertime. We'll have barbecue. We'll buy you beer. Or hookers. Or whatever it is you like to have when you're on tour. Cocaine? Prozac? Bombs? You never know.

So here's the skinny. Straight up. My grandma's book club read your book, and so did I. And, Thack, if you intended to move us, you totally did. You made us think. You made us have capital-letter Things to Say. But some of those things can only be asked of and said to the author, and since you're the author, that's you.

I'm sure authors get asked for a lot of stuff. Free books, bookmarks, pens, research papers, put me in a book, whatever. But it can't be every day that you get a heartfelt e-mail from a sixteen-year-old fan, offering you hookers and cocaine to just talk to her dying granny's book club for thirty minutes. Even if the granny isn't exactly dying.

Although I suppose you never know when your number is gonna come up, right?

Say yes.

Sincerely,
Bailey

To Whom It May Concern:

"You never know when your number is gonna come up, right?"

Is that a threat?

Listen, I don't know what your game is, or what you really want from me, but please cease and desist all contact immediately, or I shall get my lawyers involved.

R. Sebastian Thackeray III, Author

Thack (Rufus):

You can't really think I was threatening you. What

is a half-crazed sixteen-year-old going to do to you? And did you really use "shall" in a sentence? You do know this is the twenty-first century, right?

Okay, okay, okay. I'll lay my cards out on the table. I'm desperate.

I'm an orphan.

Who can deny an orphan?

You know you want to say yes. So just say it.

Bailey

Bailey:

Now this is just getting funny.

And, ah yes, I understand the game now. You are not the first fan to try to shake me down. I am a millionaire. That's what comes with putting in the time and effort and work to become famous. But of course fame comes with crazed fans who think I have a desire to share my money with everyone else, especially bottom-feeding extortionists such as you. I can only imagine you have a stun gun and ransom note at the ready.

Please leave me alone, or I will be forced to forward your next correspondence to the Kansas City Police Department.

Sincerely,
Thackeray

Sebastian:

You are so way off, it's not even funny. I have no stun gun, no ransom note, no snarling pit bull or handcuffs and doggy collar.

And I am an orphan. Not like Annie, no, but I'm still an orphan, living with my grandma, and I don't belong here.

Thing is, I don't belong anywhere.

My mom is an alcoholic. She's living here too, actually, but by "living," I mean sleeping all day and getting wasted all night, with intermittent bouts of talking crap about my father. Who probably deserves every bit of it, but the man's my dad, you know? I call him Ghost Dad, though, because he doesn't want anything to do with actual parenting. He's the one who sent me to live with my grandma when my mom was in rehab. Just sent me away like a shirt he didn't want anymore. And he said he would call all the time and stuff, but so far . . . nada. Nothing. Zilch. What kind of dad sends his kid away and never calls, not even one time, Thack?

My grandma wouldn't be half-bad, except my grandpa died a couple years ago, and she's like the walking wounded. She acts like everything's okay, but I can hear her crying in her room at the same time every day, and once she went outside and stood in front of the shed for like half an hour and then came inside without having ever done anything but stand outside. It was weird.

And her only friends in this world like to read soft porn and talk about getting it on with guys who don't actually exist in real life.

And I got naked at a public pool in the middle of the day, and I am way too fat to be doing something that stupid.

I had no prom date. I once caught my mom's puke in my hands.

My family is so fucked up. Worse than a literary novel. And if you come talk to our book club, you can use us for your next book.

Think it through. That's all I ask.

Sincerely,
The Real Bailey

SEVENTEEN

Bailey was already awake by the time Jean woke up. Jean had noticed when she'd gone to shut her bedroom door, as she always did before her shower, and a beam of sunlight had sliced through the hallway into the threshold of her bedroom. She leaned out and looked and, sure enough, Bailey's door was open, her bed empty, save for the rumpled linens and the book that always poked out from under Bailey's pillow. Jean had turned and checked the clock—surely it wasn't that late. It was just barely ten, late for Jean, but not unforgivably afternoon.

She had leaned out into the hallway and cocked her head, listening for the television downstairs. Bailey wasn't the biggest TV watcher in the world, and she'd never watched it this early in the morning, but Jean supposed anything was possible when it came to that girl. Instead, all she heard was the muffled voices coming from Laura's

TV in the bedroom next door. That TV was never turned off. It was impossible to tell what might be going on in that room. And half the time Jean didn't want to know anyway.

Maybe Bailey was hanging out with that lifeguard down at the pool again, Jean thought, and, despite her worries when Bailey had been spending time with him before, she hoped it was true. Bailey had been a little easier to get along with when she'd been seeing him. And going out with kids her own age was normal behavior, at least. At one point, Jean had even wondered whether her granddaughter had fallen in love. But something must have happened between the two of them, because it had been weeks since Bailey had gone to the pool. Jean knew better than to ask about it.

Jean finally decided to go ahead and take her shower as usual. She would assume that nothing terrible was going on, and maybe she'd be right for a change. Plus, after the scene at the book club two nights before, she really was just too exhausted to jump into the day without a shower.

She showered, slowly, her entire bedroom filling with steam, and dressed, then headed downstairs. About halfway down the stairs, she realized something was different.

It was the smoke.

And the smell.

Bacon.

Bacon?

Jean raced down the last few steps and rounded the

corner into the kitchen, to find Bailey standing over a skillet. A cloud of smoke drifted up from the pan, and Bailey squinted against it, pushing meat around with a fork that she held in a hand covered by an oven mitt. On the counter next to her was a plate full of blackened meat. She glanced at Jean and then went back to work in the skillet.

"Cooking is disgusting," she said. "I almost barfed when I had to touch it raw."

Jean stood frozen in the doorway. There were other things askew as well. A trio of glasses sat next to the orange juice container. Toast, also burned, littered the counter with gravel-like crumbs, an open tub of margarine with a knife impaling it at a ninety-degree angle nearby. Some bananas had been crudely sliced into a bowl, a half-opened can of mandarin oranges, with the can opener still attached, sitting next to it. And something grayish was in a pan next to the skillet Bailey was working on now. Were those eggs? Jean checked the sink. Yes, eggshells. She'd made eggs.

Finally finding her feet, Jean moved over to the stove, reaching over Bailey's head to switch on the fan. It was loud, but the smoke cloud shifted toward it.

Bailey swiped the meat around in the grease a few more times, then turned off the stove and pulled the bacon out with the fork, laying it so carefully across the plate, as if she were afraid she'd somehow ruin it. She wiped her hands on a towel and swiped her hair out of her face. Jean noticed beads of sweat above the girl's brow.

Bailey looked around, seeming to assess everything, and then let out a breath. "I doubt she'll eat, but . . ." She never finished the sentence, just trudged upstairs.

Jean stood in the center of the kitchen, hugging herself. In a million years she'd have never guessed that Bailey would be making breakfast this morning. The same girl who'd said such hateful things, who'd smashed the wine bottle to bits, who'd embarrassed her in front of her friends repeatedly.

Maybe there was hope after all.

After a few minutes, Bailey came back downstairs. She didn't speak, just picked up one of the juice glasses and put it back in the cabinet. She didn't need to say anything, and Jean's heart broke for the girl. How could her daughter be so self-centered?

"We have plenty," Bailey said. She piled the toast on the bacon plate, picked up the eggs, and started toward the dining room. Jean poured the two glasses of orange juice and followed her.

And nearly dropped them when she saw the dining room table.

It had been neatly made, set for three, with Jean's good plates and silverware—the ones she usually only brought out for book club. The Christmas cloth napkins—the ones she never used—had been folded into neat points and laid out on each plate. And in the center of the table, a vase was overflowing with familiar flowers.

"Are those . . . ?" Jean asked, setting down the glasses and lightly touching the petals of a Knock Out rose.

Bailey sat, still not making eye contact, and began loading her plate with food. "I saw you out there that day," Bailey said. "They're pretty."

Jean's mouth opened, but she had no words. How simple it seemed to just bring the flowers into the house. How simple it seemed to bring that thread of Wayne closer to her. Why had she never thought of it? Had she been so intent on focusing on what wasn't that she couldn't see what was?

Her fingers shook against the petal, and she dropped her hand. Slowly, she settled into the chair next to her granddaughter and gazed at the side of the girl's head. Her hair glistened—dyed and tortured, but still healthy—and her skin seemed so silky, so smooth. When she wasn't shining with anger, Bailey seemed to just shine.

Bailey shoveled a forkful of eggs into her mouth, then noticed Jean staring at her. "What?"

Jean shook her head, hoping the smile she was feeling on the inside was translating onto her face, but she feared that she only looked dazed, which she also felt.

"What?" Bailey said again, louder, more agitated, and that rocked Jean out of her stupor.

Tidily, she busied herself with unfolding the red napkin across her lap, and then took a spoonful of eggs for herself. "You're right. They're very pretty," she said.

The eggs were dry. And very peppery—Jean quickly ascertained that it was black pepper that had made them so gray. The bacon caught in Jean's throat, and the toast was so hard, it almost hurt her teeth. Yet somehow it was the most delicious breakfast she'd had in years.

The flowers didn't cause a miracle. Jean and Bailey didn't talk over their orange juice. They didn't chat about boys or college or school dances. Irritation still radiated off Bailey with every bite, with every word not said, and Jean knew that it wouldn't take much to set the girl off once again.

But there was something else there too. An acknowledgment. An opening. And Jean would be a fool not to sit there in silence and eat the dry eggs and burned bacon and love every minute of it.

"Thank you for making breakfast, Bailey," she finally murmured when they were both done and the plates sat empty in front of them.

"I screwed it all up," Bailey said.

"It tasted great to me."

Bailey braced herself with her hands against the edge of the table, and Jean was sure she was going to scoot away from the table and the spell would be broken. She didn't mind. Even a short spell was a welcome one.

After all, the girl had cut flowers for her.

"Can we go shopping today?" Bailey asked instead.

Jean was surprised. "Shopping? Do you need something?"

"I just need to go shopping," Bailey spat, but then

seemed to catch herself. She didn't look at Jean, but said to the table, "It's just been a long time since I've been shopping. You don't have to buy me anything." Jean thought the voice had taken on a childlike tone, as if Bailey were bartering. It almost broke her heart.

"Of course," Jean said. "We can go shopping. And if you need something, I'll buy it."

Bailey nodded, then scooted her chair back and stood, gathering the dishes and glasses and taking them to the kitchen.

Jean sat, stunned into motionlessness, afraid to be as excited as she felt over this new revelation. She could only stare at the flowers and wonder if Wayne was seeing this now.

As if she could read Jean's thoughts, Bailey called out from the kitchen. "The flowers have something to do with him, don't they? With my grandfather?"

Jean got up, refolded the napkins, then rethought and wadded them up in her fist. They would need to be washed. How long had it been since she'd washed these napkins? She brushed crumbs off the front of her shirt and headed into the kitchen, where Bailey was already filling up the sink with sudsy water.

"Yes," Jean said. "They do. And he would love that you think they're pretty."

"Can we go after the dishes are done?" Bailey asked.

"Sure. I'll get ready." Jean had to force herself not to run up the stairs in her excitement, but she couldn't keep the smile from her face.

Jennifer Scott

"But I don't want to take her, so we should clear out before she wakes up," Bailey yelled from the kitchen, and the way she said the word *her*, Jean knew very well that she was talking about Laura.

Jean stepped to Laura's door, splayed her hand over it, leaned her head against it. The drone of the television echoed back at her, and nothing else. *Oh, Laura, please open your eyes and see what's going on,* she thought, but she backed away from the door and leaned over the banister.

"Okay, just us," she called downstairs, and then headed into her bedroom to get ready to go.

EIGHTEEN

Jean's hands trembled around the two sodas she was carrying. She could feel the fizz dancing off the top of them and landing with tickles on her wrist. Bailey was by the microwave, pouring melted butter over a bowl of popcorn and mixing it together with her hand. Jean paused a moment to enjoy the contentment on her granddaughter's face.

Laura shuffled into the room, looking wrung out and skinny, but better than she had looked in a while. She might have even been wearing blush, Jean thought. And mascara.

"Hey," she said, and Bailey and Jean both shot glances at the clock. It was unusual for Laura to be awake and downstairs at this hour. Usually by now she was either still in bed, or back in bed, or wherever she went in between the two. "Movie night?"

"Why? You here to ruin it?" Bailey mumbled, and Jean caught herself starting to correct the girl. No. She wouldn't get involved between the two of them anymore.

"Baseball game," Jean said instead. She handed a soda to Bailey, who set it on the counter and plunged back into the popcorn bowl with her free hand. "I was going to watch, and Bailey decided to join me. Popcorn and soda seemed like a good addition."

Laura's head cocked to one side. "I had no idea you were such a baseball fan," she said to Bailey, in a way that sounded to Jean to be not terribly kind.

"There're a lot of things about me you have no idea about," Bailey growled.

"You're welcome to join us," Jean offered, opening the cabinet to get another glass. "We'll pop more."

"I won't keep you," Laura said, leaning into the open refrigerator to rummage for a bottle of water. "I just wanted to tell you something."

"That you're out of wine?" Bailey sneered.

"No," Laura shot back. She leaned against the counter and opened the water. "We're going home. We're leaving tomorrow." She said this so nonchalantly, almost flippantly, as if she were pulling one over on everyone.

"What? Why?" Bailey asked, dropping her handful of popcorn back into the bowl.

"What do you mean, why?" Laura asked, her happy expression disappearing immediately. "Because you want to. Because I'm better. Because it's time."

"Well, I don't want to anymore," Bailey said. "And you are not. What about the wine? We know you drank that wine the other night. You're still drinking."

Laura pointed at Jean. "Whoa, wait a minute. Your grandmother drank the same wine. And so did all those ladies who were here for whatever that club is."

"It's a book club," Bailey said. "And there's a difference between a glass of wine and a bottle of wine."

"Adults drink wine, Bailey. You shouldn't let your father convince you that every time an adult has a drink she's automatically an alcoholic."

"But I haven't had to wake up every adult in their car in the garage in the morning. I've had to with you, though."

"That's different."

Jean set her soda down on the counter too, the game temporarily forgotten. She had a feeling that wherever this was headed, it wasn't good, and it would most likely end with her watching the game alone—or not at all.

"How is it different?" Bailey shrieked. "It's not! You're making excuses."

"I'm trying to make amends," Laura pleaded. "Your dad is coming home too. I talked to him this morning."

"I don't want your amends," Bailey said. "I want you to leave me alone. You're good at that. Shouldn't be a problem for you."

Bailey left the room, heading straight up the stairs again. She'd stormed up those stairs so many times, Jean mused that there ought to be a path worn in the carpet by now.

Laura let out a breath and sagged against the counter. "I just can't please her," she said, almost under her breath. "She wants to go; she doesn't want to go—whatever option is opposite of what I'm planning."

Jean didn't know what to say. After what she'd seen, she couldn't really blame Bailey for being skeptical, for giving Curt and Laura a hard time. But at the same time, she felt sorry for her daughter. She could hardly look at her without seeing the child inside. *Her* child inside. Even though their relationship had been strained for years, she still wanted Laura to be happy. To be healthy. To have a good life. And she wanted to believe in Laura. Wanted to believe that she would make good on the promises she was giving Bailey.

"She'll come back downstairs," Jean said, and she hoped it was true. She really had been looking forward to watching the game together.

She hadn't asked Bailey to join her for the game. She'd simply been flipping through the channels, looking for the right one, when Bailey had sauntered into the room, awkward and shy.

"Gonna watch some soft porn to go with that book you read?" she had asked in her usual abrasive manner, but something had softened in her voice.

Jean had shaken her head. "Royals are playing. I'm not a baseball fan, but your grandfather was. Sometimes I think I just watch out of habit. I was thinking about making a bag of popcorn, though, if you want some."

"I don't like sports," Bailey had said. "Have you ever put cinnamon and sugar on buttered popcorn?"

Jean had shaken her head again. "Sounds good, though. Like dessert."

"It's the sweet-salty thing," Bailey had agreed. "Can we make two bags? One plain and one with cinnamon and sugar? Like dinner and dessert?"

"Of course," Jean had said, rushing to the pantry to pull out the bags. Bailey had searched the cabinets for cinnamon and sugar and a bowl large enough to toss it in.

It wasn't a big moment of closeness. Sometimes it was as if they were in the same room together, but not in the same room at all, both in their own worlds, each afraid to say something that would forge a relationship that might one day get ripped apart.

And all of a sudden it was that day.

"You're leaving tomorrow?" Jean asked Laura.

"That's the plan," Laura answered. "I know, can't get here soon enough, right?"

Jean shook her head. "Why would you say that?"

Laura rolled her eyes at her mother. "Mom, I'm not deaf. I hear you crying in your bedroom. I hear you talking to Saint Kenny. I hear you complaining to your friends. I get it. We're a burden. Especially Bailey."

Maybe at one point they might have been, Jean thought. But somewhere along the line, she'd begun enjoying that burden. She'd begun enjoying Bailey's snarling attitude, her rude comments, her embarrassing actions, their awkwardly silent breakfasts, and shopping excursions. She was engaged in Bailey's life now, and she didn't understand how she'd spent so many years without Bailey around.

"She doesn't want to go," Jean said to Laura.

"She's a kid. They never want to do what they're told. She'll go."

"No, but she . . ." Jean trailed off.

"She what?"

"She's finally settling in," Jean said.

"She'll settle in at home," Laura said. "She'll remember when she gets there how much she wanted to go back. Listen, so we'll pack up tonight and hit the road in the morning. You want us to wake you?"

"No," Jean said, feeling close to tears and not understanding why. Laura was right—she had complained so many times about having them there. At times it seemed like they would never leave. At times it seemed like she would break down, like the whole house would fall apart with them in it. But now that they were leaving, all she could think about was that she and Bailey had not even put the cinnamon and sugar on the popcorn yet.

"You don't want us to wake you up when we leave?"

"No, I don't want you to go."

"Why not? You're miserable with us here."

"At least leave Bailey here," Jean said, aware of the desperation in her voice but unable to do anything to stop it. "Just until school starts. You and Curt can spend a couple weeks getting things put back together."

Laura shook her head, annoyed. "No. We don't need a couple weeks to put things back together, and we're not going to want to drive across the state to pick her up two weeks from now anyway. We're leaving in the morning."

After Laura had gone to pack, Jean had stared into the popcorn bowl, not seeing the popcorn there and trying to convince herself that their leaving would be a good thing. Her book club meetings wouldn't have to take a breather after all. She wouldn't have to worry about Bailey embarrassing her in front of anyone she knew. She wouldn't have to clean up messes left behind from Bailey's tantrums. And once again the house would be silent and controlled.

But she couldn't shake the feeling that silent and controlled was no longer what she wanted, that once Bailey left, silent and controlled would feel . . . lonely. Before Wayne died, this house was hardly ever silent and controlled. She felt incurably widowish when everything was silent and controlled, rattling around the old place, nothing ever moving, nobody ever challenging her. When had silent and controlled gotten so depressing? Or had it always been that way?

She picked up the small bowl of cinnamon and sugar, the one Bailey had mixed to sprinkle over the popcorn. There were little indentations in the mixture where Bailey had licked her finger and pressed it into the granules. Jean shook the bowl slightly, until the indentations were covered over, the surface of the cinnamon and sugar flat. It was that easy to erase Bailey having ever been there.

In the end, she couldn't make herself pour it over the popcorn.

In the end, she'd turned off the TV, thrown away the popcorn and the soda, and gone to bed.

NINETEEN

Jean pushed her cart down the breakfast aisle as fast as she could. Since Bailey left, she hadn't been able to restrain herself from buying Pop-Tarts—iced cherry, Bailey's favorite. She knew it was a stupid move. She would never eat them herself. And Bailey wasn't going to be coming back anytime soon. The boxes were stacking up in the pantry, lined up like lonely pets waiting for their owner to come home. But still Jean bought them. Somehow buying Pop-Tarts made her feel closer to Bailey.

Such a silly feeling, anyway, she realized. It wasn't as if they'd ever gotten close. The morning that they'd left, Bailey hadn't even hugged her good-bye.

"Thanks for stuff," she'd said, looking at the tile in the entryway, clutching her pillow and blanket to her stomach in a mirror of what she'd done when she'd arrived at the beginning of the summer. "Tell the old biddies I said it's been real." She'd started to walk out the door, but had stopped after a step. "Tell that one old biddy that her cake was actually pretty good."

That had been it. She'd stalked out the front door and shut herself into the backseat of Laura's car. Laura had followed her out, tugging a bulging suitcase behind her. "I'll call when we get there," she'd said just before sliding in behind the steering wheel. But of course she never did. Some things never changed.

No hugs, no tears, just a normal day. Jean had stripped their beds and vacuumed their floors before lunch.

But she'd kept buying the damn Pop-Tarts.

Just as she reached the end of the aisle, she saw Janet ducking down the next aisle over. "Janet!" she called. "Hello!" Janet stopped, checking over her shoulder like a fugitive.

"Hey, Jean."

Jean rolled up to her. "Did you get my e-mail? About the club? Bailey and Laura have gone home, so I thought we could meet next Tuesday?"

Janet nodded. "Yeah, I, um . . ." Her face reddened, typical Janet-style, and she chewed her bottom lip nervously. "About that . . . I wanted to tell you . . ."

Jean's heart sank. She was afraid this was going to happen. They'd take a break, and the club would die. "Please don't," Jean said.

Just then, a blur of khaki and yellow polo whizzed around the corner from the bread aisle.

"Janet!" the man boomed, his head so shiny it reflected the overhead lights. Janet jumped—her knees bent into a crouch, as if she were going to sprint away. But she stayed put, and he strode up to her. He shook his head as if she were too useless for words. "The fish case isn't going to clean itself. I told you to clean it and I expect it to be done. At no point did I tell you to stand around and chit-chat, did I?"

Janet shook her head, refusing to make eye contact with anyone.

"Then get to it, and next time I have to come find you to remind you about your job, you won't have one."

He toddled away, down the pasta aisle, stopping to straighten a box of macaroni, which had been knocked askew on the shelf. Jean gazed at her friend in wonderment. How could she work every day with such a man?

"I'll let you go," Jean said. "But next Tuesday, okay? My house. All desserts."

Janet nodded, and Jean turned to leave, but just as she turned her back, Janet's tiny voice piped up. "Will you be home tonight? I get off at six."

"Yeah, why?"

"I need to talk to you. I'll come by."

Janet hurried off to the fish case, where Jean later found her, most of her girth stuffed down into the case as she tried to wipe the inside of the glass with a cloth. Jean made one more sweep down the cereal aisle, where she picked up another box of Pop-Tarts, thinking she would mail them all to Bailey—it would be a nice surprise, a Pop-Tart variety care package—but knowing that she would never get around to it, because there was something she loved about seeing them in her pantry.

Later, after Jean got home, Loretta came by with a magazine page she'd torn out at the doctor's office.

"This year's best discussion books, according to . . ." She studied the article. "I can't remember. According to these guys, whoever they are. There's a vampire book on the list."

Jean made a face. "Remember the last time we tried the vampire thing? None of us finished it. In fact, we banned vampires, if I recall."

"That was before I was brilliant enough to have us read it at Halloween time. We can dress up for our meeting. I've got just the vampy negligee."

"Nope," Jean answered, taking the list and scanning it. "Some of these look all right. I heard someone talking about *Where'd You Go, Bernadette* at the salon the other day. Supposed to be really good." She handed the list back to Loretta. "No costume required."

Loretta took the list, folded it. "Well, that's no fun."

"That's me. No Fun Granny. Just ask Bailey."

"How is old perky Bailey?"

Jean shrugged. She had no way of knowing how her granddaughter was doing. While she'd never been close enough to get day-to-day information out of her, she'd never missed it before. Now she felt it, like a daily blow. "I guess no news is good news," she said.

"Healthy outlook," Loretta said as she bent to retrieve a can of soda out of Jean's refrigerator. "Want one?"

"Sure."

They opened their sodas and went outside to sit on the front porch swing. The neighbors' kids were out throwing a ball at one another's feet, stopping every few minutes to argue over who was "out" in a game Jean couldn't quite decipher. Their dog stood on his hind legs and barked over the fence at them. Jean liked watching the kids, watching the game and the way they fought and the healthy way they giggled or cheered or even pouted. It was good to see someone else's happiness. It was a good reminder for Jean to have some of her own.

Jean had forgotten about Janet, so when the green pickup pulled into her driveway, at first she was confused. But when the door opened and Janet stepped out, Jean and Loretta offered a wave. Jean got up to fetch Janet a soda, but Janet waved it off.

"I can't stay," she mumbled, the blood seeping upward from her collar to her face.

"Couldn't wait for the meeting next week?" Loretta said. "You're a bit early."

Jean bumped Loretta's shoulder. "Don't listen to her. She was over here with a book list herself."

"Yes, and good news. We've chosen another Thackeray," Loretta added. "This one's titled *How All of Humanity Can Kiss My Ass.*"

Jean gasped and Janet giggled, settling herself onto the porch step a few feet away from the swing. "I can't believe you just said that," Jean said, barely holding back her own laughter. "You just get worse and worse every day."

"At my age, I prefer to think I worsen by the hour. Otherwise I'll never hit my goal."

"We are not reading another Thackeray novel," Jean said. "We'll read that vampire book first. Thackeray's officially been banned."

"Actually, that's what I wanted to talk to you about," Janet said. "Well, not just Thackeray. Rodney too."

"Who's Rodney?" Loretta asked, turning to Jean. Jean shrugged.

"My boss. Jean's met him a couple times."

Jean thought, *"Met him" might be a stretch. More like "watched him yell."*

Janet's jaw hardened. "He's such a jerk. In some ways a lot like that book. Remember in that book where the narrator says the only thing fat women are good for is moving furniture to dust underneath it?"

Loretta and Jean both nodded.

"If only he knew how wrong he is. I never dust under my furniture," Loretta said. "Though I've thought about dusting Chuck every now and then, just to make sure he's still alive."

Janet cleared her throat, and still the beginning of her next sentence came out with a squeak. "Rodney actually said that to me today. He said, 'Fat people are useless unless you need something heavy picked up or a wall knocked down.'"

"Oh, my God," Jean said. "He didn't."

Janet nodded. "He says stuff like that all the time. He's constantly yelling at me in front of customers and he calls me Two Ton Tilly and he's always saying things to really embarrass me and I'm so sick of it."

"Have you talked to anyone about it? His boss, maybe?"

Janet shook her head, swallowing miserably. Jean thought maybe she could see some tears perching on Janet's lower lids, threatening to spill over. "I'm afraid to. I'm scared they'll just laugh at me and do the same thing. Or fire me, and we really need the money right now. It's stupid—I know."

"Oh, honey, it's not stupid. You're shy. You can't help it," Jean said. Even Loretta seemed to be without wise-cracks at the moment. "But he's wrong. He needs someone to tell him how wrong he is. He needs someone to put him in his place."

"That's the thing," Janet said. "That's why I wanted to

talk to you. Because Thackeray's the same way, only he's not just saying it to me. He's saying it to every big woman out there."

"Oh, hell, it ain't only big women he hates," Loretta interjected. She took a sip of her soda. "Basically if you are penis-free, he's got a grudge."

"Exactly," Janet said. "And he's spreading that crap." She paused, blinked at the word *crap*, as if she couldn't believe it had actually come out of her mouth.

"Well, you don't need to worry. We've read our last Thackeray book," Jean said. She raised a hand. "Executive decision."

Janet pressed her lips together tightly, then said, "I think Bailey was right. We should invite him to our meeting. We should give him a piece of our minds."

Jean and Loretta looked at each other in surprise; then Loretta let out a bark of laughter.

"I can see it now. 'Dear Mr. Thackeray, Please come halfway across the country so we can tell you what a blowhard donkey's ass you are.' I don't think it's gonna fly."

"It still might be worth a try," Janet said.

"He's gonna volunteer to stop by so we can yell at him?" Loretta asked.

"Well, no," Jean said. "We don't have to tell him why we want him to come. We just have to ask if he will."

"And before he knows what's going on, we can give him a piece of our minds. I can sit on him if he tries to leave. Just like Tess does to that boy in *Blame*. He'll love the irony," Janet said, and then put her hand over her mouth to cover a laugh.

Loretta waved at Jean and Janet with her soda. "You two are crazy. It's never gonna happen."

"All we have to do is ask," Janet said. "The worst he can do is say no, right?"

"No, the worst he could do is say yes," Loretta said. "Guy's a jerk."

Jean looked from one of them to the other. She remembered that day Bailey had proposed this very thing to the group. How boldly she'd stood in front of a bunch of strangers, three, four times her age, and had levelly mapped out her idea.

They'd all but laughed her out of the room. Jean had gotten so very angry. She'd told Bailey to leave.

To have Thackeray visit now would be a slap in Bailey's face, especially with her not here to meet him and give him a piece of her mind herself. No way could Jean do it. Not now.

"We should just help you stand up to Rodney instead," she said quietly, and her heart felt heavy as she saw Janet's face fall, going from expectant to dashed. There was no chip on her shoulder as there had been on Bailey's. Bailey handled rejection with fury; Janet looked like she wanted to throw herself in front of a bus. "Loretta's right. Thackeray will never come here."

"So we shouldn't even try?" Janet asked, her voice going wobbly.

"No. We should just move on," Jean said, but she wasn't sure whom she was talking to—Janet or herself—or what she was talking about.

Was she telling herself to move on from Thackeray's book?

Or from Wayne's death?

Or from losing Bailey?

TWENTY

Jean had the TV turned up as loud as she could stand it. Not that she was watching what was on it—some reality pregnancy show that Bailey had liked—just that it was so quiet in the house without Bailey.

Jean had never noticed it before, but the pipes rattled at the oddest times. The clock in the kitchen ticked at an ungodly loud decibel. And the tree outside the den window scraped the gutter annoyingly.

How had she not noticed these things before?

The silence. It stretched. It mocked. It hurt.

She'd thought she'd been tormented by silence after Wayne's death, but somehow the silence after Bailey's departure seemed even louder, more oppressive.

Jean had taken to humming, sometimes singing aloud, old show tunes or big band classics or even Christmas carols, even though the holidays were still months away. She rattled dishes and let cabinets *thwack* closed and turned on the TV with the sound ratcheted up.

It didn't help.

She still thought she heard the thump of Bailey's feet coming down the stairs, still thought she heard the squeak of the pantry door as Bailey opened it to rummage for a Pop-Tart. She longed for some sort of nuisance to interrupt her day—some crazy stunt or Bailey antic.

She never would have guessed in a million years that she would miss those things.

But somehow, unexplainably, she did.

She sagged into the couch, cracking open a Kent Haruf book. She and Wayne had loved his books, with their soft, rural tones, their familiarity of character. Their comfort.

But just as she began reading, the doorbell jarred her.

"Who could . . . ?" she muttered to herself as she set the book down and headed toward the stairs. She hardly had a lot of visitors, especially at this time of night.

She grabbed one of Wayne's old walking sticks out of the umbrella stand next to the door and then felt foolish and put it back again. For goodness' sake, not every visitor would be out to kill her.

She opened the door and was greeted with a blast of noise—hollering and cheering that made her jump and cover her head with her arm.

"GNO!" shouted Loretta, holding a bottle of vodka over her head. Her yell was seconded by the shouts of Mitzi, Dorothy, and May, who stood behind her, waving their hands excitedly. Even Janet pulled up the rear, not yelling, but grinning shyly.

"What is this?" Jean gasped. "You scared me half to death, Loretta."

"This," Loretta said, pushing past Jean and leading everyone into the house, "is a GNO. Girls' night out," she added when Jean's face registered confusion. "Don't worry, I just learned what a GNO was a couple weeks ago myself."

"We're storming you, lady," Mitzi said, following Loretta into the kitchen.

"Be prepared for fun," May added, and gave Jean a sideways hug. "You need it."

Jean heard the clink of glasses as Loretta pulled them down from the kitchen cabinet. She shut the door behind Janet and followed her in.

"It's late," Jean said.

"Pshaw, it's barely nine o'clock," Loretta countered, pouring dollops of vodka into each glass. "Don't be an old fart." She pushed a glass into Jean's hand. "Drink up. You're already one behind the rest of us."

Jean held the glass numbly, still trying to figure out exactly what was going on here. The TV still blasted downstairs, and she didn't understand quite how she went from not watching a pregnancy show and getting ready to settle in with Kent Haruf to holding a glass of vodka with unexpected visitors in her kitchen—visitors who were each holding a glass of their own and looking at her expectantly.

May laughed out loud. "Don't look so shocked, Jean. We're all of age."

"I'm not shocked," Jean said, then reconsidered. "Actually, yes, I am kind of shocked. We've never done anything like this before."

"Here's the thing," Loretta said, leaning forward on her elbows on the counter. "It's high time we did something like this."

"You've had such a hard road lately with Laura and Bailey, we thought you could use a little fun," Mitzi said. "It's exhausting taking care of a problem child."

Dorothy held up her glass. "Hear, hear!"

"Bailey wasn't a problem," Jean argued, but her argument was halfhearted. Who could deny that problem was exactly what Bailey had tried to be?

May slid off the stool she'd been sitting on and looped her arm around Jean's shoulders. "You always take care of us. Tell us what to read, organize what we eat—"

"Oh, and we do eat!" Loretta said, lifting her glass again.

"Taking attendance," May continued. "Leading the discussion."

"It always gets derailed," Jean said.

"Well, that's Loretta's fault," May said. "The point is, you always take care of us, so now it's time for us to take care of you."

"Plus, there's not nearly enough dancing at our meetings," Loretta added.

"Dancing?" Jean repeated. She hadn't danced in . . . Well, she couldn't really remember when.

"It's a girls' night *out*, Jean. The opposite of in. We're going out. To Electric Oregano. So you should get dressed."

Jean had heard of Electric Oregano. It was the crowded nightclub downtown. "I don't . . . ," Jean started, but she trailed off. Why not? Why wouldn't she? Why continue to rattle around this old house like a skeleton? Why not get out there and have some fun with her friends for a change? Laugh a little, dance a little, drink a little. Wayne was dead, but by God, she was still right here with a pumping heart and breath in her lungs. "Okay," she said, sounding more settled than she felt. "Sure. Electric Oregano."

"Atta girl!" Loretta cheered, and she lifted her glass again. "To books!"

"To books!" they all shouted, and drained their glasses.

It had been a long time since Jean had drunk vodka, but she didn't remember it tasting like this. It had a familiar punch, to be sure, but there was something else to it. She examined the glass. "What is this?"

Loretta turned the bottle so Jean could see it. "Doughnut flavored. We're going all out tonight, Jeanie. Fancy booze." She refilled their glasses. "One more for the road." She winked at Jean. "Don't worry, I got us a designated driver. Go look."

Jean headed to the den, her head already feeling light from the vodka, and peered out the front window. Parked in the driveway was Loretta's van, a shadow Jean recognized in the front seat.

"Is that . . . Chuck?" she asked, incredulous. "You got him out of the recliner?"

"Yep! Guess the old girl's still got some feminine wiles left after all," Loretta shouted from the kitchen.

"It also doesn't hurt that the sports bar next door to Electric Oregano has nachos and big-screen TVs," Mitzi said.

"*Salud!*" Loretta shouted, and Jean heard the clink of glasses again.

If Jean had been looking for noise distraction, she'd definitely come to the right place. Electric Oregano was loud. Deafeningly so. And dimly lit, most of the light in reds, oranges, and pulsing blues that shimmered off Loretta's sequined silver top like a disco ball and erased everyone's wrinkles and gray hair. The dance floor thumped, writhing with bodies, and condensation rolled down the nearby windows.

It was fabulous.

The ladies took a table in the back, near the restrooms, Loretta noting that it'd been a long time since she'd tested the integrity of her bladder with alcohol, so better safe than sorry. Plus, it was a little quieter back there. They could talk without rupturing vocal cords, which, for some reason, Mitzi had actually been concerned about.

May ordered a pitcher of margaritas for the table, and

when the waitress brought it, it looked unbelievably huge to Jean. If they drank the whole thing, would they even be able to rouse Chuck next door and find their way to the van? Jean was doubtful and tried to remind herself to sip, sip, sip, and never be the first one to refill. Not that that would be a problem with Loretta at the table.

"I swear, Loretta, I don't know how you do it," Jean half said, half shouted over the music. "You can just about keep up with these kids." She gestured to the crowd of young adults milling around the bar.

Loretta took a gulp of her margarita and tapped her temple. "Age is all in the mind," she said.

"Hmm, I don't know," Dorothy said. She paused to let a tiny belch escape. "In my experience, age is also in the boobs."

Mitzi burst out laughing. "My goodness, Dot, if I didn't know better, I'd say you were getting a little tipsy. Let's dance."

"I've never heard this song before in my life," Jean said.

"Me neither," Mitzi said. "But I like it."

Mitzi stood and crooked her elbow toward Dorothy, who stood and linked hers to it. The two of them made their way to the dance floor, Loretta jumping up and trotting after them while shouting something Jean couldn't make out. May giggled and slowly got up to join them.

"Why not?" she shouted over her shoulder before diving into the throng.

Jean and Janet were left alone at the table, both looking out over the dance floor. Jean noticed Janet chew the side of her lip, as she had a habit of doing when she was nervous.

Suddenly Jean felt awash with fondness for Janet. The poor girl was so timid, yet she'd continually reached out to Jean. It must have taken every ounce of courage for Janet to talk herself into going out for a night on the town with Loretta and a hundred young people. Yet she'd agreed to come.

Jean drained her glass. "Let's do it."

Janet looked up, terror-stricken. "Oh. No. I can't."

"Sure you can," Jean said.

"I'd embarrass myself. I haven't ever gone dancing."

"Never?"

Janet shook her head. "I didn't even dance at my wedding. I'm just so . . ." She gestured toward her body and shrugged.

Jean was struck with a flashback of Bailey, striding across the pool deck, naked as the day she was born, not a fear to be seen. Oh, to have that confidence.

She watched their friends on the dance floor. They stuck out like sore thumbs in the sea of twentysomethings, wearing their comfortable shoes and high-waisted jeans. They looked like a bunch of old ladies bobbing around with their fingers snapping and their hands clapping to the rhythm. Even May, who was far from old, looked out of place among the sexy kids. But the ladies hooted and smiled while they danced. They leaned into one another and shouted, then threw their heads back and laughed. And nobody thought anything of it. Nobody even seemed to notice them.

"If they can do it, we can do it," Jean said, gesturing toward Loretta and the ladies.

Janet chewed her lip feverishly, then nodded. "You're right," she said. "Okay."

The two of them stood up and faced the dance floor, the lights bouncing off their faces. Jean looked toward Janet and grinned. Janet grinned back.

And they headed toward the dance floor.

"I think I broke muscles," Loretta said. "Is that possible?"

They were all back at Jean's house, draped over her couch and love seat, mugs in hand. Jean had brought the coffeemaker down into the living room and brewed the coffee right there on the end table so they wouldn't have to traverse the stairs again, partly because they were all still a little unstable on their feet, and partly because they were already all sore from the dancing.

"I can't feel my feet," Jean said. "I think I left them on the dance floor."

"You were moving pretty good during that Pitbull song," May said.

"Remind me again who Pitbull is," Mitzi said.

"I'll sing it," Loretta said.

A chorus of *No!* broke out, and someone tossed a throw pillow at her.

"I haven't been up this late in a long time," Mitzi said, checking her watch. "I think I'm getting slaphappy."

"Well, don't fall asleep or we'll put your bra in the freezer," Loretta said.

"Oh, my God, I remember doing that at sleepovers," May said. "Do girls still do it?"

"No idea," Jean said. "Do they still play truth or dare?"

"I think it's two truths and a lie now," Dorothy supplied. "Or at least the boys used to talk about that."

"What is that?" Jean asked.

Dorothy refreshed her cup and sat back. "Just like it sounds. You go around the circle, and each person tells two truths and one lie, and everybody tries to guess which one is the lie. You know how kids are. Full of too much information and calling it fun."

Loretta pulled her feet up on the couch. "Oh! Let's play it!"

"What? No," May said.

"Aren't we a little old for that?" Mitzi said.

Loretta raised her eyebrows at Mitzi. "Do I need to sing the Pitbull song again?"

"No!" they all shouted together, and settled into giggles once again.

"I think we should do it," Janet said, and everyone

turned to look at her. She shrugged. "We already embarrassed ourselves dancing like fools. How bad can this be?"

"Speak for yourself," Mitzi said. "My moves are hardly embarrassing."

"The kick thing is kind of embarrassing, Mitz," Dorothy said. "I'm in. Let's play."

Mitzi and May protested, and the ladies razzed and goaded until finally May threw her hands up in surrender. "Okay. Fine. Let's do it. Who's first?"

"I'll go first," Dorothy said. She set her coffee cup on the table and paused to think for a minute. "Okay. I can do the splits. I once snuck over to Elan's house in the middle of the night and dumped the entire cat litter box on his front porch. And I'm going to be a grandma."

"All lies," Loretta said. "You're supposed to tell two truths."

"There are two truths in there!" Dorothy protested.

Mitzi sized her up. "It's truth, truth, lie. And gross about the cat box. Hilarious, but gross."

"Nope," Dorothy said.

Loretta shrugged. "Then it's lie, truth, lie. Two lies. Still cheating."

Dorothy shook her head. "I swear there are two truths. It's truth, lie, truth. I never did the cat box thing. Wanted to, but didn't."

There was stunned silence. Jean broke it. "Forget the cat litter. You're going to be a grandma?"

Dorothy nodded. "Devon. Seventeen years old, a baby himself."

"Oh, my God, Dot, what are you going to do?" Mitzi breathed.

"What can I do?" Dorothy said, and the silence fell again.

"You can do the splits, that's what," Loretta finally said. "Or so you say. I want proof."

Dorothy groaned. "I was afraid you were going to say that," she said.

"You have to offer proof—it's the rules."

May laughed. "How do you know, Loretta? You'd never heard of this game before tonight."

"My rules," Loretta said, and started clapping. "Do it! Do it! Do it!"

Finally Dorothy got up and moved to a clear spot over by the fireplace. Slowly, she lowered herself all the way to the ground, her legs splayed one in front of her, one behind. She held her arms up in a victory pose. Everyone clapped.

"We will help you," Jean said when things had quieted again. "Whatever you need. Babysitting, diapers . . ."

"Someone to talk to," May added.

"I appreciate that," Dorothy said. "And you didn't need to say it. I already knew."

"Okay, my turn," Loretta said. Everyone got quiet as Dorothy came back to the couch. "I've never been to Electric Oregano before tonight, I once had a dream that

Flavian Munney was the produce boy and on my shopping day we did some mean things to the broccoli, and last night Chuck and I had sex."

"Easy," May said. "Truth, truth, big lie."

Loretta pointed at May. "Nope, smarty-pants. Truth, lie, truth."

"What? Hasn't it been years?" Jean asked, stunned.

Loretta winked. "Now you know how I talked him into being our designated driver tonight. Somebody else go."

"Wait, not so fast. I want to know when else you've been to Electric Oregano," May said.

"Need-to-know basis," Loretta answered. "Next."

"I'll go," Janet said. She took a deep breath. "My husband talked me into joining the club so I would make some friends, and I'm really glad he did."

"That's only one," Mitzi said. "You're supposed to give us three."

Janet shook her head. "I don't want to lie to my friends."

"Aw, that's sweet," May said. "You're off the hook. I'll go." She situated herself. "That cake that Bailey destroyed? I didn't make it. I bought it from a bakery. I got a new cat. And I met a guy a few weeks ago, and I really like him. I think he might be the one."

Jean smiled. "I've got this one. Truth, truth, lie."

"Nope," May said.

"You bought that cake? I feel so betrayed," Mitzi said, and May smacked her arm.

"Yes, I bought it."

"You told me you got the recipe off a baking blog," Jean said.

"I did get a recipe off a baking blog. And it didn't come out. So I replaced it."

"Is that against club rules?" Mitzi asked Jean.

Jean shook her head. "Only club rules are no green salads, no vampires, no Thackeray."

"So it's truth, lie, truth?" Janet asked, and May nodded.

Jean's mouth dropped open. "You met a guy? But I thought you were happy by yourself."

May shrugged. "I was. Until I met him. His name's Tony. He's a contractor. He's the one who remodeled my bathroom."

"Ooh, remember when Flavian was a contractor?" Loretta purred. "So sexy, with that tool belt."

"Tony has one of those," May said.

"You should have him wear it and nothing else," Loretta suggested.

"Already have." But she could barely get the words out before the hoots and catcalls drowned her out.

"If I didn't know any better, I'd think you were in love," Jean said.

May sipped her coffee. "Maybe," she said. "Hard to tell just yet. But I'm open to it."

Jean smiled. How things can change so suddenly. How happiness can be redefined.

"Okay, I'll go," Mitzi said. "I hate this game. I hate this game. But I liked dancing."

"Those are all true," Dorothy said, and tossed another throw pillow. It glanced off Mitzi's shoulder and nearly toppled the coffeemaker. "Just ignore her. Jean, it's your turn."

Jean thought. She wasn't used to opening up like this to anyone but Wayne. But she couldn't deny it—tonight the club had turned a corner. They were more than just book friends now. And Wayne was no longer around. She couldn't stay closed up forever.

"Just one," she said. "I miss Bailey. I didn't think I would say that, especially when she first got here and was doing the most embarrassing things. But now that she's gone, I miss her. And I don't know what I would do without you guys, because the time we're all together is the one time I can forget how alone I am. So . . . that's all. Truth."

There was a beat of silence. May leaned over and patted Jean's shoulder. Mitzi smiled at her sadly.

"To books," Loretta said, raising her coffee mug.

"To books," everyone responded, and they all drank.

TWENTY-ONE

Wayne died right smack in the middle of the day. Not too long after lunch, not that Jean had eaten any lunch. Not that she had any appetite to speak of. She'd been having to force herself to eat something in the evenings for weeks, even though nothing had taste and everything sat in her stomach disagreeably. Sometimes she was certain that living through a loved one's death without slipping into death yourself was nothing short of a wonder.

The nurse had told her about twelve hours before that it could be any minute, and Jean had kept vigil by his bedside all night, waiting until he took his very last breath. She didn't want to miss it. She didn't want to miss that chance to say good-bye, even though she had said good-bye months ago when he was still lucid. They'd both said it, her sturdy hands gripping and dwarfing his veiny, blue hands, professing their forever-love, promising to meet up again on the other side, thanking each other for a great life, even if it was cut too short. It had been one of the worst nights of Jean's life, and sometimes she dreamed it, exactly like it was, and woke up crying.

But still she didn't want to live her life knowing she had been in the kitchen making a tasteless ham sandwich the moment the love of her life took his last breath. Wayne had been in a morphine stupor for so long, he hadn't so much as opened his eyes for days. She supposed she might have been hoping for a dramatic moment, where he would suddenly rouse and call her Jeanie, pat her cheek, stare into her eyes, tell her something profound and lovely, instruct her not to worry about him, anything. But he didn't. He simply opened his eyes, turned his head, then closed them and stopped breathing. Done. Jean hadn't even been sure if he'd seen her when his head turned. He looked rather as if he were seeing something a thousand yards behind her.

Sometimes she dreamed that Wayne was being taken from her suddenly, in the middle of the night. It was one of the reasons she'd had such trouble sleeping at first. She would be in that happy, everything's-just-fine dreamland. She would be just settling in bed and the phone would ring. Her heart would leap into her throat, adrenaline coursing through her so hard she could feel it in her fingertips and on the back of her neck. And in her dream she would pick up the phone, and a voice on the other end would say, "Mrs. Vison, it's your husband. I'm afraid he's gone." She would wake up, sweating and crying out the word *no* every single time, and then she would feel silly and defeated. He was gone. He had been gone.

So three weeks after Laura and Bailey left, when the phone rang at midnight, ripping Jean out of a dreamless sleep, she wasn't sure if the pounding heart and rushing electric feeling was a dream or real. She sat up and fumbled in the dark for the phone, knocked it off the nightstand, and had to lean over the side of the bed to pick it up again. This detail had never appeared in her dream before, a realization that rattled her into reality.

"Hello?"

"Jean? It's Curt."

"Curt? What's going on? What's wrong?" She sleep-slurred the words out, laying her hand over her heart without even realizing it, as if she could hold it in her chest. As if she could soothe it back into a regular beat.

"There's been an accident," he said.

Jean pulled herself up further. "Oh, God, is everyone okay?"

She could hear a page over an intercom in a background, as if Curt were calling from somewhere public, echoey. A hospital. Of course, again a hospital. "No. I'm afraid she's been banged up pretty bad."

"Oh, no, should I come? What happened? Was she drunk again?"

"I . . . normally wouldn't ask you to come all this way again," he said, "but she asked for you. Before the surgery, she asked me to call you. She wants you here."

Jean slid sideways so that her legs hung over the side of the bed. Her feet searched for her slippers. Laura had asked for her? For *her*? "Surgery?" she asked slowly. Everything seemed so confusing and her half-asleep brain couldn't take it all in.

"She busted up her arm," he said. "They're gonna have to put some pins in it. She's still up there right now, I think. She's going to have to stay overnight too, because she hit her head and has a concussion. She had been drinking, yes, but that doesn't matter right now. She's pretty scared, so we'll deal with the drinking later. She's going to be in a lot of trouble. Thank God she only ran into a tree, and thank God she was wearing a seat belt. But it'll be a long time before she can get her license now."

Jean closed her eyes and rubbed her forehead. "They took her license. Of course they did. DWI. I suppose that's probably a blessing in disguise. Will she have to go to jail?"

"Jean," Curt said, "it's not . . . It wasn't Laura."

"What?"

"It wasn't Laura driving the car," he said. He paused long enough for Jean to hear another page over the intercom. "The person in the accident was Bailey."

TWENTY-TWO

Jean reached the hospital in record time—three hours and five minutes. She probably broke many traffic laws on the way, and may have been lucky to have made it there alive at all. But there were hardly any other cars on the road, and besides, she had brought Dorothy with her to keep her calm and alert.

She couldn't really explain what it was that had made her pick up the phone in the middle of the night and call Dorothy after talking to Curt. By all expectation, if she were going to ask a friend to come along to hold her hand on something like this, it should have been Loretta. After all, Loretta was her best friend. And Loretta seemed to really like Bailey, even when Bailey was at her worst. Loretta seemed to be able to relate to the girl.

But there was something that told Jean she could trust Dorothy to be strong at a time like this. To lend Jean strength to spare. If anyone knew about children who were lost in their own familiar worlds, it was Dorothy.

"Of course I'll go with you," Dorothy had said, her voice scratchy with sleep, though Jean could hear deep, rowdy voices in the background, as if the boys in her house had never gone to sleep. "Just let me get a few things together and I'll be right over."

On the way to St. Louis, Jean filled Dorothy in on everything, from Laura's refusal to stick around after Wayne's death, to Bailey's troubles at home, to spying Bailey in the loft of her house and saying nothing. She told Dorothy details about Wayne's last days—things she'd never even told Kenny and Laura or Loretta. About all the dignity he lost and how she always left the room when the nurse had to do something particularly humiliating, even though he wasn't coherent enough to know, just to let him keep his pride. About how he begged for asparagus with butter over and over again and how she'd finally relented and made him some, and how he hadn't kept it down, but how he'd thanked her for doing that for him, and told her it was the best last meal anyone could hope for. About how she'd taken a baseball bat to his aftershave bottles the morning he died. She had lined them up in the garage and had smashed them, one by one, until the smell consumed her and she had to go back inside.

And she told her how at first she'd been so frustrated by Bailey. How she'd been convinced that Bailey hated her, but how worried she'd been that something exactly like this would happen. And how she wanted to stay out of this mess—she wasn't comfortable with drama—but she felt a necessary part of it now. This mess was hers. She just had to own it.

Three hours and five minutes wasn't much time to get between Kansas City and St. Louis, not by a long shot, but it was plenty of time to purge a soul.

"Well, if we're going to talk kid worries," Dorothy said once Jean had talked herself out, "I've got more than my share of those." They were on a stretch of I-70 that was pretty isolated. Jean knew that soon St. Charles would bloom up on them, and that would mean they weren't far at all, but for the time being, it was just them, their thoughts, and the night road. Dorothy tucked a strand of silvery hair behind her ear. "I worry that not a one of mine will even be alive in five years."

Jean glanced at her, admiring how smooth Dorothy's skin looked in the night light. "You shouldn't say that—of course they will."

Dorothy shook her head. "Then they'll be in jail. All of them. Every last one. They're criminals. They were bad before Elan left, but now they're just . . ." She turned her head to the window and shook it again.

"They're boys. They'll turn around," Jean offered.

"I doubt it," Dorothy mumbled. "Although Noah did keep a job this whole summer. I was shocked."

"Which one is Noah?"

"Second-to-oldest. He's lifeguarding at your subdivision pool."

Jean's eyes went wide. "At the Bay Ridge pool?" she asked.

Dorothy turned to her. "Yes. Why?"

"What does he look like?" And while Dorothy described him, the image of the handsome boy at the deck table plucking a soaked pair of Bailey's shorts off his chest formed itself in Jean's mind. She couldn't help herself. She burst out laughing.

"What?" Dorothy asked. "What's so funny?"

But it was several moments before Jean had the power of speech again, her stomach aching from laughter. She took a few deep breaths and told Dorothy the whole story, from the striptease to the slow walk to the car.

"Well, now I know why he was taking so many shifts," Dorothy finally said. "Boy was probably in love. Or at least in lust. Who would have guessed: my problem child and your problem grandchild, a love connection."

"Bailey did spend a lot of time at the pool," Jean agreed, and they fell into giggles again.

Finally, when they were laughed out, Dorothy wiped underneath her eyes and pressed her back into the car seat. "It's good to have someone who understands you can't always control them," she said.

"Ever," Jean corrected. "You can't *ever* control them." Not even, apparently, when they were forty years old and raising children of their own.

"I suppose in the end they'll be good people. It's just hard in the meantime. I feel so . . . judged."

"Oh, honey," Jean said, squinting in the headlights of an oncoming car, "you shouldn't feel judged. We've all got our stuff. Until recently, Loretta's husband hadn't touched her in years, Mitzi needs Prozac, and Janet's boss treats her horribly. And then there's me." Jean gave a sardonic chuckle and head shake. "There's my family."

"Wait. Janet's boss treats her horribly? Why?"

So Jean told Dorothy about what she'd seen at the supermarket, and by the time she was finished talking, they could see the arch up ahead.

"You know the book club is probably the only social thing she ever goes to, right?" Dorothy asked as Jean directed her car toward the hospital. She'd gotten quite used to the route by now.

"Who?"

"Janet. She's so painfully shy. The club is good for her. Even if she doesn't ever talk."

"You think?" Jean turned into the hospital parking lot.

"It's good for all of us," Dorothy said. "I think it was one of those serendipitous things that came up right at a time when we all needed it. Think about it. Your husband dies right at the same time that mine cheats on me? Right at the same time that May's got all these date disasters? Right when Mitzi most wants to hear herself talk?"

Jean laughed. "And don't forget. Right at the time Loretta discovers Flavian Munney."

"Oh, God, don't remind me." Dorothy giggled, holding her stomach. "His abs are so chiseled, you could break a tooth on them. She knows they're painted on, right?"

"Break a tooth—that's too funny. You should send that to the author. She might use it. After all, she had his butt literally bust through a pair of jeans at a rodeo. You remember that one?"

"Oh, yeah," Dorothy said, pointing at Jean. "He nearly killed the horse with that weapon."

But the laughter dried up as Jean pulled into the underground garage, all lit up with sickly orange lights that made everyone look green, no matter how well they were. Jean found a parking space and pulled in.

"I suppose you're right," Jean said. "About the club, I mean. I know it's good for me. I don't know what I would've done if you hadn't gone with me tonight."

Dorothy patted Jean's arm. "I don't know what I would've done if you hadn't asked," she said.

Dorothy stayed in the main lobby while Jean raced up to the third floor, where Bailey had apparently just come out of surgery and been brought back to her room. Visiting hours were long over, and the halls and rooms were all dark and sleepy. Jean's vision felt grainy, her eyes dry and scratchy, as she headed up in the elevator. Yet somehow she felt energized, as if a weight had been lifted from her, and she couldn't quite pinpoint it, but she couldn't shake a delirious feeling of being . . . necessary. And not just for Bailey. Or even for Laura. But also for Dorothy, and maybe even the others as well. Dorothy was right—maybe the club was about more than just books and food and a good time for *everyone*, not just for her.

The elevator doors opened, and right away Jean knew she was in the right place, by the sound of huskily whispered arguing voices coming from down the hall. She headed toward them and found herself in Bailey's room.

She took one look at Bailey's shaved and nicked-up head, and sucked in her breath. "Oh, my God." She pushed right between Laura and Curt and went to Bailey's bedside. "Her concussion was that bad?"

At first Curt and Laura looked at each other confusedly, forgetting to fight for a minute. Then it seemed to dawn on Curt what Jean was talking about.

"No, believe it or not, that haircut is my daughter's idea of fashion."

Jean gazed at her granddaughter in wonder. She'd shaved her own head? When had she done that? And, more important, why? She could see a few scabs crusted over on the dome of Bailey's white head, along with a new cut just above the left eyebrow, swollen and puckered around some stitches. Her left eye was bruising, and she had a smaller cut high up on her left cheekbone. The whole effect was grisly, making Bailey look as if she'd just come back from the brink of death. And maybe she had. Maybe she was still trying to—in more ways than one.

Jean ran her fingers over Bailey's newly casted arm, which was lying across her stomach while she slept, drifting up and down with the motion of her breath. She turned back to Curt.

"What happened?"

"He's what happened," Laura said, gesturing at Curt, and Jean thought she recognized a glassiness to her daughter's eyes. "I go out for one night, and he lets Bailey get bombed and take off in his car."

"Whoa, whoa, whoa," Curt argued. "First of all, I did not *let* her get bombed. In case you haven't noticed, our daughter is a willful—"

"Is she drunk, Curt? Is she?" Laura demanded, hand on swaying hip.

"You are," he responded. "That much is clear. And I told you a thousand times, I'm not going to talk to you when you've been drinking."

"Please. Like you ever talked to me before. You just don't want to admit that this is your fault."

"Oh, really? So where did she get the booze, then, huh? Because I sure as hell didn't buy it. I don't have bottles stashed in my boots in the hall closet. Oh, you thought I didn't know about that? Because, what, I'm blind? I'm stupid?"

"Don't even ask me what you are. Because right now I have a list a mile long."

"Would you keep your voice down? People are trying to sleep in here. I know that doesn't fit with your Center of the Universe complex . . ."

Laura scoffed. "I'm the center of the universe now?

Me? I don't think so. You couldn't handle your own kid for even a few weeks, so you shipped her off. First you leave. Then you force me out. Then you send her away. Are we that much of an inconvenience to your life? And now look at her." She waved her hand in Bailey's direction, narrowly missing hitting Jean in the chest.

"It was your idea to send her to your mom's," Curt cried.

"Because you were calling me every day, whining about how you couldn't handle it."

"How many times do I have to say it? You had things in such a bad mess, financially, I couldn't keep missing work. And she set fire to my apartment!" Curt hissed.

"She put a cigarette out on your pillow, Drama Queen. She didn't—"

"Enough!" Jean barked, loudly enough that Bailey's eyelids fluttered open and both Curt and Laura stopped midsentence and turned toward her. Jean lowered her voice. "I've had enough," she said. "You two are . . . ridiculous, and . . . and toxic. Have either of you stopped looking at each other long enough to look at your daughter for five minutes?" She held her hand out toward Bailey, as if presenting her to an audience. "Look at her! This fighting is why she does the things she does. She's trying to get noticed, and it's not working, so she just tries harder and harder, and . . . she is in trouble, and neither of you give enough of a . . . a shit . . . to even notice. How can you not see it? You're so busy blaming each other and blaming her, you never even consider what you can do to make things different. You never even try to listen to her or make things better. She is hurting and neither of you care. You should both be ashamed of yourselves." She swallowed, feeling her face burning over, of all things, her use of profanity in a public place. "Right now I'm ashamed of you."

Curt at least had the decency to look duly chastised, to appear embarrassed by his behavior. But Laura cocked her head to one side and placed her hand back on her hip. "No offense, Mom, but this is none of your business."

"The hell it's not," Jean said. "I got a call in the middle of the night saying that Bailey was asking for me. Did she ask for either of you? I've tried to mind my own business when it comes to your life, but now I'm making this my business, because that child needs to be somebody's business, and you're clearly not making her yours."

Laura's face scrunched up, making her look ugly and somewhat monstrous in the dim light. "How dare you? Go ahead and join the Judging Laura party, Mom. Curt will be glad to have you. But the fact is, nobody is complaining when Laura Butler is bringing home the paychecks and taking care of the fund-raisers and baking countless cookies for PTA bake sales."

"That's not true," Jean said, and again she swept her hand toward Bailey. "She complained. And she is still complaining. That's what this is. That's what she's doing right now. Every time she breaks something or does something crazy, she's complaining, and if someone doesn't start to pay attention, she is going to kill herself trying to make her complaints heard."

Laura shook her head, her eyes pointed up toward the ceiling. Jean could smell alcohol in the air, but she wasn't sure whether it was coming from Laura or Bailey. "Go ahead," she said. "Blame me. Fine."

"How can you not see it?" Curt said, but then seemed to rethink speaking. Instead, he just loped over to the chair next to Bailey's bed and slumped down in it, shaking his head.

Laura looked from him to Jean and back again. "So what do you expect me to do?" she asked. "Make myself disappear? Is that what you want?"

"No, of course not," Jean said. She reached for Laura, but Laura ducked away from her touch. "But you need help for your drinking."

Laura lifted her palms up and tipped her head back. "What? Rehab again? Are you serious? I thought we'd been through this before."

"It didn't work," Curt mumbled from his chair.

"Shut up!" Laura shouted, and immediately Jean heard the squeak of shoes coming down the hall toward their room.

"Laura, you've got to keep your voice down," Jean said. "They'll make you leave. You'll wake Bailey."

Laura threw her hands in the air. "Yet another thing I'll have done wrong! The list just keeps growing and growing. Hey, maybe next I'll cause a flood or a hurricane or . . . the goddamn Apocalypse! Right? Because, oh, Laura's a drunk, Laura needs rehab. I'm so sick of hearing it!"

"But it's true," Jean said, though she heard her voice getting smaller and smaller.

"Excuse me, ma'am?" a nurse said from the doorway. Jean did not recognize her from before. "Is there a problem?"

Jean shook her head, but Laura barreled over her. "Nothing anyone here can fix," she said, aiming a steely gaze at Jean and then over at Curt, who was still looking down at his shoes.

The nurse shifted her weight. "Well, we need you to keep your voices down so our patients can rest."

Laura's clenched jaw pulsated a couple of times. She looked much more in control of herself than she had when Jean arrived, and Jean found herself wondering just how much she'd had to drink. Maybe not much after all? Maybe Jean had unfairly accused her?

"I'll do you one better," Laura finally said. She leaned over and grabbed her purse out of the chair by the door, and pushed past the nurse, disappearing down the hallway, her heels clacking on the floor.

Everyone stood still, even the nurse, until the heels stopped reporting and there was the sound of the elevator opening on their floor. The nurse slowly faded away from the doorway, and Jean and Curt sat quietly in Bailey's room, listening to the faint hisses and beeps and the occasional murmur of the machines stationed all over the unit.

"You think she'll come back?" Jean eventually asked, breaking the silence.

Curt shrugged. "No idea what she'll do anymore." He was quiet again, then, "We're getting divorced."

Jean nodded, even though he wasn't looking at her. "I figured you would. It'll probably be for the best."

"I tried," he said, and Jean could have sworn she detected a catch in his voice, and it occurred to her that he really had tried. Living with Laura had never been easy for anyone; they'd all just pretended it had been because she gave them no choice. When a person looks to all the world like she has it together, who wants to be the lone naysayer out there? Laura gave such a strong impression of perfection, even those she was most imperfect with bought the act. "I failed," he said. "I tried, but I failed."

Jean thought about Wayne. About all the times they had failed each other. The trip to Yellowstone. The arguments about the children. The rough patch after Kenneth moved out. They had tried, and they had sometimes failed, and by the end, none of it mattered anyway. In the end, someone always ended up alone.

"You tried," Jean said. "Nobody would blame you."

"Bailey blames me."

"Bailey blames everybody," Jean said. "She's hurt. Someone needs to acknowledge that. She's a smart kid." She shifted in her seat. "You know what you should do for her?"

Curt looked up, one eyebrow cocked higher than the other.

"You should find her a book club," Jean said. "She loves books. She reads all the time." She thought about Dorothy sitting down in the main lobby, probably flipping through magazines or maybe dozing with her head propped on one chair. "You'd be surprised how much good book clubs can do."

"Bailey? A book club?" Curt asked skeptically. "I can't even get her to go to school. I don't even know if she can read."

"Of course she can read," Jean said. Then she added under her breath, "Sometimes more than I wanted her to."

"Well, you'll forgive me if I'm not really into finding an enrichment activity for her at the moment," Curt said. He pulled himself to standing. "And since Laura has decided to take off, I guess that means I'm on the night shift. I should get some coffee. You want any?"

Jean shook her head. "I'm just going to sit for a while."

Curt headed out, and Jean leaned forward, studying her granddaughter in her sleep. She looked so peaceful, and without all the anger, her face appeared so much younger. Pretty, even, if it weren't for the cuts and bruises.

As if she knew she was being watched, Bailey opened her eyes.

"Hey," Jean said, leaning forward and reaching to put her hand on Bailey's good arm but feeling self-conscious and taking it back at the last second, resting it in her lap. "How are you feeling?"

Bailey tried to scooch up to a better position, but

winced and eased against the pillow again. "Like I've been thrown into a windshield." She touched her cheekbone gingerly.

"You look a little like you've been thrown into a windshield too," Jean said. "You had me scared to death."

"At least someone was," Bailey said, glumly. She lowered her hand and pushed her head back into the pillow again.

"Oh, honey," Jean said. "They were scared. They're your parents."

Bailey chuckled, then winced again, touching the ribs on her left side just as gingerly as she'd felt her face a moment before. "Yeah, you can stop lying now. You heard them. The only thing they care about is themselves."

Jean couldn't argue that, could she? After what she'd witnessed coming into this room, how could she for an instant say Bailey was wrong about that?

"I heard what you said," Bailey said. She fiddled with the wire to the remote. "All the things you said about me? About me being smart? That stuff?"

"Oh." Jean quickly wracked her brain for memory of what else she'd said. And, worse, for what Curt and Laura might have said. What exactly had Bailey heard?

"Thank you for that," Bailey finished, and Jean could have sworn she saw tears gathering in the corners of Bailey's eyes. "'Cause I was a pain in the butt at your house, and I wouldn't blame you if you didn't want to stick up for me."

Jean leaned forward, and this time she did put her hand on Bailey's arm, a gesture that felt strange and warm and right all at the same time. "Everything I said was true. I don't know how long you've been going through all this . . . stuff . . . but just from what I've seen, I know it hasn't been easy. You're very strong."

Bailey's chin crumpled, just like a small child's, and the tears spilled over. "I've been acting so stupid," she said, her voice cracking. "I could've died tonight. I'm lucky I didn't." She turned her eyes up to Jean's, and Jean thought she could see a lifetime of heartache in them. "I don't want to die," Bailey said. "I don't want them to do that to me."

Jean squeezed Bailey's arm. "Then don't let them," she said, and then she was reminded of something her therapist had said to her one time before Wayne died, when he started really going downhill. "You can't control what's going on with someone else. The only person you can control is yourself," she said, reciting his sentence word for word.

"I thought I was," Bailey said. "I thought I was doing everything I wanted to do, and they couldn't stop me because their lives were so messed up. But it turns out I was only doing what they didn't want me to do. They were still calling the shots, even if I didn't know it. I'm so stupid."

"You're not stupid," Jean said.

"My haircut is stupid," Bailey said.

Jean paused, then nodded. "Okay, the haircut is kind of stupid," she admitted, and they both laughed.

"I want to come live with you," Bailey said after a beat. "Like, permanently. I don't want to go back with them. Either one."

But before Jean could answer, Curt came into the room, carrying a cup of coffee. He paused when he saw the two of them talking.

"Everything okay?" he asked, his body silhouetted in the doorway.

Jean and Bailey gazed at each other for several moments.

"Everything's fine," Jean said, finally. "Actually, everything's looking better than it has in a long time."

TWENTY-THREE

Dear Mr. Thackeray:

My name is Jean Vison, and my book club recently read your book *Blame*. Several members of our club have expressed an interest in trying to speak with you directly as part of our book discussion. We have already spent an entire meeting discussing it, but we would be more than open to discussing it again if you were there to shed a little light on your inspiration and what exactly you were trying to say with this book.

We know that you don't normally make visits to book clubs, but we were wondering if you'd be willing to make an exception this one time. We have taken up a collection and could cover your airfare and a rental car.

We will meet at my house, 1155 Mount View Road,

at one p.m. on the nineteenth. Please feel free to stop by.

I hope to hear from you soon.

Sincerely,
Jean Vison

Dear Bailey,

You are fooling nobody. I suppose this Jean Vison is the dear old granny you have been talking about in your e-mails. You should tread carefully when it comes to misrepresenting yourself and pretending to be someone who you are not online.

At any rate, it doesn't matter. I was planning to come anyway. Your last e-mail had me at "story." But the money is, as they say, icing on the cake.

I am allergic to eggs, strawberries, and am fairly lactose intolerant. Also, I don't care for olives and prefer to eat organically whenever I can, because a green society is the only society an intelligent individual would tolerate inhabiting.

See you on the nineteenth.

Sincerely,
R. Sebastian Thackeray III, Author

TWENTY-FOUR

It took Bailey only two days after being released from the hospital to get entirely packed and ready to go. Like, more ready than she'd ever been for anything in her whole life. Her grandmother had loaded everything into bags and boxes from the grocery store. What she couldn't fit in her car, she'd taken to the post office and shipped, assuring Bailey that it would all arrive within just a few days.

Bailey didn't really care. The box full of her books had made it into the car. A new copy of *Anne of Green Gables*, which her grandmother had brought to the hospital, was tucked in her backpack. Everything else was just stuff.

They'd loaded up on snacks and drinks—way too many for such a short trip, in Bailey's opinion—and Grandma Jean had bought her a new iPod so she could block out their boring old-lady talk from the backseat. Not that Bailey thought it was always all that boring. But she wouldn't say that to Jean and Dorothy.

Bailey's arm was in a cast. Her shaved forehead was scabby and sporting the tiniest bit of fuzz in some places, and was dwarfed by a giant gauze bandage. Her eye was blackened, and she wore a pair of old pink sweats that she used to wear back in seventh grade, before things got so out of control, and a plain white T-shirt that used to belong to her dad. She looked terrible—shocking, even. But she didn't care.

She had only one more thing to do.

Getting into the rehab center had been no easy task, especially as strung out as she looked, but once she got past the nasty desk nurse who treated her like trash, she walked down the hall until she found her mom's room. Her mom was in there, sitting on the edge of the bed and staring out the window.

"Hello," Bailey said.

Laura jumped, looked like she wanted to stand up, but thought better of it and eased back down on the mattress, which let out a small plastic gasp.

"Bailey," she said, "look at you. How's your arm?"

Bailey looked down at her wrist, momentarily forgetting about it, and then back at her mother. "I'm fine. I just wanted to tell you good-bye." Laura's eyebrows twisted up, and she pressed her lips together. She looked flummoxed. "I'm going to live with Grandma Jean," Bailey continued. "I didn't know if Dad told you."

Laura shook her head. "He didn't. I haven't talked to him. You're sure? That's a long way from your friends."

"I'll manage," Bailey responded with a hint of bitterness. Like she had any friends. And why did her mother still not know that? Why did she insist on living under this delusion that everything was okay?

"It's a long way from me too," Laura said, and for a second Bailey almost felt sorry for her mother, especially when she saw a single tear slip down Laura's cheek. Had she ever seen Laura Butler the Great cry? She couldn't think of a time.

But then Bailey remembered the million times she'd been hurt by her mother, and her resolve hardened. "I know," she said.

At least Laura had the decency to not look crushed. "What about your dad?" she asked, whisking the tear away efficiently.

Bailey shrugged. What about him? He hadn't argued at all when Jean and Bailey approached him. He may have actually looked relieved. Which was a pretty crappy thing to do to your daughter, but Bailey supposed she couldn't blame him. She'd directed heaping amounts of crap toward him, and he hadn't had the alcohol to take him away like her mother did. "I don't know," she said to Laura. "We haven't figured out all the details yet. But he doesn't care. He never did."

"He did," Laura said. "He does. He's had a lot to deal with. Give him time. He'll show it."

Bailey nodded, scraped the toe of one shoe down the side of the toe of the other. Silence stretched between them too long, but just before it became so long as to become uncomfortable, Bailey blurted, "You're a horrible mother." Laura didn't react. She was steely, almost as if she hadn't heard Bailey speak at all. Bailey took a breath. "But you haven't always been. So I came to give you this, because I don't need it anymore, and maybe you do."

Bailey took two steps into the room, leaned forward, and dropped *Home for a Bunny* on her mother's bed. It was worn, the pages curling at the corners, the cover illustration rubbed off, and the binding loose. How Bailey had loved that book.

Bailey took those two steps back into the doorway again as Laura laid her hand on the book. "I won't die for you. I won't ruin myself to save you. You understand that?" she asked.

Laura swallowed. "Of course. I wouldn't expect you to."

"Good," Bailey said, and turned to leave.

"Bailey?" Laura called, halfway pulling herself up off the bed again. Bailey turned and locked eyes with her mother. "I'm going to get better. I'm going to stay here until I'm better. And then I'll come get you."

Bailey wiped her cheeks with the palm of one hand and said, "Right."

And then she turned and left.

TWENTY-FIVE

The ride home was much quieter than the ride east. Dorothy and Jean both felt wrung out, having spent three days in a seedy motel, neither of them getting any sleep. Jean had spent most of her days at the hospital, sitting quietly while an aggravated and sore Bailey cussed out anyone who dared look at her wrong: Curt, the nurses, even the poor volunteer who stopped by to see if she'd like a second blanket. Jean winced every time Bailey opened her mouth, but she understood this to be part of Bailey's demons, part of what she needed to get out. And she understood that these demons were part of why Bailey wanted to come live with her. She knew that Bailey also hoped they wouldn't follow her there.

In the evenings, after dinner was brought and Bailey got sleepy, Jean would go back to the motel, only to find Dorothy on the phone with a lawyer or a bondsman or with her ex-husband, trying to work out this problem or that.

Together, they would grab a quick bite, and then head to Laura's house, where they systematically packed up Bailey's things, cramming them into old banana boxes Jean had gotten from a grocery store. Dorothy covered Bailey's hanging clothes with trash bags and hauled them to the car in armloads while Jean wrapped knickknacks in tissue paper and placed them under soft pajamas and T-shirts. They were moving her out completely, at Bailey's request, as if she expected to never return to her old life, not even for a day.

Curt hadn't argued at all about Bailey going to live with Jean. Not that she'd expected him to. In fact, she'd have been shocked if he had.

I think that's what's best for all of us, he said, and though cynical Bailey clucked her tongue and said, *Translation: It's what's best for Curt,* Jean couldn't help but feel that he was saying what he really believed. Throughout everything, the man never left his daughter's bedside—not even to go home and change clothes—and if that didn't speak for some sort of dedication, Jean didn't know what would. Curt was doing the best he could.

Every night, Jean expected to sleep like the dead, but as soon as she and Dorothy turned out the lights, her mind would start racing. What would Wayne have said about a grandchild coming to live with them? Would he approve? Could she do this? Was Bailey just coming to live with her because she figured she could get away with her outrageous antics there? Would she steal from Jean, hurt her? She could hear those last questions in Wayne's voice.

And soon she would hear Dorothy's voice over the noise of the highway outside their window, drifting through the pitch-dark motel room.

"Jean?"

"Yeah?"

"You awake?"

"I can't sleep."

"Me either."

There was a pause; then she heard the rattle of the air-conditioning in the unit next door coming on.

"Jean?"

"Yeah."

"I miss them. The boys. Can you believe it?"

"Yes, of course I can."

"They're not all bad. I know people think they are. But they can be so loving too. They're my boys. Do you know they make me breakfast in bed every year on my birthday? Every year. Never missed one. Bad boys wouldn't do that, would they?"

Jean thought it over. One of the many things she'd learned over the past couple of months with her daughter, and Curt, and especially Bailey, was that nobody was ever all bad. "I can see that," she said. "Noah's a good lifeguard."

Dorothy chuckled. "It's easy to be good when you don't have anyone to actually save. I don't know how he even got the job. I had no idea he even had a lifeguard certificate. I wouldn't be surprised if he faked one."

Jean turned to her side and fluffed the pillow up under her cheek. "Oh, God, that's terrible."

"But it's not, really. Noah would never let anything bad happen to an innocent person. He'd drown with them."

"Well, ideally, nobody drowns," Jean said, though in the back of her head she was thinking how swimming was a lot like life that way. Nobody expected to be the one at the bottom of the pool, reaching for a hand to pull him up for air. Nobody expected to be the one who didn't make it.

On the third day, when Bailey was released, Curt found Laura at the Blue Serenity Rehabilitation Center again. She was in bad shape, they told him. She was at her rock bottom, they told him. She wouldn't see him, they told him.

But Bailey had requested to visit her mother one last time, and Jean had taken her. When Bailey finished up there, she was in no mood to talk, so they'd gone ahead and hit the road. Bailey didn't say good-bye to Curt; she just leaned over against the car door and fell asleep. She remained that way the entire ride home.

Likewise, Dorothy fell asleep within an hour. Jean stopped at a gas station, picked up a bag of candy-coated licorice, and kept herself awake with talk radio and sweets, her excitement and fear growing every mile they got closer to home.

This time, Bailey didn't stand around in the entryway, pouting. She grabbed the largest suitcase and her pillow and blanket and headed right up to her bedroom. She came back down and got her other things, one box at a time, and hefted each one up on her own.

Jean drifted into her bedroom and opened Wayne's top drawer. She sifted through the treasures inside until she found what she was looking for: a photo of Wayne holding baby Bailey, a stern-faced Laura peering over his shoulder. Jean could remember the day so clearly. Whereas she worried about silly things like how the word *grandma* made her sound old, Wayne was nothing but proud to be a grandfather. He handed out chocolates to his friends; he told every cashier and waiter along the way to St. Louis that he had a new grandbaby and that she had his eyes. He couldn't wait to hold her.

Of course, Laura had Bailey's naptimes so carefully controlled, they scarcely got to see the child, and this was the only photo of Wayne holding her. He'd kept it in his top desk drawer. He'd looked at it often.

He would approve of Bailey's new living arrangement. Jean knew that now.

"Hey," Jean heard, softly, from the doorway. She turned to find Bailey standing just outside.

"Is something wrong?" Jean asked, lowering the picture into her lap.

Bailey shook her head, then nodded. "I don't know," she said. "It's weird."

"What's weird?"

"This. Moving in with someone I don't really know, and I'm, like, really far away from my mom, and I don't know if I'm supposed to love her or hate her or . . ." She shrugged again.

"Or miss her?" Jean asked, and Bailey nodded. "For what it's worth, it's a little weird for me too," Jean said, and when she moved her hand, the photo caught Bailey's eye. She stepped into the room and tentatively lowered herself next to Jean on the bed.

"Who's that?" she asked.

Jean frowned. "You don't remember Grandpa Wayne?"

Bailey squinted at the photo. "Maybe," she said. "He had glasses, right?" Jean gave a sheepish grin, and Bailey took in a short breath. "Oh, right. I forgot about that. Those were his. Can I see?" She held out her hand, and Jean passed the photo to her. Bailey ran her fingers over the image. "I was tiny," she said. "At least I think that's me. Am I right?"

"Our only grandchild," Jean said. "He was very excited."

Bailey looked for a moment more, running her fingers over Laura, and then using her forefinger to blot out Laura's face. "At least someone was."

"Bailey, I know your mother loves you. She's just . . ." Jean trailed off. She didn't know how to finish the sentence. Laura was "just" so many things.

"Selfish?" Bailey finished for her, and Jean had to admit, at least to herself, that *selfish* was one of the traits she would use to describe her daughter. *Entitled* was another.

She nodded. "Yes, I suppose she is."

"But she's also wonderful sometimes," Bailey said.

"Everyone wants to be like her. I wanted to, for sure. But not anymore."

Jean could see tears glisten in the corners of her granddaughter's eyes once again, and could see Bailey tremble with the effort to keep them in. She wondered what it must have felt like to be Bailey—to be in constant pain and always trying to control it, always trying to maintain it.

Actually, Jean realized, she knew exactly what that felt like.

She stood and walked to the dresser, motioning for Bailey to join her. Bailey got up and crept to the drawer, peering in timidly.

"You know what this is?" Jean asked, and Bailey shook her head. "This is my Crying Time drawer. These are the memories I keep of Wayne, and once a day, for one hour, I get them out and I look through them and cry over him and I just allow myself to feel terrible. But when my hour is up, I put them away and close the drawer. Crying Time over. The rest of the day is all about getting on with my life."

Bailey reached in and touched some objects. She picked up the pinky ring and turned it over in her hand. She felt his wallet, wore his glasses. While she did, Jean rifled through the old photos until she found half a dozen of Wayne with Laura. She held them out to Bailey.

"If you want, you can have a Crying Time too. It might help you decide how you really feel about her. And it will be okay for you, for that one hour a day, to miss her. And to cry for her."

Bailey seemed to stare at the stack of photos for an incredibly long time. So long, in fact, Jean was sure she wouldn't take them and would leave Jean standing there, holding them forever. But just as Jean was getting ready to put them back in the dresser, Bailey reached out with a trembling hand and took them.

"Thank you," she whispered, and Jean could see that the tears had finally spilled over. It broke Jean's heart to finally see the tough exterior on her granddaughter begin to crumble. She had seen lots of emotions on her granddaughter—defiance, insolence, anger, hatred—but this was her first hint of sadness.

"You're welcome," she said.

Bailey started back toward the door, sniffling and swiping at her spilled tears with one hand while staring down at the photos that she held in the other. She left the room, and Jean closed the drawer, feeling a pang of loss over having given the photos away, but not necessarily a loss that wasn't balanced out by a huge gain.

Just as Jean closed the drawer, Bailey came back down the hall and leaned in the bedroom doorway.

"Can I ask you for a favor?"

"Sure. Anything," Jean said.

"Can I redecorate my room? Those bears are really stupid."

Jean laughed. "Of course you can," she said. "It's your room now."

TWENTY-SIX

"Stop fidgeting," Bailey whispered, leaning over to Jean, who had barely touched her wine.

Mitzi broke away from Loretta and Dorothy's conversation. She turned the stem of her glass between her thumb and forefinger. "What are you so nervous about, anyway?" she asked.

"I've never had a celebrity in my house before," Jean said, and her stomach rumbled. The roast lamb that she'd made for the special occasion had overcooked, and the longer it sat on top of the stove, resting, waiting, the worse Jean feared it would taste. Dry. It was going to be dry. Rubbery. Tough. She should have known better than to try something fancy. What on earth had she been thinking? She was hardly a chef, and to try to imagine herself as one was ridiculous. She should have stuck with her capers.

Even Bailey had tried to talk her out of it. "Don't

make anything special for him," she'd said. "Serve bologna sandwiches. On stale bread. He'll probably like having something to complain about."

But had Jean listened? No, of course not. And now a Pulitzer Prize–winning author was going to be chewing on cardboard lamb in her dining room. Correction: a Pulitzer Prize–winning author was going to first have to step over the purplish stain and wine-bottle dent on her kitchen floor before chewing on cardboard lamb in her dining room. Dear God, why had she agreed to this?

By this time, Dorothy and Loretta's attention had been grabbed too.

"He's just a normal person," Dorothy said. "Pants on one leg at a time and all that, you know."

"Speaking of pants," Mitzi said, "I saw your boy Leonard the other day. Had his pants hanging half down his ass. You should tell him to pull those up, Dot."

"Oh, trust me, not a day goes by that I don't. But, hey, if you think you can reason with him better than I can, I wholeheartedly invite you to try." Jean caught a flick of Dorothy's eye and remembered the conversation they'd had in the car on the way to St. Louis. Was Dorothy feeling judged right now? Most certainly. But was she letting it roll a little too? Jean thought so.

"Who said anything about reason?" Mitzi said. "I'll just come up behind him and give him a wedgie till he sings soprano."

Dorothy laughed. "His dad used to sing, way back in

junior high. I remember. His voice was so high, and we didn't have enough sopranos, so they had him sing with them. It was the funniest thing. He was so embarrassed, and all the boys in school gave him so much trouble over it. They called him Elaine instead of Elan."

"See? I'd just be helping Leonard relate to his dad on another level. Leonetta and Elaine." She leaned over the table and clinked glasses with Dorothy, triumphant.

"This is ridiculous," Mitzi said, checking her watch. "I'm starving over here. I say we should eat. He's not the pope."

"Even if he was the pope, you'd still eat," May said.

"Only after saying the blessing," Mitzi answered. "Come on, Jean—everything's getting cold. What if he doesn't show up? He's just the type to not show up."

They all looked at their hostess, who was growing paler by the minute. She'd fidgeted with her book so much, she'd torn a corner of the cover off, and then had been beset with fear that he would notice and would lay into her for not respecting his book. Why? Why, in the name of the universe, had she let Bailey talk her into this?

Bailey scooted her chair back and stood up. "I don't have any problem with eating. Show up late, don't get food—that's my motto."

"He'll be expecting us to eat all the food anyway," a voice said from the end of the table, and everyone stopped and peered down at Janet, who was shaking with terror at having spoken aloud. She mashed her lips together a few times, chewing on the bottom one, then said, "He thinks women are all fat useless creatures. I mean . . ." She paused, swallowed, and Jean had an urge to go to her, to put her arm around her and tell her it was okay, she could keep talking. "It's all in the book. You just have to read between the lines."

Loretta made a *pfft* noise. "Not too in between, and, yes, I totally agree with you."

Mitzi leaned her elbows, clad in a brown and maroon embroidered jacket that looked more like tapestry than clothing, on the table. "What do you bet his mother is fat? Or whoever raised him. I agree with Janet—he's got a vendetta. If you read between the lines in this book, he's basically saying all women are whores until they become moms, and then they're fat, lazy whores, screwing not for money, but for timeshares and expensive cars and designer onesies for their babies. Nobody who was raised right really believes that, do they?"

Dorothy, who had been standing, plopped back into her chair. "Hell, even my boys don't believe that. Even Topher, when he's not in prison, treats his girls like queens."

"I was more struck with Thackeray's interpretation of Josie, the bandleader. Could he have described her as being any uglier?" Mitzi complained.

"He had gnats swarming her in that one band camp scene, for goodness' sake," Loretta pointed out, and Mitzi nodded in agreement.

"See? Who does that? He hates women. He's going to

take one step in here, sense our ovaries, and hiss and melt into a pile of bloody goo, like a vampire in sunlight."

"Mmm, yummy description, Mitzi. Let's eat," May said, and they all stood up and made a beeline for the buffet. Jean hurried in to cut the lamb and arrange it on a tray, and was pleased to see a little juice and blood run out onto the china as she did.

But before she could get herself a plate, there was the sound of a car door slamming, followed by the clack of dress shoes coming up the front walk, then a man's cough. Jean's heart seized, and she stood motionless, a serving fork in one hand.

Everyone else had just gotten settled when the doorbell sounded.

"He's here," Jean heard Bailey say, and then heard the scrape of Bailey's chair being pushed back. On one hand, Jean was grateful to her granddaughter for answering the door, as she seemed to be frozen in place and completely incapable of doing anything other than listen to her heartbeat at the moment. But on the other hand . . . Oh, Lord, Bailey was answering the door.

Jean heard the door pull open, and heard hushed whispers coming from the table, along with intermittent scraping and clanging of forks on china (yes, she had even brought out Grandma Vison's good china for the occasion— plates she'd only ever used on Thanksgiving and Christmas), and then the hum of a male's voice heading toward the kitchen. Jean noticed some of the ladies craning their necks to catch a glimpse of the Great R. Sebastian Thackeray III as he made his way into the kitchen.

Jean dropped the fork she was holding with a clatter onto the dish below it. She jumped into action, rushing to the man and holding out her hands as if to take something, which he did not have.

"Welcome," she said. "I'm Jean."

The man, who was incredibly short and stout, a block of pudge and excess skin balanced on two fire hydrant legs, came in, scowling. Bailey was following, a smug smirk on her face. Jean dreaded to think about what might have already been said, and silently pleaded with Bailey to say nothing more. The man's eyes darted around balefully, his swollen lips overly wet.

"Smells like a short-order cafeteria in here," he said. He wrinkled his nose. "Old grease and unfounded opinions all balled up into one oppressive feast for the senses."

Jean's mouth flapped shut. She wasn't sure how to respond to that. Was he insulting the smell of her house? She honestly couldn't tell.

"You can take my jacket," he said, pulling off his sport coat and holding it out toward her between his index and middle fingers, as if he might drop it at any second, and if she wasn't prepared to catch it, God help her.

Jean grasped the jacket and hung it on the coat hooks on the kitchen wall, her hand bumping up against the little vase that sat on the shelf above, nearly knocking it off. She stopped its lazy roll with one palm.

"Please help yourself to some dinner," she said. "Plates are over there. And we have wine on the table. Or would you like something else?"

He sneered. "Mmm, supermarket wine, how could I resist? Twist top, I presume?"

Jean blinked. This time she was sure he was insulting her. She cleared her throat and tried again. "Did you have any trouble finding us?" she asked, going through every Polite Hostess effort in her repertoire. Bailey disappeared into the dining room. The author picked up a plate and proceeded to serve himself, fastidiously, almost daintily.

"I once traveled through Turkey for two weeks, alone, with nothing but an American Express and a pocketful of lira," he said in a recitation voice that boomed so loud, even the soft noise in the dining room stopped. "I have lived twenty years in New York City, and never once have I gotten lost." He spooned some of Mitzi's hash brown casserole onto his plate, then glanced up with a grin that was not altogether friendly. "I think I can handle suburbia with aplomb," he said.

"Oh. Okay," Jean said, and, not knowing what else to say to or do for this curious little man, she edged into the dining room, loitering in the doorway until he finally made his way over, his plate nearly overflowing with food. He had taken some of everything, Jean noted, except for her lamb.

"So," he said, settling into a chair and scooting up toward the table. Mitzi leaned forward and poured him a glass of wine. "What have I missed? Gossip, no doubt. Whom are we hating today? Supermodels? The Real Housewives of Missour*ah*? One another?" He crammed a huge bite of potatoes into his mouth.

"You," Bailey whispered at Jean's side, and Jean shot her a look. Bailey went wide-eyed and shrugged.

Thackeray didn't notice. He ate another spoonful, and then another, everyone else around the table pausing to stare.

Finally, he licked his lips, swilled some wine, and gazed around the table. "So, are we here to talk or what?"

Uncomfortable, Jean shifted, knowing there was no way she was going to eat any of the food she'd put on her plate, not that she'd brought her plate into the dining room anyway. In her haste to make everything perfect for Thackeray, she'd accidentally left it on the kitchen counter. She cleared her throat. "We actually read *Blame* a couple months ago. But we had such a lively discussion about it, we thought it would be interesting to get the author's viewpoint on the story."

He motioned to Jean with his fork. "Yes, your granddaughter told me as much. You don't look so bad for a dying woman, by the way." He shoveled more food into his mouth.

Jean glanced over at Bailey, who blushed deeply. "Sorry," Bailey mumbled. "I kinda lied to get him here."

"It didn't work," he said. "I knew she was full of shit from the moment I read the first e-mail. She had that certain adolescent entitlement about her, that certain fuck-you-ish-ness that makes teenagers so very charming to be around."

Jean could see Bailey's face transform from blushing embarrassment to glaring anger. She knew that look all too well. Until recently, it was the only look Jean had ever seen on her granddaughter. She knew that Thackeray had better watch his step, or he would find out just how much "fuck-you-ish-ness," as he so indelicately put it, Bailey had in her.

"But . . . I have to appreciate anyone who will offer up her family on a silver platter to a word whore such as myself. A voyeur of strife. A stealer of pain. I'm hoping, though not hopeful—and yes, there is a difference—that she wasn't lying about that. Where's the alcoholic mother?"

At this point, Jean and the others were so confused, they could do nothing but exchange puzzled glances, but Jean felt Bailey stiffen next to her.

"She's in rehab," Bailey said.

"Oh, ho!" Thackeray crowed, throwing his head back. "It's too perfect! The drunkard mother can't be properly denigrated because she's in rehab, drying out. I couldn't have written it better myself." He pointed to Jean again with his fork. "And I am assuming this . . . dying grand-mother . . . of yours is the one whose husband died?"

Jean sat up ramrod-straight. What all had Bailey told him about her?

Bailey nodded, her mouth working silently around words only she could hear.

He shrugged. "Kind of a boring story. People die all the time. But I suppose I could use your extreme passion for the boring and ordinary for a twist. To never leave the dead one's side, to pine until you'd pined yourself into a pine box. To forget how to live because you watched him die. Oh, how beautifully poetic. The dramatic irony is killing me." He gulped more wine, closed his eyes as if to enjoy whatever scene it was he had set in his mind. "Do they actually call people 'widder' in Missouri, or is that just how I imagine it to be? As in 'Widder Jones'? Ah, never mind. I can make it work even if they don't really say it. I can make the whole world believe it, that this Widder . . . What was your last name again?"

He snapped his fingers at Jean, and she answered, the response popping out of her mouth before her brain could even unscramble everything he was saying. He spoke in such riddles, she had a hard time making sense of it all. "Vison."

"The old Widder Vison," only he said it *vah-son*, "rattling around her drafty house, desperately alone and lonely, only to discover that her Mr. Perfect—or should I say Mr. Perfectly Dead—had a long-term affair. Tell me, Widder Vison, how well do you think you know your dear, old, dead husband?"

"Very well," Jean responded icily. This time she understood perfectly what he was getting at, and she felt something dangerous well up inside her, felt herself sit up straighter, defensively. This man knew nothing about her, about Wayne. Who was he to suppose anything about their lives?

"So how did it feel when you discovered that Mr. Perfect had taken a gay lover?"

Jean gasped. "He never did!"

"Ahhh, the dear widder has a touch of the bigotry," he said, elongating his words in a crude interpretation of a Midwest accent.

Jean tried to chuckle, but what came out sounded so mirthless, she couldn't really classify it as much of anything more than a grunt. "Oh, please," she said.

"Not a denial, Widder," he retorted, gleefully tucking a deviled egg into his mouth.

"Stop it," Bailey said, and when he started talking again, she said it louder. "Stop it!"

At first, he looked amused. His eyebrows shot up into his thick black hair. Then his mouth drew down into a thin line. "I do believe you got me here under false pretenses, Bailey. I do believe your promise of letting me use your, in your words, 'fucked-up family' for a story went uncleared by the powers that be."

"What?" Jean breathed, turning to Bailey. Bailey looked down into her lap, fiddling with the cloth napkin there.

"Well, that's a shame. Not even the absent father for me to whet my teeth on."

"Okay, that's enough," Loretta said. She had an uncharacteristically steel glint in her eyes. "She's a girl. Leave her alone."

Thackeray mimed wiping tears from his eyes. "Oh, well, since she's a girl . . ." He propped his elbow on the table. "She happens to be a very manipulative girl. These weren't things I pulled out of her—she offered them. I am human to take her up on her offer."

"No, you're not human. You're a monster," Mitzi said. "We knew it by page five. It's about time you caught up with us."

Again with the cocky, unkind smirk. "Oh, so that's what this is about. You recognized yourself in my work, and it's Attack the Author Day. Spare me the colloquialisms. You paid a lot of money to get me here. Offer me an argument." He took a bite of potato and then made a face, reached up to his mouth, and pulled something out. "Jesus, is that a hair?"

"Here's an argument," Mitzi said. "You have mommy issues."

Thackeray laughed, a mirthless sound. "And is that your professional opinion, Dr. Nobody?"

"It's all of our opinions," Dorothy said. She held up the book. "This book sucked. We couldn't believe you meant it to sound like it really sounds. But after listening to you talk, I can see that you did. Why?"

"Because it's the truth," Thackeray snarled, tossing his fork down onto the plate and chipping a piece from the edge. Jean cringed. It had been important to Grandma Vison to keep these dishes—all of them—in the family. "That's what you people want, right? You book readers, isn't that what you're always after? The truth? Well, here's a truth for you. Sometimes stories are just stories, and *you* are the ones supplying the so-called truth. And then, when you don't like the reality your own brain has supplied, you blame the author. You come after my blood because you don't like how the reflection of your own misgivings made you feel. How dare you question an artist about his art? You are clearly both tacky and stupid."

"I'm not the one sitting at someone else's dinner table, eating someone else's food, and insulting everyone around the table," Dorothy said. "If you want tacky."

Mitzi piped in. "Here's a news flash. You're a far cry from perfect."

Loretta nodded. "You have the nerve to criticize people for their size, and you're Chubby McHamburglar."

"You're definitely no artist," Mitzi added.

"How many awards adorn your walls, my dear?" Thackeray responded.

"How many friends adorn yours?" Loretta shot back.

"I'm betting zero," Mitzi said. "I'm betting negative on the friends list."

"Let's have it, then," he said, tossing his napkin into his plate and leaning back in his chair, crossing his arms triumphantly. "You want to criticize the book? Go ahead. Criticize."

"Well, for starters, we're not created by our mothers alone," Bailey said, her voice shaking. She stood. "There are fathers too. And there is personal responsibility. You want to know something about personal responsibility? Ask any kid of an alcoholic. Responsibility is all we know. We're practically choking on it. You act like we're doomed to repeat our mothers' mistakes, and that's not going to happen. It's bullshit."

He rubbed his chin thoughtfully. "Ah. So you're afraid you're going to be doing the twelve-step line dance in the future, is that it? You don't like the central theme of responsibility for how our future generations are shaped? You have issue with that? Maybe you should turn on your Internet and text out a bomb threat. That's what your generation knows best."

Bailey shook her head, her eyes slitted in such a way that Jean hadn't seen since spotting her up in the loft at her old house. "You don't know anything. I will not be like her. She doesn't shape me; I do."

"Well, I hate to be the bearer of bad news, Pollyanna, but statistics say you will be exactly like her. And your daughter exactly like you. And on and on until the world is populated by an unhealthy proportion of drunk Visons who eventually kill themselves off with the hooch. Darwin at his finest."

Bailey opened her mouth, but another voice cried out from the end of the table. "That's not true." Janet had pushed herself out from the table and was perched on the edge of her chair.

"Really, now?" he mused. "What do you say we make a bet, then? I'd like to wager that your mother is fat. That she's such an important role in your life, she can't practice even a modicum of self-restraint, and she clearly taught that to you. Am I right?"

Jean noticed a tear streak down Janet's face, but she made no move to wipe it away. "No. That's not true," Janet said again. "But what is true is that you're a scared little man."

"And you are the embodiment of my main character, Blanche. A self-righteous, quivering mound of excess flesh, too into your own sensibilities to care anything about anyone else's." He swept the ladies with his gaze. "You all are. You are all proof that once again I am right. Look into the mirror, ladies. You will see loads of awards in it, with my name on each and every one. You are the very characters, with your binge eating and your affairs and your illegitimate babies, who win me accolades and make me rich."

And then the room erupted. Mitzi jumped out of her seat; Loretta clenched her fists at her sides; even sweet May shook her head disgustedly. They all talked over one another, slinging insults and barbs, inviting him to do things to himself. And he shouted back, superior and haughty and predictable.

Jean didn't yell. She didn't know what to say. This meeting had not gone as she'd expected at all. She'd thought maybe he'd explain why he wrote the things he wrote, that maybe they'd give him a little piece of their mind, that he'd hear it and they'd adjourn over pie. Instead, she watched as the larger-than-life, intimidating celebrity she'd imagined morphed into a bitter, ugly little man as full of bile as his books were.

But when she looked to her left, she saw Bailey, shrunk back into her chair, her feet pulled up to the seat, her face buried against her knees, her shoulders shaking with tears. She turned her face to Jean. "I'm not going to be her. I swear I'm not. I can't be," she cried, and Jean couldn't take it anymore.

She stood. "That's it!" she yelled, her voice edging through everyone else's, cutting them all off in midsentence. "That's it!" she repeated. She turned to Thackeray. "Get out of my house."

He stared at her in mute shock.

"Get up, get your arrogant opinions, get your cheap suit coat, and . . ." She paused, clenched her fists. "Get the hell out!"

It seemed to take a moment to sink in on Thackeray that Jean's sudden outburst was directed at him. But when it finally did, he angrily pushed his chair out, stood, and swept into the kitchen in one motion.

"I should have known better than to think that a bunch of doughy Midwesterners would have the brainpower to understand my work," he muttered as he hurried to his coat.

Jean followed him, and was followed in turn by each of the ladies, who filled the kitchen doorway like a posse running a bad guy out of town.

"And another thing!" he said, yanking his coat off the

hook a little too harshly. The vase Jean had nearly knocked over earlier, and which she had only settled without pushing it properly back up on the shelf, made two teetering swoops and rolled off, shattering on the floor at Thackeray's feet. Out of it tumbled Noah's weed, which Bailey had been stashing all summer.

Everyone stared at the marijuana that had showered over Thackeray's shoes.

"Is that . . . ?" Loretta asked, and Bailey burst out laughing.

"That's pot!" Thackeray exclaimed, doing a disgusted little jig to shake it off.

"Where did that come from?" Jean gasped, mortified.

Bailey, disabled with giggles, choked out, "The pool."

Dorothy rolled her eyes. "For God's sake. Noah."

And then Mitzi let out a snort.

Jean held her hands out toward Thackeray, desperate. "We don't do that here. This is a mistake. I had no idea." She looked at Bailey for help, but Bailey was nearly doubled over at this point, her eyes watering from laughter now instead of tears. "Dammit, Bailey!"

"Language, Jean," Bailey said between racking laughs, and then Loretta joined in.

Thackeray looked from the dope to Bailey, to Jean, and back again. "You are all insane," he said, and stormed out of the house, shrugging into his sport coat as he clacked down the sidewalk. "I knew I would regret this. I—I have no words."

Jean could barely hear the sound of his car squealing out of the driveway over the laughter in her kitchen. Even Janet was holding one hand over her mouth with glee. Jean faced them. "You all think this is funny?" she cried.

Mitzi nodded. "Kind of. No, more than kind of. Come on, Jean. It's hilarious."

May giggled. "You know his next book is going to star a bunch of drug-smuggling book nerds, right?"

"Oh, God," Jean wailed. What would Wayne have thought of this debacle? He would have never wanted to show his face again. "This is illegal. There are illegal drugs on my kitchen floor."

"We should get T-shirts," Loretta said. "'Drug-smuggling Grannies Who Read.'"

Bailey pushed her way through the knot of friends and snaked her arm around her grandmother's elbow, her face shining with tears and glee. "You should be proud of me, Grandma Jean," she said. "I didn't smoke it."

"Well, at least there's that," Jean said, and she too succumbed to laughter.

"Besides, did you hear what he said?" May asked. The ladies shook their heads. "He said he had no words."

"We rendered the great R. Sebastian Thackeray speechless?" Mitzi said.

"It's exactly what we wanted," Dorothy said. "To shut him up."

Bailey's eyes grew wide. "My plan worked!"

And they all cheered.

TWENTY-SEVEN

They all met in the supermarket parking lot. Janet was in her smock, as always, and as always looking a little green around the gills with the stress of being forced to be social. But she was there, twisting her apron, rubbing at the line where her forehead met her visor, casting worried looks at the front of the store. But she was there nonetheless.

After her outburst with R. Sebastian Thackeray, the day that Jean liked to think of as the Best and Most Humiliating Day of Her Recent Life, Janet had seemed to come out of her shell a little more. They'd decided to have another meeting the next week, to make up for their botched one, and she'd actually started the conversation, her fingers shaking around the pages of the book she held open in front of her, but her voice a little clearer, a little bolder.

That was when they'd decided to meet again today.

"I've got goodies!" Mitzi called, coming out of her car, shopping bag first. Everyone had worried about Mitzi's unending strong opinions. Everyone had rolled their eyes and sighed about her at one time or another. But one thing they could all agree on—for her harshness, there was a certain place in the group for Mitzi. She kept them in line, but she was also their biggest fan. There was no one in the group, Jean had realized, more loyal than Mitzi. And Jean also knew that Mitzi never judged anyone more harshly than she judged herself.

She loped over toward them all, Dorothy climbing out of the passenger side of the car and following behind, a big grin on her face.

"We ready for this?" Mitzi asked, breathlessly.

"I think so," Jean said, and at the same time, Bailey said, "Hell, yeah!"

Jean glanced at Janet, who shrugged miserably. "Not really," she said.

"You'll do great, honey," May said, patting Janet's round shoulder. "We've got your back."

"And speaking of backs, I've got a surprise," Mitzi said. She set the shopping bag on the ground and bent over it, then stood, pulling a black T-shirt up over her chest and holding it out for everyone to see. "Ta-da!"

"'OBWB'?" Jean asked, squinting at the shirt.

Bailey laughed, a hand over her mouth. "'Old Biddies with Books'!" she said, pointing at the smaller letters beneath the big ones.

"I got one for each of us," Mitzi said. "I thought it could be the official name of our book club. What do you think?" She passed one to each of them, then pulled out a pink T-shirt and held it up to Bailey. It read: AYT: AND A YOUNG'UN TOO.

Bailey clapped her hands and took the shirt. She reached out to hug Mitzi. "I love it!"

"We thought this would give us some authority," Dorothy said. "Like a uniform or something. Plus, it's just fun."

The ladies stretched their new shirts on over the shirts they were wearing, then paused a moment to admire themselves.

"We look like Hooters girls," Loretta said, craning her neck to peer down at her shirt. "Only our boobs are lower."

"Speak for yourself, Lolo," Bailey said, and Jean smiled. Bailey had been making such great progress, and Jean knew she had Loretta to thank for part of it. Bailey had really taken to Loretta—called her "Lolo" and spent many afternoons in La Ladies' Lounge, gobbling up Flavian Munney books like candy. *Man candy,* Bailey called the books, and both she and Loretta worked hard to convince Jean that reading them was an integral part of Bailey's homeschooling work. *It's part of health class,* they'd argued. *No, no, anatomy.*

"Should we get this over with?" Janet asked, holding her T-shirt in one hand. It wouldn't be allowed as part of her uniform.

"You ready?" Jean asked, and again Janet shrugged.

"I have to be," she said. It had been her idea. She understood the risks. But she'd said it was worth it and that hearing Thackeray's opinion reminded her how people saw her. Standing up to him had reminded her that she was important too, and if she didn't take care of herself, nobody would.

"Let's do it," Mitzi said, and confidently led the way, grabbing Janet's sleeve as she passed and pulling her across the parking lot.

As soon as the front doors whooshed open in front of them, they stopped and stood still.

"You've got to lead the way from here," May said. "We don't know where to go."

Janet gave one last pleading look to each of them, then squared her shoulders and marched through the doors.

All the customers turned when they came in, and the cashiers paused. It wasn't every day, after all, that six women, all wearing matching shirts, pounded through the front doors of the supermarket, looks of determination etched on their faces.

They ignored the stares and followed Janet, across the front of the store, through an Employees Only doorway and up a flight of stairs to a smoky common room where several employees in various states of uniform smoked cigarettes, read the newspaper, and picked through lunch bags, their shoes off and their feet stretched out on couches. A snowy tube TV was on in one corner. Jean noticed that one whole wall was a bank of windows, what appeared to be mirrors on the other side. It dawned on her how many times she'd been watched from within this room, how she'd been monitored unseen. It was an unsettling feeling that only added to the anticipation of what they were about to do.

"Hey, Janet, I thought you were working at five," a woman said from over at one of the tables.

"I am," Janet said. "Is Rodney in his office?"

The woman made a face. "Better not mess with him, though. He's in a mood."

"He's always in a mood," Janet mumbled, in a surprising show of sass that Jean was totally not expecting. Janet headed ever faster toward a door in the corner of the room, the ladies following her. She knocked on the door, and then pushed it open without being invited in.

There sat the bald guy that Jean had seen lay into Janet twice. He was bent over his desk, writing.

"Did I say you could come in?" he droned without even looking up. "I'm busy. Get out."

"We said we could come in," Mitzi said, stepping up next to Janet and throwing an arm around her shoulder in a show of solidarity.

Rodney looked up from what he was writing, his pen still poised over the paper. His mouth hung open just slightly, showing elongated front teeth that Jean hadn't noticed before. His beady eyes magnified out from behind his glasses, giving him a rodent look.

"What is this?" he asked, and Jean's natural inclination

was to shrink back, to apologize for intruding, to leave the way she'd come. But then she remembered how he'd embarrassed Janet in front of her, how he'd treated her like trash, and she forced herself to stand tall. She even shuffled a step or two toward Janet's back.

"We're here to get some things straight," Mitzi said, and then nudged Janet's shoulder as if to cue her. Rodney's giant eyes flicked from Mitzi to Janet.

"Okay?" he said.

Loretta stepped up on the other side of Janet. "She has some things to say to you," she said. "Right?" She too glanced at Janet, who seemed to have been struck with stage fright.

"I heard you the first time," he said sourly, and when Janet still didn't speak, said, "I don't have time for this. Just leave. I'll deal with you later. This is my office, not a place for field trips."

But instead of leaving, Janet stepped toward his desk, breaking free of Mitzi's and Loretta's arms.

"No," she said, her voice tiny, then again, louder. "No. I'm not going anywhere. Until . . . until you hear me out."

This time Rodney put down his pen and folded his hands on top of his desk. "This ought to be good," he said. "Please, do tell me everything that's on your mind."

Janet glanced over her shoulder at Jean, who gave her a nod. "First of all, I don't like the way you talk to me. You're mean and you yell for no reason and I'm a good employee."

"Pacifiers are in aisle two," Rodney said, oh-so-sympathetically.

"Shut it, chrome dome," Dorothy said. She linked elbows with Loretta. Bailey stepped up and linked Loretta's other elbow.

"Hey, now, you have no right to come in here and—"

"And number two, I don't like it when you call me names. Rotunda, Frieda Fatty-pants, Large Marge. Those are harassing names, and I could sue you."

He held out his hands. "Whoa, whoa, whoa. Nobody's talking about lawsuits here."

"I'm a lawyer and I'm telling you right now, she could sue your bald little balls off," May said, stepping up and linking elbows with Dorothy and Mitzi, and even though it was a lie—May was a librarian, and they hadn't said the word *lawsuit* even once before coming today—it was a very, very convincing lie. "So you'd better stop talking and start listening."

"Third, if you yell at me in front of a customer one more time . . . ," Janet said, and then she faltered, seemingly unsure how to finish the threat.

Finally, Jean stepped up and linked her elbow through Bailey's remaining one. "I will never shop here again. And I will tell everyone I know to stop shopping here too. And, trust me, I know a lot of people." Jean smiled, satisfied with herself. She'd just sounded exactly like Wayne. Quickly, she glanced up at the ceiling, sure she'd see him smiling down at her from above.

Rodney looked nonplussed. "Are you all done now? Fine. I'll baby your friend here. But not because I'm scared. Because I'm a nice guy." He swished his hands at them as if ushering them out of the room. Slowly, they each let go of one another's arms and turned to leave, shuffling forward a few steps, the whole meeting feeling a little too easy and thus anticlimactic. The way they'd talked at the last meeting, still high from their demolition of Thackeray, Jean had expected . . . more.

But just a step or two short of the door, Janet pulled up. "No," she said, looking at the ground and bringing her fists together across her body in a double aw-shucks move. She shook her head. "No," she repeated. She turned, held her head high, and yelled, louder than Jean would have even believed Janet to be capable of. "No, you will not quit because you're a nice guy. Because you're not a nice guy. You're going to quit because I'm bigger than you and I will kick your ass!"

A cheer erupted, Mitzi, Dorothy, and Loretta all pumping their fists. Mitzi and Dorothy patted Janet heartily on the back. Janet smirked, her smile growing wider as it became obvious that Rodney wasn't going to respond at all to her threat—and, in fact, he did look scared—and they all tumbled out of the office in one rising, laughing, matching-shirt-wearing pile.

TWENTY-EIGHT

They'd all gone for pie after Janet's confrontation with Rodney. They had stormed Gingham Kitchen, known for its buttery crust, and had each ordered a different kind of pie—strawberry, rhubarb, lemon, blackberry, banana, French silk, mincemeat. When the waitress came, they pushed all the plates to the middle of the table and each took forkfuls from every one until the plates were scraped clean and Bailey had licked her finger to pick up the crust crumbs.

They were giddy. Silly. Best friends.

Janet worried aloud that she would get fired, and Mitzi reminded her that having to get a job with a better manager might not be a bad thing, anyway.

"Besides, you finally stood up for yourself. Doesn't that count for anything?" Mitzi had added, and Janet had smiled, flushed with happiness. She had a crooked front tooth—in two years of club meetings, Jean had never seen that before now.

"Yeah," she said. "Actually, it counts for a lot."

"Okay, okay," May had finally said when Loretta mentioned needing to get home. "But we need to decide on our next book."

"Flavian is in training for a marathon right now," Loretta suggested, and someone threw a wadded-up napkin at her.

"A looove marathon," Bailey said in a low, sultry voice, and giggled.

"There's a Jeremiah Manning biography out," Dorothy said. "I just started it. It's really good."

"Jeremiah Manning," Jean repeated. "Where have I heard that name before?"

"He's that congressman, you know, the one with the hair?" May said, pantomiming big fluffy hair.

"He's the one who cheated on his wife with a whole bevy of frat boys," Mitzi added. "A real bonehead. Why in the heck are you reading that drivel, Dot?"

Dorothy shrugged. "Because he's an idiot. It's like a train wreck. Gotta watch it."

"How are his abs?" Loretta asked.

"Ew. No," Dorothy said.

"We could read it and then get him to come to our meeting," Bailey suggested, and this time she was hit by several wadded-up napkins. "You're right," she said, giggling pointedly at Jean. "We don't have enough pot for visitors."

Bailey was like a new person, Jean noted. She still had her moments. She screamed at her father on the phone pretty much every time he called. She wrote dark and depressing poetry on her bedroom walls with a Sharpie marker. She slept too late and ate too much and never cleaned anything.

But she was trying. And given the girl that she had been at the beginning of the summer, trying was the best Jean could hope for.

They came home after the pie and went to their separate corners as they so often did. Bailey disappeared into her room, and Jean into hers. Out of habit, Jean kicked off her shoes and went straight to Wayne's top drawer. She pulled it open and fished out an item—this time, a love letter from when they were in college. The paper it was written on was yellowed and fragile, the ink of his pen softened with age.

She carried the letter over to her bed and leaned back against her pillows, unfolding the paper and holding it to her chest. She didn't have to read it to know what it said. She'd memorized it months ago:

> My Lovely Jeanie,
>
> Last night when I proposed, I honestly wasn't sure how it would go. We'd never even talked about marriage. I had no idea how you felt about it! Maybe you were one of those women who only worried about doing it all for

*herself, and didn't want to get married. Maybe
you wanted to get married, but not to me.
Maybe you wanted to get married, but not now.
I was taking a huge risk! Putting my heart out
there, leaving it for you to step on and squash.*

*I knew this, but in the end I decided it was
worth it to find out if, by chance, you were one
of those girls who did want to get married, and
maybe even married to me, right now.*

*I am over the moon that you said yes. Say
it again—yes and yes and yes. Say it on our
wedding day. Say it in our home. Say it in
every way you can, and say it until death do us
part. And even then, say it again. That's all I
ask.*

I love you.

> *Your future
> husband,
> Wayne*

Jean circled her hands around the note and pressed it
to her chest. "Yes and yes and yes," she whispered, just as
she always did when she revisited this particular letter.
"Yes, yes, yes."

She checked the clock and waited for the tears to
come, for Crying Time to begin.

But they didn't. It didn't.

She had said yes and yes and yes. She had said it on their wedding day and in their home and in every way she could and until he died and even then again. She had done what he asked. She had been the wife he wanted.

She was finally, just now, sure of it, and the tears never came.

And she knew with a certainty she'd not felt since that first day when that first doctor had looked across his desk at them so solemnly, that her Crying Time was finished. It was time to move on.

And someday it would be finished for Bailey too. And Jean would be there when it was.

TWENTY-NINE

Dear Margaret Wise Brown:
My name is Bailey Butler and I'm sixteen years
old. I wrote to you a long time ago, but what I
didn't know then was that you were already
dead. I just discovered that right now when I was
looking for your e-mail address. You can't e-mail
dead people, so I'm just going to write this one
longhand. I have no idea where I'll send it. I
wonder where my mom sent my letter all those
years ago? Maybe nowhere. Also, I hope it's not
rude to call you "dead." I'm still learning from
my grandma what it's okay to say about people
who've died and what isn't. I think "dead" is
okay, though, in this circumstance, especially
since you won't actually ever read this.

You know how sometimes people will ask
you what is your favorite book of all time?

Jennifer Scott

When people ask me that question, I lie. It's pretty easy to do. I read all the time, and I really love a lot of the books I read. I used to think I was Ramona Quimby, and I learned spells and stuff like Hermoine, and I have read <u>Anne of Green Gables</u> more times than I can count. And each of those books, if you had asked me at the time that I was reading them, I would have told you were my absolute favorite. Or maybe I would have made up something like <u>Catcher in the Rye</u>, which I've never read, or <u>The Grapes of Wrath</u>, which I actually hated, just to sound smart and impress people.

But all of those answers, the true ones and the false, would have been lies.

Your book <u>Home for a Bunny</u> is my favorite book of all time. I've always known that.

I was obsessed with it when I was a kid. That bunny felt real, like a part of my family. Like the pet I never had. Sitting on my mom's lap and listening to the story was the coziest I've ever felt. Like nothing bad could ever happen to me. Like nothing bad could ever happen to us.

I will admit, I always wondered why the bunny didn't have a home. Why was he searching? Where was his family? What had happened to his home? And why didn't he seem upset about it?

It turned out bad things could happen to me. Bad things could happen to us. I wouldn't be cozy forever. I wouldn't be in my mom's lap forever, and it has finally dawned on me that sometimes bunnies just don't have homes, and they have to go looking for their version of the fluffy snow-white bunny who will take them in at the end. Maybe that was what you were trying to say with your book? Maybe it wasn't just about a cute woodland animal and words that are fun to read aloud?

I carried that book with me everywhere I went. Nobody knows this, but I even kept it in the front pocket of my backpack every day that I ever went to school. And it would be in my backpack again this year, my junior year, but I'm homeschooled now. But even if I wasn't homeschooled, I wouldn't be carrying it, because I gave it away to someone who needs it more than I do. I have found my white bunny to take me in and make me cozy. And now I think I understand the bunny completely.

Thank you for giving me . . . well, everything.

Love,
Bailey Butler

Jean knocked on Bailey's door, jarring Bailey out of a nap.

"You ready to go?"

Bailey sat up, spilling her comforter onto the floor next to the bed. She wiped her eyes, feeling cobwebby. She wasn't sure how long she'd been lying down. It seemed like only a minute. Yet she'd had enough time to dream that her mother had shown up looking pink and healthy and scrubbed clean, asking Bailey if she was ready to go home. She'd had that dream a lot lately. It was always followed by Bailey telling her mother that she was already home. But in the end, Dream Bailey climbed in the car with her mother, feeling sorry and sad and thrilled and hopeful all at the same time. She hated that dream.

"Took you long enough," she grumbled, stepping into her flip-flops and opening the door. "I've been ready forever."

Her grandmother studied her face and grinned. "I can see you were waiting anxiously. You have a handprint on your face. Was it a nice nap?"

"Whatever," Bailey said, picking up her string bag by her bedroom door and looping it over her shoulder. She couldn't help smiling too. "You get lost on your way to change?"

"I tell you every day, it takes a long time to work up the courage to get into a swimsuit when you're my age," her grandmother said. "Plus, I had to call Loretta."

"You look fine in your swimsuit." Bailey jogged down the stairs. "Kind of hot, actually."

Grandma Jean laughed as she followed Bailey down the stairs. "Now it's my turn to say 'whatever.'"

It was still hot outside, even though it was September, and for that reason the pool had been kept open past Labor Day. Most days Bailey got her schoolwork done on the computer before lunch was over, and she and her grandmother packed up bags of cinnamon sugar popcorn and cans of soda and headed down to the pool before the neighborhood kids got out of school and flooded the place.

"Is she coming? Loretta?" Bailey asked as she plopped into the car, her grandmother handing her the overstuffed pool bag and two towels. She felt dwarfed, as if she could barely see through the windshield, but she didn't mind. It kind of reminded her of when she was a kid and hid in blanket forts. Back when she enjoyed being invisible.

Her grandmother groaned as she lowered herself behind the steering wheel. "Doesn't want to pull herself away from La Lounge today," she said.

"Rave DJ Flavian? Still? I thought she'd finished that one. Don't tell me she installed black lights into that chandelier like she threatened."

"Most likely, she did. But she's moved on to Cruise Captain Flavian. Now she's navigating the seven seas in nothing but a sailor hat and a compass that always points north. Or at least that's how she put it."

"Gross," Bailey cried, bursting into a belly laugh. Every so often her grandmother did that—surprised her with something really funny or silly—and she was almost shocked by the sound of her own laughter.

They drove the four blocks to the pool and piled out of the car, Bailey trying to juggle the pool bag and towels while her grandmother signed them in. Noah was working the lifeguard table, like always, gazing out into nothing while gnawing on a thumbnail as if his life depended on it.

"Hi, Noah," Bailey said as she walked by.

"Hey," he said. He still hadn't totally warmed up after the cell phone incident, and Bailey felt a pang of guilt every time she saw him pull out an old janky phone, look at it as if it were useless, and sullenly tuck it back into his swim trunks pocket. She didn't know how to apologize to him, and besides, she wasn't an apologizing type of person. But she felt bad, and if it counted for anything, she still considered him a onetime friend that she sometimes wished she could hang out with again. Not that Grandma Jean would ever let her hang out with him again, anyway, after the whole pot incident. So she settled on saying hi and leaving it at that.

They went straight to their usual two chaise lounges, the ones they had sat in the very first time they visited the pool, back when Loretta's raunchy talk had grossed her out completely. The lounges were tucked under a patio umbrella, which Bailey always immediately wound to an open position. If Bailey pulled her feet up, she could be totally shaded. If she stretched out, she could get some sun on her legs. Grandma Jean just preferred the shade.

"You talk to your mom or dad today?" Grandma Jean asked as soon as they got settled. Same question every day.

"Nope," Bailey said, moving around to get comfortable on her towel. Same answer every day. She supposed one day the answer would change, but she tried not to think about it. She rehearsed in her head all the time what she would say to Curt or Laura Butler if she ever heard from them again, but part of her was scared that she'd never have the guts to actually say it. A part of her feared that, just like in her dream, she would go to them, because they were her parents, and as much as she hated them, she missed them sometimes too. The old them. The ones who laughed when she popped out of her blanket fort, no longer invisible.

And just like every day, she asked her grandmother the same question. "You hear from them?"

Grandma Jean slowly shook her head as she reached into the pool bag. "Not today."

And Bailey hated it, but that answer always came with a little stab of anger and hurt that, for just a second, made her want to do something crazy like vandalize a car or . . . take her clothes off in the pool. Sometimes she gave in to that anger—there was a closet wall in her bedroom so full of holes she could see insulation behind it—but more and more often she tried to fight it. To not let them do that to her.

Her grandmother pulled out a bag of popcorn for each of them and handed one, along with a can of soda, to Bailey, who immediately tucked it into her lap. She then pulled out two matching books—a lengthy period novel that Bailey was surprisingly into—and handed one to Bailey.

"Where are you?" Grandma Jean asked, crinkling her bag as she dug out a handful of popcorn.

"Adelaide just found out that John has come home from the war," Bailey said.

"Oh, don't tell me any more. I'm not there yet. You read so fast," her grandmother said.

Bailey shrugged. "Lots and lots of practice, I guess. You better hurry up, though. Book club meets next week."

She pulled her feet up and propped the book on her knees. Her grandmother munched on popcorn and flipped to her bookmarked page. Noah stared off into nothingness and chomped on his thumbnail, and the water softly lapped against the sides of the pool.

And side by side, they read.

Photo by Lacey Crough

Jennifer Scott is an award-winning author who made her debut in women's fiction with *The Sister Season*. She also writes critically acclaimed young adult fiction under the name Jennifer Brown. Her debut YA novel, *Hate List*, was selected as an ALA Best Book for Young Adults, a *VOYA* Perfect Ten, and a *School Library Journal* Book of the Year. Jennifer lives in Liberty, Missouri, with her husband and three children.

CONNECT ONLINE

jenniferscottauthor.com
facebook.com/jenniferscottauthor

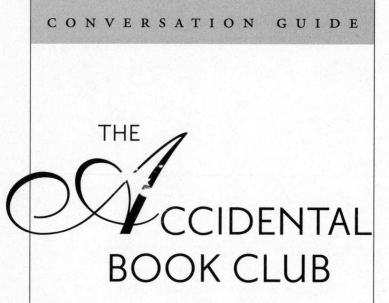

THE ACCIDENTAL BOOK CLUB

Jennifer Scott

This Conversation Guide is intended to enrich the
individual reading experience, as well as encourage us
to explore these topics together—because books, and
life, are meant for sharing.

A CONVERSATION
WITH JENNIFER SCOTT

Q. The Accidental Book Club *focuses on both the relationship between a grandmother and her granddaughter and the relationships among the members of a book club the grandmother creates. How did this story begin for you? Did some characters speak to you more than others? Were some harder to write than others?*

A. I am often asked to visit book clubs that have read and will be discussing one of my books. And I'm thrilled when I can join them, because book clubs tend to be very open and honest with their opinions. I love that honesty, and always welcome the opportunity to learn from them.

The idea for *The Accidental Book Club* came when I began wondering, however: What would happen if a visiting author *didn't* welcome that honesty? What if, in fact, he responded quite rudely? And what if the book club wasn't asking him there to pick his brain, but to pick a bone with him instead? Something about that setup intrigued me, so I ran with it.

Loretta really spoke to me. She was the member I would most want in my book club, if I had one. She's a chronic reader, but she doesn't take it all so seriously. In fact, she doesn't take much of anything seriously. And she doesn't have a very good filter, which makes her flinchingly hilarious at times, and someone I can relate to. I also really connected with Bailey. I felt so sorry for her, and I understood her anger and her antics. I was rooting for her the whole way through.

Mitzi, however, was the most difficult for me to write. She and I have fairly different viewpoints in life, and I found myself at times not really liking her much. It wasn't until she began to admit that she wasn't perfect, and that maintaining the appearance of perfection was exhausting for her, that I began to understand and appreciate her a little more.

Q. Jean Vison, the founder of the book club, remarks that the group came to be as much about the events in their lives, the food they brought, and the wine as the books themselves. Have you been a member of a book club? Did you find this to be the case?

A. I have never been a member of a book club, but I would sorely love to be. But I have noticed over the years of visiting book clubs that they almost all have one thing in common: food. There are always prized dishes that are fawned over, experiments that are test-driven, and regulars that everyone loves (the most common regular: dessert; most common dessert: brownies). In fact, for most of the clubs I've visited, nothing happens until everyone gets a plate. Another constant in the book clubs I've visited is wine. Lots and lots of wine. With margaritas as a close second.

Of course, once you get booze and chocolate flowing, the conversations loosen and real friendships are born. I once visited a book club meeting during which we discussed my book for about ten minutes, and then segued into a discussion about childhoods and fathers that was deeply intimate. It was a wonderful experience. The discussion was not about the book at all . . . yet, in a way, it was the deepest book conversation I'd ever been a part of.

Q. Bailey, the granddaughter, has written to authors of books she loves from a young age. Do you have books that serve as touchstones for you in your life? Could you tell us a little bit about them? Did you ever write to one of the authors the way Bailey does?

A. So many books were touchstones in my life, and their authors sometimes felt like more than just authors to me. They were my heroes, for sure, but almost, in a way . . . they felt like friends as well. Beverly Cleary, Judy Blume—it's no coincidence that Bailey writes to the authors she does. The Ramona books defined my early childhood. Judy Blume helped usher me into adolescence, and her books *Blubber, It's Not the End of the World,* and *Are You There, God? It's Me, Margaret* each touched me particularly deeply. I have never written to any authors, but if I did, I imagine I would write to the authors Bailey wrote to and would say something very similar to what she said.

Q. *The author of the book* Blame *receives great critical acclaim, and yet his ideas regarding women seem derogatory and outdated (to say the least!). What inspired you to explore this conflicted version of the artist-writer?*

A. I don't know if I was really exploring a critically acclaimed artist-writer so much as I was exploring the critically acclaimed in general, be it artist, author, performer, comedian, sports star, politician, actor, or otherwise. How we treat the famous is a very interesting study in contradiction to me. We put some celebrities up on pedestals and then put impossible pressure on them to behave perfectly, to think as we think, and to never voice an opinion otherwise. So many of the famous have found themselves in the midst of terrible, scathing critical firestorms and, at times, career-ending hate over a misspoken word. Yet at the same time, other celebrities frequently behave deplorably, and we still continue to happily consume their brand. It's as if we are willing to overlook the willfully dreadful behaviors of some while at the same time refusing to allow any slack for the mistakes of others. And it seems so random who gets that free pass and whose career will end. So the exploration of R. Sebastian Thackeray, III, wasn't the exploration of authors, readers, and critics so much as it was the exploration of the famous and their fans.

Plus, it was just really fun to create a nasty, vile little man and then beat up on him a bit.

Q. What would you most like readers to take away from reading The Accidental Book Club?

A. Well, first, foremost, and always, enjoyment. I want my readers to feel as if they've spent time with friends after spending time with Jean's book club. I know I felt like they were friends while I was writing it.

But I think what I'd most like readers to take away is the feeling of empowerment behind human connection. The same that Janet felt when they marched into the supermarket, or that Bailey felt when she asked to live with her grandmother. Whereas R. Sebastian Thackeray's novel was all about blame, judgment, and disconnect, *The Accidental Book Club* is all about acceptance, forgiveness, and connection, and the great power that comes from those things.

In some ways, that theme of reaching out in love and connecting with the humans around you, no matter how different you are, is a theme found in all of my books, because I think learning that is the most important, and most difficult, of all life's assignments.

Q. You've now written two works of women's fiction, The Sister Season *and* The Accidental Book Club. *Was the writing process similar for both? Did you feel one came easier than the other?*

A. In terms of process, I would say they're fairly similar, with the exception that I wasn't writing *The Sister Season* for anyone but me, whereas I knew going in that *The Accidental Book Club* would be published. With *The Sister Season* there were no expectations, no deadlines; it was just me hanging out with my favorite hobby. I also have very strong emotional ties to the setting of *The Sister Season*, so in those two regards, it may have been slightly easier to write.

That said, there were times that I had so much more fun writing *The Accidental Book Club*. The GNO scene, the confrontation with Thackeray, the initial pool scene—I got so much enjoyment out of writing those. And I truly loved Bailey's character and watching her transform and grow.

In the end, comparing writing processes for different projects is like comparing apples and oranges. My books are like my children—they all have their strengths and their challenges, their good days and their bad, and in the end I love them all equally, and miss each and every one of them when I'm done.

QUESTIONS
FOR DISCUSSION

1. *The Accidental Book Club* opens with the scene of Jean Vison, the founder of the book club, cooking a dish for the club members and struggling to make it "book club–worthy." How does food become a bonding mechanism throughout the story? Do you think this attention to food detracts from the ultimate experience of the book club?

2. A complicated character, Jean is, among many things, a widow. As the story progresses, we learn of Jean's different ways for dealing with her grief. What are they? Do you think some of them are more productive than others? Have you used similar coping mechanisms in your own life?

3. Bailey, Jean's granddaughter, arrives at Jean's bearing a lot of attitude. And yet through the story she undergoes an interesting transformation. How does she change as the story

progresses? What are the most important things she learns? What do you see for her in the future?

4. As a mother, Jean Vison is surprised, perplexed, and dismayed when her daughter is diagnosed as an alcoholic. In some ways she feels responsible. Do you think mothers can and/or should be held accountable for the actions of their children—either young or adult? And how does this connect to the book *Blame* that Jean reads for the book club?

5. The other members of the book club—Loretta, Dorothy, Mitzi, Janet, and May—all have different struggles and issues they are trying to resolve concerning men, children, and bosses. Which member did you relate to the most? The least? Why?

6. Books play many roles in this story—sometimes they are touchstones to which the individuals turn for solace, sometimes they are publicly praised but have questionable ideas, sometimes they are used for wish fulfillment and escapism, and sometimes they contain new ideas that challenge the characters to act differently. What books have made significant impressions on you? Which are your favorites and what do they give you?

7. Discuss the different kinds of romantic love depicted in this book. Do Jean, Loretta, and May all see love similarly? How does this affect the choices they make and the books they read?

8. When Bailey has the idea of inviting a famous author to

the book club, she gets him there by dangling her family's dirty laundry in front of him and telling him he can use it in his next book. The author takes the bait—which leads one to ask: Is it fair of authors to use the material from the lives of their friends and family in works of fiction?

9. Standing up for yourself and taking responsibility for your life are two significant themes in the book. How do the various characters accomplish this? Think of Bailey and her revelation in the hospital. Of Janet and her confrontation with her boss. Of Jean and the way her relationships change with her children and granddaughter throughout the book.

10. In the "Conversation with Jennifer Scott," the author states "that theme of reaching out in love and connecting with the humans around you, no matter how different you are, is a theme found in all of my books, because I think learning that is the most important, and most difficult, of all life's assignments." Where do you see this within the book? What connections grow between the different characters and how do things change in their lives as a result?

11. What did you most enjoy about *The Accidental Book Club*? What will you recall from it six months from now?